First
Night
of
Summer

First Night of Summer

A NOVEL

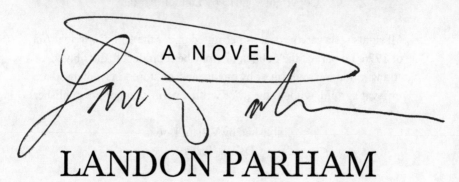

LANDON PARHAM

Published by Valiant Books
Dallas, Texas.

Printed in the United States of America

First Edition

Library of Congress Control Number: 2012924326
First Night of Summer / Landon Parham. – 1st ed.
ISBN 978-0-9888025-1-3
ISBN 978-0-9888025-2-0 (ebook)

To Lauren, without whom, I would simply be . . . without.

Author's Note

Disassociation from reality is the most deplorable act a society can commit. Sweep all the taboo unpleasantries of life under the rug, and there they will reside, just as dangerous, forever lurking beneath the surface.

In the United States alone, a child goes missing every forty seconds. While most are recovered alive and unharmed, many are forced to suffer the indignity and pain of abuse, often sexual.

Each year, approximately one hundred of these children are brutally murdered at the hands of their abductors. Countless others are never added to this statistic because they remain lost, never to be found or heard from again.

Prologue

J ason Smith, a freckle-faced four-year-old, curled his bare toes against the grainy surface of his rooftop. Six inches from the edge, nothing but thin air standing in the way of a two-story plummet to the green grass below, he showed no signs of fear.

A cool spring breeze came down the Rocky Mountains and rustled his curly red hair in the New Mexico sunshine. A pair of faded black sweatpants, two sizes too small, hugged his chunky legs with a baby fat spare tire hanging over the waistband. His cape, a turquoise bath towel safety-pinned around his neck, completed the homemade superhero ensemble.

Inch by inch, gripping with his feet, he crept closer to the drop-off. One more step, and that would be it. The mid-century, Craftsman-style home had no safety features to offer once he ventured beyond the eave.

The visual of a pudgy boy wearing a heinous costume was humorous. His intentions, however, were not. The rambunctious child had recently embarked on a string of wild hair endeavors. None ended well.

The entire Ruidoso Valley floor was visible from his perch. He felt free in view of the expansive landscape. Trout streams, granite walls, aspen, and pinyon-covered mountains were spread out before him like some magical, Wild West adventure.

"Watch me fly!" he shouted for the world to hear.

He puffed up his pale, naked chest, and turned his head to face the sky. The proclamation ricocheted and echoed off the surrounding slopes.

Jason held his arms wide. Ten toes hung over the shingles, each scrunched in tightly like an eagle's talons clutched to a limb. There had never been a braver hero—nor a more foolish one.

"I'm here to thave the day!"

The situation was serious. Otherwise, his childish lisp might have been comical. A superhero with a speech impediment was the ultimate paradox. Imagine Batman with a voice like Foghorn Leghorn. He would be impossible to take seriously.

But Jason was no Batman. He was a little boy with a wild imagination and a knack for mischief.

Before there was time to act, before anyone could threaten him with cruel and unusual punishment, his knees bent beneath the weight of his chubby body and he leapt. The ratty cape followed him on the ride down. His proud expression suddenly turned sour as imagination faded into reality.

He shrieked like a banshee, a high-pitched tone that only children are capable of, and disrupted the quiet little street. But at the last moment, before colliding with the earth, a tablecloth stretched out beneath him, saving the overzealous child from his folly.

Part One

God, forgive those whose atrocities are so great—I will not.

Chapter One

Six Days Later

A pepper spray canister and a .45 Heckler & Koch pistol banged against the wooden deck. Handcuffs, two extra magazines of ammunition, and an ASP tactical baton joined them.

Isaac Snow was playing a game of keep-away in the side yard with his two daughters, Caroline and Josie, when he heard the noise. He was "it" at the moment and turned to see who their company was.

"Charlie!" he greeted. "Hey, girls, look who's here."

Charlie Biddle, Ruidoso's chief of police, had parked his cruiser on the curb. He hung his gun belt on the deck railing, pulled the tan shirttail from his forest green pants, and ambled out into the grass.

"Uncle Charlie!" both girls shouted in unison.

Josie made it to him first, leaped into his arms, and squeezed. He quickly had to shift her to one side because Caroline was right behind. She also jumped up and gave her best bear hug.

"Hey, kiddos!" He was all grins. It didn't matter what kind of day he was having or what went wrong at work; the eight-year-old twins had a way of lighting him up. "Having fun?"

"We're playing keep-away, and Dad's it," Josie explained.

"Well, that doesn't sound too difficult, now does it?"

"Let's see how you do against them." Isaac threw a soft punch into Charlie's rotund belly. "They're getting faster every day."

Both girls squirmed to be put down. Caroline grabbed his hand and gave it a tug toward the lawn. Josie got behind him and started pushing.

"Come play! Come play!" they begged. "Please, Uncle Charlie."

He looked at Isaac. "How can I resist?"

He removed his cap with "Ruidoso PD" embroidered across the front and hung it on the rail with his tactical gear. Sunlight glinted off his exposed scalp from a receding hairline.

"Should we play teams or just keep it away from your old man?"

"Teams," Josie declared.

"Who are the captains?"

"We are," Caroline said in a way that implied a meaning of "Duh."

"All right but just a game or two. Your Uncle Charlie needs to take a load off."

By the time two games were finished, he was leaning over, hands on his knees, and glazed with perspiration. This is how it had been since the sixth grade. Isaac was the tall, handsome athlete, and Charlie, the polar opposite.

"That's it for me." He made the timeout sign with his hands. "I'm out."

"I told you they were getting faster."

He nodded and headed for the porch. Through the railing, he could see a blue Igloo cooler and had high hopes that something cold and crisp was inside.

Up the steps and onto the deck, Isaac pulled two chairs from the table and faced them toward the yard. He popped the tops on two longnecks from the cooler and handed one to Charlie, who graciously accepted and wasted no time in quenching his thirst.

"Long day?" Isaac asked.

Charlie paused until he finished swallowing. "Not really, but it's still good to be off work."

Isaac leaned back on the chair legs and stretched his own out in front. He crossed one over the other and rested them on the railing. His tanned skin was exposed below a pair of shorts. Strong, shoeless feet were stained green from running in the lush, fescue lawn.

Josie and Caroline continued playing while everyone waited for supper to be ready. They sent a Frisbee back and forth, trying to catch it while jumping in the air. There was an endless amount of giggling and squealing. To the casual observer, they looked identical. But there were differences. Some, only Isaac and their mother, Sarah, could see, but they were still there. Caroline was a half-inch taller. Josie's green eyes were slightly darker. Her ears were pierced, but Caroline wanted nothing to do with it. And even though they shared clothes, each had subtle ways to be an individual.

"Hey, I meant to tell you," Charlie said. "I saw the girls on the news the other night. Pretty cool stuff." He kept his gaze on Caroline and Josie. A stream of pride ran through him.

"Yeah, it was pretty cool."

"How'd it go?"

"It was interesting. A Channel 6 crew came all the way down from Albuquerque and did the interview right here. Between that and the VFW giving them an award—"

"Hometown heroes."

"We're still not sure who called it in, but they thought the reporter was a lot of fun."

"Oooh, yeah." Charlie shifted in his chair. "I saw her. She as good looking in person as she is on TV?"

Isaac laughed at his bachelor buddy. "Yeah, she's pretty, all right. But way too high maintenance. I'll guarantee you that. Flashy, oversized hair, bright red lipstick, and the whitest teeth I've ever seen. That all takes work."

"A trophy wife," Charlie mused.

"I think we have her card in the house if you're really interested." He cocked an eyebrow and waited for a response.

"Nah." A thoughtful look was on his face. "She'd probably think I work too much."

"Yeah, I'm sure that's exactly what she'd think."

Charlie got tickled. His belly bounced up and down with laughter. "Well, good for them." He toasted with his beer and motioned toward the neighbor's house where the calamity had unfolded. "If they hadn't thought of anything, that boy could be laid up with two broken legs right now."

Isaac thought of little Jason Smith and how lucky he was that circumstances played into his favor. Charlie was right. Had it not been for Caroline and Josie, there was no telling what his condition might be. It brought back memories of when he himself was a boy.

*   *   *

Isaac's childhood had been fantastic. His parents took him all over the United States, exposing his young mind to limitless possibilities. And on one of those trips, he found his dream. It happened at a Cannon Air Force Base air show in Clovis, New Mexico. Watching the fighter jet pilots go through their paces had been mesmerizing. His destiny was sealed.

Charlie, on the other hand, grew up neglected and tossed aside by parents who were only into themselves. A few times, he had even shown up at the Snow's doorstep in the middle of the night because his mom or dad was on a bender. The people who should have cared the most cared the least.

But Isaac and his parents, Tom and Helen, had cared and were there for Charlie when no one else was. Now, at only thirty-five, Charlie was the youngest chief of police in Ruidoso history.

* * *

"So, you guys going to do anything to celebrate?"

Isaac crossed his legs the other way. "Like what?"

"I don't know. Maybe go to Disneyland or something?"

"I'd love to, but you know how it is. My schedule is going to be hectic, at best, this summer. Hopefully we'll have a wet year, and I'll get some time off. I don't know if we'll be able to swing anything long enough for a trip like that."

"Yeah, I know." Charlie paused. "Sometimes I don't think this town could get by without me. But then I remember that it was here long before me and it will be here long after I'm gone."

"True, but you're the boss man. What you say goes."

"Humph! I'm a simple public servant, and if I'm not seen serving, I can kiss my salary good-bye. Then what am I going to do?"

Isaac rubbed his face. His thumb and fingers made a scraping sound against a dark, five o'clock shadow that matched his head of thick, black hair. "I haven't really thought of it that way."

"At least you have other pilots to fill in for you. I, my friend, am just one man. No Charlie equals no chief of police."

Isaac was a forest fire patrol pilot for the state of New Mexico. His flying credentials from the air force were impeccable and helped land the position. Growing up in the local culture and knowing the terrain also contributed.

"You know," he said, "I guess we are taking a trip the first weekend in August. Sarah's doing her Susan G. Komen Walk for the Cure in Albuquerque. While she's doing that, the girls and I are flying up to Taos and staying with Mom and Dad for the weekend. I'll tell them it's their surprise for saving Jason."

"But don't the three of you take that trip every year? I mean, while Sarah's doing the cancer walk?"

Isaac smirked. "Yes, but I'll see if I can get away with it anyway."

"Oh, c'mon. Two little girls—without a moment's notice, I might add—tried to use a picnic tablecloth to catch a four-year-old boy who jumped off the second-story roof of his house. Not only did they try, but it actually worked. After a twenty-two-foot drop, the kid doesn't have a bruise on him."

"Look, I'm as proud as anyone. But they're still in school, and I have work. End of summer. That's the best I can do."

Charlie shook his head, a sarcastic show of disappointment. Finally recovered from the keep-away exertion, he tilted his head back and looked at the blue sky. He loved it there in Ruidoso with friends close by. Evenings like these were his favorites. The mountains truly were majestic. *What a place to work. What a place to raise a family. What a place to enjoy one's life.*

"So, what's for supper?"

"I think she's cooking spaghetti."

Charlie patted his belly. "That sounds great."

"Didn't we have that last week when you were here?"

"Yeah . . . well . . . Sarah knows it's my favorite. I've been eating spaghetti in that kitchen since your mom used to cook it. Besides, you never complain when putting a third helping on your plate."

"So true," he conceded. "Do you remember when we were in high school and Mom had to double the recipe? We ate so much that Dad thought our legs were hollow."

Both men were startled when a hand was placed on their shoulders. Surprised by the touch, they turned around to see that Sarah had joined them on the porch. She looked so much like the twins. Or, rather, they looked so much like her with the same blonde hair, the same green eyes, and the same good looks.

"Hey, hon."

"Hey, Sarah."

"Who's hungry?" she asked.

For a big man, Charlie was surprisingly quick getting to his feet. He tipped back the beer and slugged down the last couple sips. "That would be me." He waved at Josie and Caroline. "Come on, girlies. Uncle Charlie's hungry." Within two seconds, he was through the door, not bothering to hold it for anyone, and seated at the table.

Outside, shadows between giant pines were blending into one dusky shade of gray. The pillar-like trees cast their black silhouettes as sentinels around the neighborhood. Evening was nearing its end. The air was peaceful and calm. In the distance, two mountains stretched into the heavens, their peaks reaching for the stars.

Isaac held the screen door open for Sarah and the twins as he took in the last vestiges of a resplendent day. As a parent and a husband, he felt on top of the world. He and Sarah were settled in a town they loved, had two good girls, friends, and plenty of money to support a comfortable way of life. They didn't feel the earth tilting on its axis, but it was. The chaos had not yet begun, but it was coming. Soon.

He stepped into the house and turned his back on the final moments of light. Darkness approached in more ways than one. Someone was watching.

Chapter Two

A dangerous man, hidden within the shell of a refined, non-threatening citizen, fantasized over the lithe movements of Caroline and Josie Snow. Ricky Doors suppressed his perverse urges while watching their game of keep-away. In the fading sunlight of evening, long shadows stretched around him. He was in the gray area, concealed from view, exactly where he liked to be.

The girls enamored Ricky. He sat poised, eyes wide with adoration, watching them run to and fro. Their golden blonde locks rippled in the breeze and shone like celestial bursts of light in his real-life fantasy. Even from his distance, through pocket-sized binoculars, their green eyes were as bright as the spring grass. Their supple skin, so peachy smooth.

Not for ten lifetimes could I search and find their equal. Purely evil, he put sexual urges aside. He focused on the moment at hand. The scene was so cheerful, not like his life experiences.

Sure, there were moments of excitement but no true joy. His thrills came from all the wrong things, all the wrong places. As the years rolled by, his moral gray area quantified, further separating darkness from the light, further separating *him* from the light.

He was in awe of the twins' boundless energy and lust for life. He loved the purity in which they played games, rode their bikes, and slept at night. He felt moved by their innocence and how they carried it upon their shoulders each day, light as a feather. Their minds were pure without even trying. *What a wonderful feeling that must be.*

He leaned his head against a tree trunk and drifted off into peaceful nothingness. The girls continued playing in the distance, and he took pleasure in their laughter, their squeals of delight. The whole setting was picture-perfect. Spring was quickly leaving and making way for summer's warmth. The light breeze across his face, the rustling of leaves in his ears, and the cool earth beneath him were like little gifts. True pleasure was in the details, the nitty-gritty, sticky details.

Tree bark pressed into his scalp. He used the discomfort to sharpen his senses and stay in the present. He was there to watch, to observe. Reconnaissance was the only mission, the place where he needed to keep his mind. The other stuff would come. It all came in due time.

He took a drink of water from his canteen and screwed the lid back on. People who drank bottled drinks, especially water, disgusted him. Nature was the last unspoiled thing on earth, and for his part, he was determined to keep it that way.

Isaac and Charlie were sitting on the porch, and he wondered what it might be like to have a real friend. Briefly, he contemplated what would happen if he stepped out of the woods, walked to the porch, and sat down. *Isaac looks like an active guy. Maybe we could do some working out together. Charlie, well, he looks like the type that would be fun to watch football with.*

The thought passed as suddenly as it had come. Sure, they might accept him for a while, but only until they found out who he was, or worse, what he did. And really, the twins meant more to him than anything else, any friendship, in the world.

No buddy or pal could ever give what he planned to take from them.

He put a pair of Swarovski binoculars to his eyes. He liked being up close and personal, and the binoculars were the best money could buy. They came directly from the factory in Europe. To look through the lenses was to be drawn into a brighter, clearer world. Even at twilight and dusk, they could collect enough light to miraculously illuminate any landscape, and with a price tag near two thousand dollars, they were well worth it. Again, it was all about the details, the priceless details.

Ricky studied his subjects. The lenses followed every move they made. He was looking for character traits, things that might give him an opening. When one got close enough, and studied long enough, the unnoticeable became noticeable.

He also honed in on Isaac. To know how closely a father watched his children was imperative. *Is he attentive or withdrawn? Does he keep a continual eye on the girls or check in with them periodically?* All pieces of information were necessary to create a solid plan.

He put the binoculars in the pouch of his hooded sweatshirt. The neighborhood backed right up to the forest and offered plenty of cover. There were trees everywhere, ridges to hide behind, and mountains to disappear in. He had hidden in the forest now for over two hours, and no one knew he was there. But sitting and watching didn't get the fox in the henhouse. Finding a gap to crawl through, a way to weasel in without being noticed, was the trick.

Patience. Patience. Time will bring me the answer. His thoughts were slowly turning from business to lustful pleasure. A new excitement was building, creating a giddy anxiousness.

When, not if, the operation took place, Caroline and Josie would be his first set of twins. The thought made his stomach jump with anticipation. The high was coming. He could feel it. He had to feel it.

Remarkable that they were capable of saving a life. What special, special little girls. A black backpack sat on the pine needles next to him. He removed a leather journal and pen. It was time to make note of some specifics, add a few words to his collection of filth. *My hall of fame has a special place just for you two.*

He wrote down every thought and observation he could recall. The journal, though, was not just for practical purposes. It was his book of memories and filled with pages dedicated to his previous victims. This particular book of secrets was already halfway full, and there were others in a hidden spot back home. In fact, there were many, many others.

As he finished writing, there was a shift in the environment. All was silent where there had just been the sound of children at play. He ended the entry and looked up. Once again, binoculars pulled him into someone else's world, a world he longed to share.

Charlie had just disappeared through the screen door and into the house. Next, Caroline and Josie came running up the patio steps and into the kitchen. And finally, holding the door for his lovely wife, Isaac gave one last appreciative look around the neighborhood.

"A detail man," Ricky murmured.

He didn't know what Isaac was looking for. He could tell the father was seeing beyond the obvious, noticing the often-overlooked essence of his surroundings. But there was more to it than that. He could sense it. Isaac's dark eyes were scanning, probing. It came across as more instinctual or habitual than anything. There was no cause for alarm, but from someone who lived by life's subtleties, Ricky noticed a profoundness and depth to the action.

"I like detail people. They know how to live."

He stood from the hiding place, packed the binoculars and journal, placed the backpack straps over his shoulders, and turned into the thicket. It was a half-mile to the jogging trail and another quarter-mile to the parking lot. Distance was no problem. There was no spare weight on his lanky, almost meatless frame to tire him out.

When he arrived at his van, the night was brand new. The boldest of stars were shyly peeking out from their homes. The absence of light revealed a darker, hidden beauty. He drove away, and the mountain swallowed him whole. He was the invisible man.

There was nothing to it.

Chapter Three

On a Friday evening, more than three weeks since Josie and Caroline had saved little Jason Smith from his failed attempt at flying, Isaac returned home from work. He parked his restored 1955 Chevy truck in the detached garage and ran along the flagstone sidewalk and up the patio steps, trying to escape the downpour. He was still in uniform. A plaid, unbuttoned flannel shirt hung over a T-shirt. Blue jeans and a pair of leather work boots rounded out his on-the-job attire.

He had been gone for two days when the New Mexico drought broke. Normally he flew patrols Wednesday through Saturday, but dispatch sent him home early. There was no risk of wildfires popping up over the next twenty-four hours. The entire state was getting soaked. And besides, flying in the storm was too dangerous.

He called Sarah from his cell phone to let her know he was coming home sooner than expected. When she promised him a surprise, coupled with his enthusiasm for extra time off, he hustled to finish up.

Isaac enjoyed his job. The flying could get monotonous, but compressing work into a four-day period was the best part. To have three days of uninterrupted time for family every week was priceless. Being away and having to stay in a hotel was the downside. Above everything, though—there was no more killing. He had his wish: a quiet life and family.

He swung open the kitchen door and stepped onto the rug. It didn't take but a second to realize something was missing. No pitter-patter of feet came running to greet him. *Funny since they knew I was on my way.* Then an aroma hit his nose and immediately reminded him of days gone by . . . one day in particular.

"When you said 'surprise,'" he told to Sarah, "I had no idea." He shook off the rain and closed the screen door, letting the sound and freshness filter into the house. "Were you already planning this? Tell me you didn't run out and grab everything after I called."

She stood over the sink. A hot pink apron slung over a gray tank top and a pair of white skinny jeans nicely complimented her figure. Her slender hips shook ever so slightly as she mixed the contents of something not visible. Her ponytail swished back and forth.

"I've been planning it. Actually, it was for tomorrow, but since your home a night early, I thought we might as well celebrate."

"Sounds good to me."

She stopped, came across the room, gave him a quick hug and kiss, and went back to work. The front of her kitchen apron read, "I cook. You clean." But he wasn't looking at her apron. The wiggle in her walk was driving him crazy after being away for two days.

"Where are the girls?"

"Over at the Smith's."

"What are they doing there?"

"I asked Anna to watch them for a while."

Anna Smith was their next-door-neighbor and Jason's mother. But the fact that Sarah had asked her to watch the kids told Isaac everything he needed to know. The special meal and the alone time, all of it was by design. Indeed, this was going to be a special evening, and he didn't see any reason to waste time. Being parents with two eight-year-olds in the house occasionally interfered with spontaneity in the sex life department. The running joke between them was to be half-lover, half-ninja. Stealth was the name of the game.

He moved across the floor, scooted up against her, and pressed in close. Both muscular forearms wrapped around her waist and brushed against the bottoms of her breasts. His chin nestled into the crook of her neck.

"Do you mind?" she said playfully. She continued to stir. "I'm trying to cook here."

"Absolutely not," he moaned into her ear. "I don't mind at all."

One of his hands slid up and caressed her bosom. A firm, round breast filled the cup of his palm. Her chest swayed so sweet, and he tightened up his grip. She wasn't wearing a bra, and the stirring motion drove him nuts.

"Easy, buster." Her voice was calm, not discouraging. "I didn't go to all this effort to let it get cold."

He moved his groping hand out to the tapering tip. "Did you say cold?"

She smiled, almost giggled, but didn't pull away. The encouragement wasn't lost, and he pressed his pelvis firmly against her bottom. His other hand went to her free breast. He now had two handfuls, the perfect balance between size, softness, and firmness. *Oh, these are the finest things I've ever felt.*

"Okay, okay," she said and wiggled loose from his grip. "That's enough."

"C'mon, baby," he coaxed and wrapped his arms back around her waist. He knew she wanted it, just not before dinner. But he was fully wound up and willing to work for it.

"I mean it. I worked hard to make all of this. If you wait, it will be worth it." She turned back to the sink.

Undeterred, he leaned back against her butt and allowed the shaking motion to work its magic. He filled his face with her hair.

It smelled like strawberries and cream, so soft. He was about to whisper something when his thoughts were abruptly cut off.

Living alone in DC for several years had prompted Sarah to take self-defense classes. She didn't know if she had ever become proficient enough to actually stop an assault, but the knowledge made her feel safer. She recalled a move to dissuade an attacker coming from behind and decided to try it out.

Slowly, her hips moved forward. Then, without warning, she thrust them backward, popping Isaac directly in the crotch. It wasn't hard enough to damage the family jewels, just enough to let him know she was serious.

He immediately let go, stepped back and groaned.

"I told you to knock it off."

"Dang, baby," he complained. "I'm burning up here. Do we have to wait? I promise it won't take long."

She turned around, mock distaste written across her face. "Yeah, that's exactly what I want to hear. 'It won't take long.' You started this, and now you have to live with it." She pointed a wooden spoon at the area below his belly button.

"I don't want to wait," he muttered under his breath and sat at the table.

She pouted her lips out. "Oh, poor thing. Did you get all worked up?"

"You think?"

"Serves you right. I told you I was trying to cook and didn't want the food to get cold." Again, she used the wooden spoon to point at his crotch. "Looks like more than the food is cooling off."

"Why you little—" He flew across the room. Isaac had her by a good ten inches and seventy pounds. He wrapped her up and began tickling unmercifully.

She screamed, writhing as she tried to beat him away with the spoon. "No! No!" she protested. She continued to squirm and scream. "Stop! Stop! Stop!"

Finally, after he was satisfied with his revenge, he quit and kissed her on the forehead. He spun her around to the sink and smacked her on that fine backside.

The mystery dish ended up being a bowl of made-from-scratch mashed potatoes. She was whipping the hell out of the spuds when he arrived, and the motion of her ocean started the whole ordeal.

The potatoes accompanied a pile of freshly steamed Maryland blue crabs, his favorite. The smell, taste, and task of cracking the shells truly did take him back in time. It was what they ate on their first real date.

The meal was incredible, as was the mess. But that was just part of seafood, especially crabs.

Sarah was prepared to bargain. "If you'll start cleaning, I'll get the girls' beds ready. I imagine they'll be asleep, and I told Anna we would come get them before midnight."

"That's not for two hours."

"I know." There was coyness in her words.

Isaac quickly scooted his chair back and got to his feet. "Deal!"

Sarah disappeared into the hallway, and he carried everything to the sink. An ex-military man, and therefore trained to the utmost in efficiency, he removed the trash can from the pantry and placed it directly beside himself. He scraped the trash in the can on his left, rinsed each dish in the sink, and put them into the dishwasher on his right. It wasn't just dishes he handled this way. It was most things. He didn't think anything of it, but their friends always got a kick out of watching.

He was turning and burning, laser-focused on the task. The faster he finished, the faster he could go back there with Ms. Plaything and have some fun. But in the middle of his rhythm, he stopped. He could feel a presence, an energy. Someone was there, watching him. He was sure of it. Every ounce of his body could feel it.

He slowly turned to his right, put a plate in the dishwasher, and used his peripheral vision to scan the room. His mind was not playing tricks. Someone *was* there.

Sarah's slender, delicately curved figure was nothing short of heart pounding. The deepness and clarity of her aqua green eyes never failed to make Isaac short of breath, especially when she put that sultry look to them. And could she ever do that. Her long, naturally wavy hair was let down with one side over the front of her shoulder. It looked like she had taken the time to style it. Her feet were bare. Toned, sun-kissed legs ran all the way up to a black thong. The front piece of satin fabric was so tiny, it barely served a purpose.

A black silk camisole covered her firm, slightly upturned breasts. The fabric was thin, especially in the cool air. Twins had not damaged her body. She had worked hard to get back in shape, but what had once been a knockout figure was actually improved. Childbearing seemed to have put more of the right stuff in the right places. Her silhouette could make a man's bones ache.

To complement the flowing curves, a flat stomach peeked from under her shirt, just above the hipbones. All her weight was on one leg. The other she had bent and pulled in close. Her arms were crossed, slightly higher than normal, elevating her ample cleavage.

Isaac was instantly back to when the whole evening began. "What got into you?"

She was close now, deeply invading his private space. She bent her knees and ran the satin thong up his lean, rigid thigh. Her pelvic bone pressed into his muscle as the fabric glided along oh so smoothly.

"The same thing that's been into me all night. Waiting for you to get home."

He dried his hands quickly on a dishtowel and placed them on her exposed cheeks.

"They're warm." She slid herself up and down his leg another time. His hands moved with her all the way. "It feels good."

"I would have taken it before dinner, but I do believe this was worth waiting for."

"I told you it would be."

He grabbed the string of her thong and pulled closer. His leg was between hers. She leaned in with her lower body and back with her upper. The silk-covered mounds pointed directly at his face. He explored the generously presented forms. They had been married for nine years, and it never got old.

"You want to come back here with me?"

"If I say yes, will I sound too easy?"

She shook her head and slowly took his hand. If she was yin, he was yang. She was so smooth and delicate, but not fragile. Isaac, on the contrary, was ruggedly refined. He was well groomed, but had an edge, a roughness to his dark features and olive skin. His eyes were black, fiery, and comforting all in the same.

She led him down the hallway to their bedroom. He watched as the slender string of satin slipped up and down between the cheeks of her firm derriere. Each musical swing of her hips fueled his overwhelming desire.

It was the beginning of a long, long night.

Chapter Four

At two o'clock on Saturday morning, Ricky Doors backed his white van into concealment, put it in park, and killed the engine. Kenneth and Joan Howard's empty carport was perfectly located, adjacent to the Snow's, assisting in his next kidnappings.

He was not aware of the Howard's taste for traveling. He was, however, aware that they had left on the rainy Friday morning with two large suitcases. People didn't pack that much if they were planning to return the same day. It made for the perfect staging ground.

He slipped into the cargo area and prepared for the task ahead. He had rehearsed the sequence of events in his mind to the point of memorization. Now it was down to action. He dampened a handkerchief with a concoction of homemade chloroform. The Internet was so useful. Information truly was a keystroke away, making the obscure ordinary. He sealed the elixir in a Ziploc and stashed it in his back pocket. Two eight-inch pieces of duct tape were torn from a roll and stuck to the thigh of his loosely fitting black jeans.

His long-sleeved T-shirt matched the pants. A pair of thin, leather gloves protected his fingerprints from being left behind, and a black, knitted ski mask disguised his face. Even with the mask, his peaceful-looking eyes appeared innocent. The watery blue irises shone tranquil, but really, they were swirling pools of greed and malevolence draining into the depths of a twisted mind. Since childhood, he was known as the boy with the baby blues. The camouflage served him well.

With everything set, he was ready to go. He had removed the lightbulbs from all dome fixtures inside the van. Nothing could blow his cover like a yellow glow in the middle of a black night. Light showed the truth. Blackness, on the other hand, cloaked and offered assistance to deception. And deception was not just a hobby for Ricky Doors. It was life.

He exited through the side sliding door and left it open. His arms were going to be full when he came back. *Two little ladies all to myself.* The thought was inspiring.

He made his way from under the carport and headed across the few feet of driveway until his boots hit plush, wet grass. From there, he continued forward, striding easily, nearing his targets with each swift step. It wasn't raining anymore, but he wished it was. Anything that provided background noise was good. He looked up and gauged the conditions. The sky was overcast and starless, but not a drop of water fell.

Josie and Caroline had two windows in their bedroom. One faced the side toward the Howards' home; the other looked over the backyard, detached garage, and forest beyond. For days he had hidden within the trees, watching every move, learning every schedule and regularity. And on Friday morning he received a lucky break.

It was early when the Howards stowed their suitcases in the trunk of their Lincoln Town Car and pulled out of the drive. Upon their departure, elated at the opportunity and happy to get out of the rain, Ricky left his observation post and went back to a little motel on the outskirts of town. He had to make final preparations.

He leaned against the cream-painted brick next to the side window he planned to use. It was closest to the van and offered the quickest escape. The back window provided more cover from the street, but the girls had a child-sized table and chairs set up just inside. He knew. He had looked through the window and seen it on more than one occasion. If he were to knock it over while entering or exiting, along with all the little plates, saucers, and teacups, the ruckus would ruin everything.

The cool night was damp and pleasant. Sarah let the girls sleep with their windows cracked to breathe in the fresh air. She and Isaac did the same. In the small community of only ten thousand people, many families slept with their doors unlocked and windows open. But Ricky had not noticed many families . . . only theirs.

A sharp pocketknife flayed the mesh screen and exposed a sliding frame. Ever so gently, he lifted the window. It slid up without squeaking, and he exhaled relief. Windows were tricky business. At any moment, they could grind on the tracks and make a terrible noise. The less he had to move it, the better. Still, it had to be open enough to snake through.

Silently, his heart pumping and perspiration building despite the mild temperature, he crawled inside. Arms went through first; his torso followed. He used his hands to hold the weight of his skinny body above the floor. One leg was pulled through and then the other. His whole body was inside, resting on all fours, completely frozen. On full alert, he allowed himself a smile.

Planning was difficult but safe. Actions, on the other hand, were incriminating. There were always a few moments in any operation when everything had to be put on the line. Now, not daring to move a muscle in the dark space of Josie and Caroline's bedroom, he was on that line.

He pulled a black aluminum flashlight from a belt holster and shined it around the room. *Piece of cake. Nice and quiet. And don't wake Sarah.*

On his feet, he went to Josie's bed. She was lying flat on her back, hair spread across a pink pillowcase. Her mind was at rest, a peaceful, serene look on her face. He slipped the dampened handkerchief from his pocket, deftly placing it over her nose and mouth for several breaths. Contented, he peeled a strip of duct tape off the thigh of his jeans. The adhesive silently relinquished its hold on the denim. He stuck it across Josie's mouth and pressed down. She was out cold from the chemical, but one could never be too careful. *Details. There was no substitute for the details.*

At Caroline's bed, he repeated the process. The second piece of duct tape peeled off his jeans as quietly as the first. Redundancy had thus far kept him off the radar and out of prison. He wasn't about to start taking shortcuts anytime soon.

He was growing more confident by the second, but before leaving, he had to check two things. For ten seconds, he pressed his ear against the wooden door leading into the hallway and listened. There was nothing but silence, a good sign. At the open window, he craned his neck outside and looked around. It wouldn't look good if Mr. Night Owl Neighbor was on a midnight stroll with Fido and caught him right in the middle of a kidnapping. But nothing was stirring, not even a dog walker.

He needed both hands to lower the girls out of the window so he clicked off the flashlight. The shaft slid into the belt holster, and he let go. Silence lasted for one more brief moment before a loud thud echoed through the room. Nothing could pull people out of a dead sleep quite like a sudden and unexpected noise. Ricky's confidence immediately turned to fear as he stood statue still. Getting caught would ruin everything. His mind raced. This was not part of the plan. It was bad.

The flashlight handle had not properly aligned with the holster pouch and fell straight to the hardwood floor. At almost a pound, it might as well have been a gunshot in the dead of night. Regardless of how much he wanted it, the tiny error could not be undone.

His senses, mainly hearing, were now in detection mode. As hard as he listened, there was not a squeak of the floor or shuffling of feet from down the hall. Time was of the essence, and he had to go now.

He plucked up the flashlight and nervously clicked it on. One mistake might be forgiven, but two, certainly, would not. He scanned around the room with particular emphasis on the floor. Stepping on a toy that squeaked or a talking dolly would add insult to injury. He put the flashlight to his belt and deliberately made sure it was properly seated. The perception of time was flying by while he seemed to be moving in slow motion.

Caroline's bed was nearest the window. He quickly ripped back the sheets and picked her up. Normally, this would have caused his urges to come into play. He liked to take his time, touch, caress, and savor every little thing, but urgency was more important.

His bony frame was surprisingly stout, and Caroline's weight was nothing. The muscles in his arms and legs were thin but wound like strands of cable.

At the window, he pushed her body outside. He eased it down, holding on by the wrists until her feet hit the grass. When he couldn't lean any further, he let go, and her body flopped onto the lawn.

Josie was next. He tossed back the covers and scooped her up. He made it to the window in four steps and looked down to Caroline's body. *Two minutes and we're out of here.*

He turned sideways, one arm under Josie's knees, the other behind her back, and maneuvered her feet out the window. A soft yet noticeable click stopped him cold.

Chapter Five

"What was that?" Sarah sat halfway up in bed and rested on her elbows.

Isaac rolled over and faced her. With eyes still closed, he said, "Nothing. The girls are probably building a tent. Go back to sleep."

"What was that loud thump?" she persisted.

Unlike most kids their age, Caroline and Josie preferred to undertake their construction projects in the middle of the night. They would go to bed in the evening and be found the next morning, asleep on the floor with sheets stretched between their mattresses. Time and again, Sarah tried to put an end to the late-night charades, but all attempts had thus far been futile.

"Sounded like they dropped a flashlight." He pulled the sheet over his shoulder.

"Don't you think you should go check?"

"I thought . . ." He yawned. "That's why you bought the flashlights in the first place. So we don't have to go in there anymore."

She let out a heavy breath. "I did."

Sarah was usually grumpy when first woken. But that was how it had always been. She was great at helping with homework in the evenings and putting the girls to bed. Isaac was the breakfast chef and morning motivator.

"It's their first night of summer. They're probably too excited to sleep. They'll be fine."

"Then I'll go see."

The words were out, but she didn't budge. She stayed perfectly still, knowing he would get up and do it. He was so well trained.

He pulled away the covers and slipped his pajama pants over boxer shorts. He didn't want his daughters to see him in his skivvies.

He scooted his bare feet across the smooth, wooden floor of their bedroom and opened the door. Caroline and Josie's room was at the exact opposite end of the hallway. The doorways faced each other. Just as his swung back, a beam of light swept across the threshold down the hall. A weak smile played across his lips. He was right. It was a flashlight, but he couldn't turn back now. Sarah would pester him until he checked it out.

A chill from an overhead vent cooled his shirtless torso. Goose bumps formed, puckering his skin. The thermostat was directly to his right, and he pressed a button to light the screen. *Sixty-eight degrees.*

There had been no more lights shining under the twin's door, and he guessed they were finished with their big top. He wanted to get back to bed. Sarah had worn his ass out with the sexy lingerie stunt.

Slowly, he eased down the hallway. He didn't want to frighten the girls by barging in. Instead, he pressed his ear against the door and listened. There was movement. The floor squeaked once, and he could feel weight shifting in the wood of the old house. Then silence.

His plan was to go in, help finish the wigwam, and tell the little Indians to pipe down. That would satisfy Momma, and he could get some sleep. But it probably wouldn't go that fast.

They usually wanted him to lie down on the floor and see their masterpiece. He rarely had the heart to say no. They were always so proud, their brilliant imaginations running wild.

He twisted the doorknob gently so it wouldn't scare them and stepped in. There was a fleeting moment of confusion before realization took hold. A faint glow from outside came through the open window. A man's silhouette was outlined in the space. He had no features or colors, only the dark, menacing figure of someone who shouldn't be there.

Chapter Six

T here was calm before the storm. Like fire and water, the inferno in Isaac's eyes reached across the room and lit the violent waves dwelling in Ricky's baby blues.

Not a split second lapsed between realization and reaction. There was never fear or hesitation, only a primal urge to protect his family. A threat cannot be posed if it does not exist, and he fully intended to eliminate the threat completely.

He raced to the window and noticed that both beds were empty. That was what training at speeds well beyond the sound barrier did. It honed an ability to think and work at the same time, in the blink of an eye, blending thoughts and actions into instinct.

The man in black must have known what was going to happen. He dropped the girl from his arms and simultaneously sprang in the opposite direction. The window was open, but not enough to accommodate the violent exit.

The child's body hit the floor, followed by a crashing of glass. Like it was nothing more than a soap bubble, the window shattered, taking half the frame with it. The masked man fell to the lawn in a storm of debris.

Isaac was in hot pursuit, about to jump out the mangled opening. But the body, which he recognized as Josie's, was in the way. *Where is Caroline?* He put his palms on the windowsill, broken glass lacerating them, and looked out. Not three feet away was the intruder. As quickly as he had flown through the window, he got to his feet and ran. And there, lying motionless on the rain-soaked lawn, Isaac found the answer to his question.

Shards of glass covered Caroline's body. The bastard had landed right on top of her, smashing jagged pieces between their bodies.

Isaac was prepared to hurl himself out the window and give chase. Backing down was not in his nature. He had killed before and knew he was capable of doing it again. And this time, he really wanted to. He was about to do so when the bedroom lights turned on.

"What's going on in here?" Sarah demanded. She stood in the doorway, wearing a pair of his boxers and a baggy shirt. "I heard glass—"

"Call nine one one!" he barked.

"Josie!" Her face was stricken with horror as she rushed forward. "What the hell happened?"

"Call the police. Now! Someone tried to kidnap them. She's fine," he said, meaning Josie.

In fact, he didn't know for certain that she was fine. He had, however, noticed the strip of tape over her mouth. Dead people didn't scream, so he assumed the best. She was alive but knocked out or drugged. There was no time to stop and see.

Sarah was frantic. Her eyes searched the room for Caroline. "Where's Caroline? Where is she?"

"She's out the window." He watched the masked man run away. "Now please, honey. Get the phone, call nine one one, and come back."

With his hands still on the windowsill, disregarding the little cuts and stabs, he vaulted through the open space. He landed over Caroline with one foot planted on either side of her. The blades of grass were soft. The fragments of glass, however, were not. They drove into his feet like nails, but he put the pain aside. His focus was too solitary to allow interference.

The bedroom lights lit the small patch of lawn where she laid, and he knelt. Outside of their island, the night consumed everything. He was about to run after the son of a bitch who had just disappeared behind the Howard's home, but he stopped short. Caroline's white sleeping shirt was stained crimson all around the neckline and chest. Had Sarah not flipped on the lights, he never would have seen it. She was hurt badly.

He heard Sarah's feet pound down the hall and into the kitchen. In a few seconds, she was giving the operator an address and explaining the situation.

In the back of his mind, Isaac thought, *I should go after him.* But he couldn't force himself to leave his little girl. *Even if I catch him, what good would it do if Caroline bleeds to death?* His world had shrunk to a tiny space in the great big mountain night. Outside of that, nothing mattered. Everything else was diminished. He could faintly hear Sarah asking Josie to wake up and the distant sound of an engine revving to life.

Caroline wore a pair of cotton pajama pants with different-colored hearts. The fabric was pulled up around her knees and exposed several scratches. A bead of blood ran down one calf. It was nothing compared to the stain growing around the collar of her shirt.

Moving someone who had just suffered a trauma injury was the last thing you were supposed to do. But Isaac had no choice. The way she was laying, he couldn't see where all the blood was coming from. He gingerly rolled her flat and almost vomited at what he saw.

The side of her neck was completely sliced open. Blood literally poured from the flesh. The flow was constant and unrelenting. The gruesomeness of the laceration was not the cause for Isaac's sickness. He had seen much worse. The gut-wrenching heave came from a sobering realization that she might be broken beyond repair. The cut was too deep, too wide, and in the wrong spot. A pool of red was already spread beneath her. The essence of her life slowly covered the green grass. He clenched his teeth and shut off emotions. His baby was dying. He had to do something.

Her shirt was thin. He ripped at it, trying not to jostle her body more than necessary. But nothing else was within reach. He rolled the T-shirt into a tube and firmly pressed against the cut. The harder he pushed, the better it stopped the bleeding. But if he held it too solid, her windpipe would collapse. The blood just kept coming, and he made up his mind. At the rate it was flowing, she would bleed to death faster than she would suffocate. So he pressed, willing the hole to close, willing her body to hang on, and praying it would work.

He still desperately wanted to exact some kind of violent justice. The men he killed before were terrorists, enemies of the United States of America, responsible for the deaths of countless women and children. But his past actions had been on orders, and he didn't have to look into their eyes as he rained fire on them from the cockpit of his jet. It was a job, a duty. This, however, his flesh-and-blood child dying in his arms, was personal. Maybe the man in black wasn't from a sect of radical Islam, but he was definitely a terrorist. Killing him would be a necessary pleasure. His teeth clenched in anger. Hoping for the opportunity, he prayed it would be a very up close and personal experience.

In the end, though, it didn't matter. He couldn't abandon Caroline for the sake of retribution. He had been there when she came into the world, all five pounds and two ounces of her. If these were her last moments on earth, he was going to be there for every second. She might be leaving, but he vowed not to let her do it alone. Determined, pleading with God to save his little girl, to take his own life in place of hers, he pulled his broken child into his lap and snuggled in closer. With his right hand, he tried to keep the life pressed into her. With the left, he peeled the duct tape away from her lips and softly stroked pieces of hair over her ears. There wasn't much hope, but wanting to do it while the spark of life was still in her body, he leaned down and kissed her forehead.

Just in case she could feel him, just in case she could hear him, he said, "I love you, Caroline. Daddy loves you so much. If you can, please hang on. Hang on, baby. Please. Daddy loves you. I'm so sorry. I'm so, so sorry. "

In the island of light, he rocked back and forth. No one else existed, just a brokenhearted father and his bleeding child.

The last thing he remembered before the ambulance and police showed up was the van. A white flash sped out of the Howard's driveway, and tires squealed onto the street. Its taillights disappeared around the bend.

Chapter Seven

Isaac rode in the front passenger seat of the ambulance. He buckled his seat belt as the siren blared to life and pierced the silent night. Red and blue flashes reflected off mailboxes, windows, and street signs as they raced down the serpentine street and toward the hospital.

A towel covered the floorboard beneath his feet. Cuts from glass, pieces now deeply embedded, dripped steadily. The pain had not been that bad initially, and he wanted to walk. But the EMTs knew better. Adrenaline was going to wear off, and there would soon be no shortage of discomfort. Concern for himself was not currently high on his list of priorities, but penetrated glass severing a tendon was a real possibility.

They were now on the main drag running through Ruidoso, and he used the straightaway to check on his family. All three of them were in the back, over his shoulder. Sarah sat along one wall with Josie lying across her lap. She was calm. A tear shimmered down her face in the fluorescent glow, and she used a hand to pat Caroline's leg. Josie was still asleep and seemed stable. Isaac couldn't help but wonder what she had been given and how long the effects would last.

Caroline's head was toward the front. He was only a couple feet away and could see a red handprint on the side of her face.

It was his hand and her blood. He had accidentally put it there while cradling her in the lawn. His hands, arms, and shirtless body were also covered, drenched from the wound. He willed himself not to feel sad. That would be to surrender, and he wasn't ready. He would never be ready. There was hope as long as Caroline had some fight left. He told himself that she was not past the point of no return, but deep down, it sure felt that way.

Two techs frantically worked a length of tubing. One began inserting it down Caroline's throat while the other hooked his end to a respiratory apparatus. They were having the same trouble Isaac had had. She was breathing, but to put enough pressure on the cut and stop the bleeding was to also close her windpipe. Blood covered the techs' surgical gloves. A huge wad of gauze, already several layers deep, was completely soaked from her jugular. The EMT applying pressure had to ease off momentarily so the tube could be shoved down her windpipe. When he did, a scarlet curtain spilled from beneath the gauze, onto the gurney, and to the floor.

"Shit!" He immediately placed both his hands back on the gauze. "We've got to trache her," he said. "I can't take enough pressure off to get the tube down."

The other tech in his navy blue pants and crisp, light blue shirt made no acknowledgment. He simply worked faster, trying to get air into the desperate little girl's lungs.

Isaac felt his composure slip a notch. He looked to Sarah. She was still sitting there, unwavering, with Josie in one arm and her other hand stroking Caroline's leg. He thought he could hear her whispering, but the siren drowned it out.

Finally, the ambulance turned into the ER parking lot. The generally calm atmosphere of the small Lincoln County emergency room was in an uproar. A team of the best medical professionals on duty had been advised of the situation and turned the facility into a hive of frenzied activity. All attention was focused on Caroline. Her body was in need of repair and replenishment.

They came to a screeching halt under the port-cochère. Two nurses awaited their arrival. They pulled out the gurney with one tech moving alongside and holding pressure on her neck. A hustling, chattering group of staff quickly went to work and passed through a set of automatic glass doors.

Josie was handled differently. With a strong pulse, regular breaths, and no immediate threat to her health, the second EMT took her from Sarah's lap and carried her in. This was not procedure, but neither was anything else. Time was of the essence, and staff was limited.

Sarah raced after the girls. First, she tried to follow Caroline. Then she tried to stay with Josie. A nurse, Allison McFarlane, an acquaintance of Sarah's and a high school classmate of Isaac's, was there to restrain her.

"Let me go." Sarah struggled against Allison. "Let me go. I have to go with them."

"Sarah." Allison wrapped both arms around her friend and pulled their bodies close together. "Sarah, listen to me. You can't go with them. Not right now."

"Please." She tried to shake loose, but the effort was halfhearted. Her voice was low now, barely above a whisper. "They need me." She watched them go and stopped fighting.

Allison put an arm around Sarah's shoulders and guided her to an empty, waiting room chair. "I'm going to get Isaac." She squatted in front of her. "Okay? Just stay here, and I'll be right back."

Sarah nodded, pulled her knees to her chest, and wrapped both arms around them. She tried to hold her physical self together because, on the inside, everything was busting loose.

The ambulance driver was helping Isaac out of his seat and into a wheelchair. Droplets of blood covered the floorboard towel. Fragments of broken glass protruded out the bottoms of his feet, and the pain was becoming very real. But the flesh and nerve damage on the soles of his feet was nothing compared to the helplessness and agony of defeat as he sat there, watching his family being carted into the hospital. *If I can't protect them or save them, what good am I?*

Allison wheeled him to the waiting room and parked him next to Sarah. She was still there alone, wrapped up like a frightened child.

"It's going to be okay." Isaac reached for her hands. Tears not yet spilled filled his eyes. "It's going to be okay."

"Isaac, I need to get you a room so we can start working on your feet." Allison tried to put a reassuring look on her face. These were not just people she was helping. They were her friends. "I'm going to see what's happening and be right back."

Time rolled on, but the progression went unnoticed. Stark walls, smooth, laminate floors, and windowless corridors blended into one, a world void of texture, color, or dimension. There was no past, no present, and no future . . . only the moment they were in and the wait that lasted an eternity. Allison had not come back. The night's explosion of events and suddenly induced fear that held them prisoner was hard to fathom, hard to perceive.

From the lobby, and without realizing it, they could hear the busy laboring and muffled chatter of people performing their duties. The sound filtered through the operating room doors. They were working to save Caroline. In the noise was an unconscious peace of mind, a knowledge that the battle still raged. Then, without warning, it ceased. The silence was cold and intense.

A parent should never have to endure certain things. To watch your child fight for their life while you sit on the sidelines, definitively unable to assist or protect them, is one. Another is to bury a child, the vessel of which a parent pours the spark of their very life into. Bone of their bone. Flesh of their flesh. To watch that vessel, a life that has been cared for so tenderly, shatter and spill all the energy it contains, only a parent can fathom the excruciating ache of a wound so penetrating.

A door hinge squeaked, and Isaac saw a man he knew coming toward them. Allison was at his side. Dr. Pearson, a longtime resident of the Ruidoso area, had treated many of Isaac's ailments and injuries as a child. He was typically a jolly man, fulfilled to assist in the health of a community. But as he neared them, all jovial appearances were absent. His head was bent. His face, somber.

"Sarah," he said. "Isaac. There's good news and bad news. Josie is fine. She's still sleeping but fine. We're running some tests right now. Something has her knocked out, but she'll come around."

The doctor took another breath and made a sideways glance at Allison, wishing he didn't have to say any more.

"Josie," he went on, "needs both of you." His eyes moistened. He had children and grandchildren of his own. No matter how many times he had practiced this scenario over the years, the words were impossible to master. "We did . . . everything we could. Caroline lost too much blood."

He stared down into the hopeful faces of a family. Isaac sat motionless. Sarah shook her head back and forth, tucking her lips into her mouth in an effort to hold on.

He hated himself, but he had to say it. "We couldn't save her."

Chapter Eight

The mood inside the van was anything but pleasant. Ricky sat in the driver's seat, safely concealed behind his garage door. Both hands clasped the black plastic steering wheel. He shook it back and forth in rage. His body jerked with force. A pair of red ears matched his mood.

How did it happen? How did I fail? The answer was simple, and he knew it. When putting the flashlight back in the holster, he had been careless. The motion was so simple, so repetitive, that he didn't focus on it, and the price for neglect was steep.

He struck the steering wheel with the palm of his hand. "It's a wonder I didn't wake up the whole damn neighborhood!"

Up until that point, during the nine-hour drive home, he had relentlessly beaten himself up over the mistake. But the more distance he put between himself and Ruidoso, the more a larger question loomed. The oversight had actually been the first mistake.

"Why the hell was Isaac there? Why was he there?" He went another round with the steering wheel. "He was supposed to be on duty."

For over two weeks, he watched, learned, and schemed, trying to find a reasonable way to disappear with the twins. It was difficult. Other than school, there was never a time when they were alone. But there was another possibility.

Isaac always left for work on Wednesday morning and returned Saturday night. Breaking and entering was definitely not something Ricky usually considered, but the notion was far less scary knowing the only adult in the house would be Sarah. He felt confident that, should things go awry, he could easily dominate her.

The plan was workable, minus one major component. A place to park was necessary. The street was close enough but too conspicuous. The jogging trail he used as a spy corridor was another option, but the parking lot was three-quarters of a mile through the woods. Even if he could manage to carry Josie and Caroline that far, too much time would pass. A quick escape was nonnegotiable.

Desperate for options, a break came his way. On Friday morning, during surveillance, Kenneth and Joan Howard drove from their house with suitcases loaded in their car's trunk. The empty carport was perfect. Coupled with Isaac's work schedule, Ricky was elated. Not only did he have a place to park, he could get out of the rain for the remainder of the day, rest, and make plans for the long night ahead.

Now, sitting in his garage with only the overhead light to see by, realization hit like a lightning bolt. *Isaac came home early because it was raining. Of course. Why would he patrol for fires in the rain?*

It all made perfect sense. He had checked numerous times that the twins kept their windows cracked. The Howards were gone, at least for one night. But Isaac came home early, and Ricky should have known it. Dropping the flashlight was his second mistake. Leaving, not staying to observe the house for the rest of the day, was the first. He should have been there to see Isaac come home.

The garage door light timed out and saturated the space in blackness. He tried to calm himself. Anger and frustration weren't going to help get the twins. Cool, collected, well-thought-out planning was the only means to have his day with Caroline and Josie. No matter what, to let this be the end was not acceptable. He was an addict, and they were his heroin. No cost was too great for the high.

Curious beyond all measure, he desperately wanted to know how things had played out after the pandemonium. *Am I in danger? How are the girls? I wonder what they're doing right now. I can't wait to see them again, every last little peachy inch.*

Chapter Nine

A t dawn on Tuesday morning, the eastern sky blazed to life. Soon, darkness was burned away. It was the day of the funeral, and Isaac wished for his own sun to rise, a desperate yearning to have the inescapable shadow washed away.

He began the day much as he had spent the night, awake but barely present. Daggers to the heart, the weight of a thousand tons upon his shoulders, were unrelenting. No drug, drink, words of encouragement, or prayer could take it away. No distraction was powerful enough to occupy his one-track mind. Caroline was dead. Period.

No matter how many well-wishers arrived at their quaint residence with casserole dishes, hams, desserts, and drinks, kind as they were, or how many heartfelt letters came tucked into elaborate flower arrangements, reality was reality.

The weekend had been a blur of activity. Teams of forensic experts, the FBI, state police, and local cops invaded the once-peaceful house on Valley View Lane. Yellow tape marked everything off. Only people in uniform or cheap suits with badges were allowed through.

News crews and their vans lined the curb. Caroline and Josie's recent exposure over the Jason Smith incident had made them local celebrities. Now a tragic story replaced the happy one, and reporters were drawn like buzzards to a rancid carcass. They hovered close by, ready and waiting for an opportunity to question anyone who might know about the attempted abduction and murder. They didn't care or bother to confirm whether the information was accurate or not before regurgitating it into a microphone and flooding the airwaves.

Time, for Isaac and Sarah, became a flurried balance between moments of anguish, sessions of questions by authorities, and making funeral arrangements.

In their quiet kitchen, a cyclone of efforts behind them, coffee was drank but not enjoyed. Isaac's parents, Tom and Helen, were there, sitting with their steaming mugs of black liquid. They had driven from Taos to Ruidoso during the dark hours of the tragic Saturday morning. Now, back in the same house they had raised their only son in, they again played a role of support, striving to make the best of a situation that felt simply unmanageable.

The natural light of day filtered in, and everyone gathered around the sturdy, wooden table. A meaningful discussion was taking place regarding the investigation. They all found that time passed more graciously with a purposeful task.

Charlie was due to arrive any minute. The chief of police had plenty of other duties, but all were put second to his friends' crisis. Personal ties or not, crimes like this were next to nonexistent in Ruidoso. The outrageous events were not just a priority. They *were* the priority.

The front door latch opened and caught everyone's attention. Like usual, Charlie showed himself in. This time, though, he did not remove his gun belt and get comfortable. He was on duty. The belt stayed where it was.

He moved through the antiquishly modern living room and into the kitchen where everyone was seated. The sixty-year-old hardwood floors creaked beneath his weight and boots. Tom stood to shake his hand, and Helen gave the man, whom she had loved since his childhood, a tight hug. He was not their son, but he was as good as.

"Good morning, Officer," Helen said with pride. Recognizing his accomplishments was her way of doting. She smoothly ran the inside of her hand along Charlie's baby-faced, blushing cheek.

"Hey." He loved the motherly affection, but he was never sure how to handle it. His own had never bestowed one morsel of positive reinforcement. He backed away and sat in an empty chair.

"What's the latest?" asked Tom. He poured a coffee, set it down in front of Charlie, stepped back, and leaned against the counter. "Any solid leads?"

"Same things but more information," he said matter-of-factly. "Whoever this guy is, he's real careful. Fingerprints would have been the easiest to trace, but gloves prevented that. Other than Isaac, there are no eyewitnesses, and no one around seems to have noticed anything out of the norm."

All eyes were intent on Charlie, hanging on every word he said.

"There hasn't been anything like this going on here, and it would appear completely random. However, abductions rarely, if ever, are." He held Sarah's expressionless stare and noticed Isaac's forced attention. "That's why we've had you go over everything again and again." He rubbed his face. The first sign of dark circles were showing up under his puppy dog eyes. "Whoever he is, he knew the Howards were gone and, more than likely, the bedroom windows were unlocked."

"He cased the joint?" Tom asked.

"It's a good bet. His plan was good enough that if he hadn't made any noise—"

Isaac was paying attention, but his mind kept flashing back. *What if I hadn't gone to check on them? What if Sarah hadn't asked me to go?* From there, the imagination became a dead sea of harrowing possibilities. It was hard to fathom that their situation could be any worse, but it could. Caroline and Josie could both be gone right now, in the hands of someone who would surely kill them but only after having his way. The thought made bile rise to the back of Isaac's mouth every time it flashed through.

Sarah didn't blame anyone, especially her husband, for what had happened. She simply felt drained of feeling, half alive, just wishing her little girl was back.

Over the past three days, each had given his or her story a dozen or more times. The state detectives gave the first formal questioning; the FBI followed. Charlie and his police force had several sit-down meetings, albeit much less rigid than the others. The Ruidoso cops were more familiar with the town and used their knowledge to try to find something out of place. The state boys worked forensics, along with the FBI, and the FBI put together a profile based on specifics of the case. Information was king, and everyone scurried to collect it.

"As of right now," Charlie explained, "the best leads we have are the description of the van, a DNA sample, and an FBI profile."

"That's great." Helen sounded encouraged.

"Well, here's where we stand." He shifted in the chair. "The FBI ran down the tread pattern left on the Howard's driveway. Dunlop makes the tires in question, and the van, judging by the wheelbase, is probably a Ford. That, coupled with Isaac's account, gives a pretty firm picture of the vehicle we're looking for. The flip side is, in New Mexico alone, there could be anywhere from several hundred to over a thousand white Ford vans. And without plates, we don't even know if the van is from in state."

"But the DNA," Tom reminded. "That's dynamite, right? I mean, isn't that what they call undisputable evidence?"

Charlie wanted to tread lightly. The DNA was a big deal, but having a sample and nailing the guy were two different animals.

"DNA is as ironclad as it gets with a crime scene," he assured. "The lab sent back results from all the pieces of busted glass. They found a sample of skin on one, large enough to test. It's not Isaac's or Caroline's."

"It's his?" Helen asked.

"Almost certainly. However, it's not registered in any of the databases, so it doesn't give us an identity."

Isaac and Sarah remained placid, but Tom and Helen were alert and in tune. Their faces sank when they heard that the sample didn't belong to any known person.

"Don't let that discourage you though. See, now we have a DNA profile to match against any future suspects."

If Charlie knew anything, it was that one stand-alone piece of evidence rarely solved a crime. An accumulation of information solved them. A puzzle of small, carefully put together pieces was how cases typically took shape. One factor, like the DNA, might become the deciding item, but only because all the others led to a probable person. Clues like descriptions of vehicles and tire patterns were just as important.

Tom wanted more. "You said the FBI was working on a profile. What's that looking like?"

"Yes. By incorporating all the specifics, they can build a pretty accurate description of who they're looking for. According to them, the person in question is obviously a male and Caucasian. He's between the age of thirty to forty-five and single. He's physically fit, probably a bit of a recluse with an above-average IQ."

The FBI had other things in their profile, but Charlie wasn't going to share those, at least not at the moment. It didn't make a pretty picture and would do nothing to help ease their minds.

He tried to go on, but there wasn't anything else of substance to mention. Silence dominated the room. Part family, part investigator, and part friend was not a position easily filled. He didn't know whether to stay and visit or leave them in privacy.

Helen sensed his discomfort and wanted to ease the tension. If there was one thing she knew, it was appetites. And Charlie had one of the biggest she had ever seen, even from the time he was a little boy. The way to his heart truly was through his stomach.

"Charlie." She reached across the table and set her hand on his. "We have more food than we can possibly eat. If someone doesn't take it, it's going to go bad. I would feel better if you'd have some. You look like you could use it." She knew just how to phrase it.

Charlie, always a little embarrassed about his weight, had a habit of turning down food in front of others. On the other hand, he also had a soft spot for people's feelings, especially Helen's. The woman had been everything to him that his real mother wasn't. If he thought eating would lift her spirits, he wasn't about to say no.

"Well." He leaned back in his chair. Both hands ran over his belly and down to his belt. A tan uniform shirt was pulled tight against his stomach. The utility belt rode low beneath the paunch. "I haven't had breakfast."

"Good. I'm also going to send some with you. I know the boys down at the station won't complain about it."

Charlie looked to Sarah to make sure the gesture wasn't too much. She nodded and gave a halfhearted, tight-lipped smile, encouraging him to take it.

He left with two sacks of food. There was still an endless pile of to-dos before the afternoon. He was sitting as a member of the family at Caroline's funeral and couldn't be late. Once more, the struggle between friend and professional nagged. But there was nothing to do except get in the cruiser, go slog out more cop work, and try to find the enigma they were all chasing.

Chapter Ten

The time was marked when a black, funeral home Suburban parked out front. Together and strong for the moment, Isaac stepped onto the spacious front porch with Sarah and Josie. Helen and Tom came last. Like one being, there was a unified inhaling and exhaling of breath. The march down the sidewalk was the start of an unfortunate ritual. A life had to be remembered and told good-bye forever.

Isaac sat in the middle seat with Sarah and Josie on either side of him. He held both their hands. They were going to get through this together. There was no other way of passage. His parents were in the third seat, silent and brokenhearted over more than Caroline. They felt dejected at seeing their son mourn with his family.

They rode to the mountainside cemetery without a word. It had rained more over the weekend, and the grass was soggy. Across the meadow, headstones, old and new, all grayed by weather, dotted the setting.

Chairs for the family were neatly lined up in front of Caroline's child-sized, open casket. The girls were sandwiched in the middle. A halo of protection and strength surrounded them. On the far end, next to Tom, Charlie took a seat. Excluding him, the five of them were the only surviving family.

Friends, teachers, acquaintances, little girls in dresses, and little boys in suits were spread around in a semicircle to hear the preacher deliver the final words of compassion to a daughter, a sister, a granddaughter, and a friend too short-lived. All was quiet and calm as her final blessings were bestowed.

Without any instruments, voices young and old offered a song to a precious little girl.

> *Amazing grace, how sweet the sound*
> *That saved a wretch like me*
> *I once was lost, but now am found*
> *Was blind, but now I see*

Those sweet words echoed across the cemetery and down the valley. The mountains stood tall, and the breeze rustled in the aspens. Caroline's spirit could almost be felt as the air spiraled and moved on to places unknown. Only her body remained. Her eyes were closed, and she was wearing her favorite dress. A lacy scarf covered the fatal wound. A ribbon and pendant hung loosely around her neck. If she could have spoken, she would have told them to not be sad. She was in a better place and patiently waiting to see them again.

"No one can hurt me now."

When it was time, Sarah leaned over, kissed her forehead, and let quivering lips linger. She would gladly have died a thousand painful deaths to trade places. Isaac pressed his lips to the same place. He felt sadness and anger but mostly failure. It was his job to protect her, and he had failed. There was no second chance. The stakes were life and death. A do-over did not exist. Tears dripped onto Caroline's face from the tragic reality. He wanted to pull her from the casket, carry her home, and never let go.

He felt a small hand squeeze his fingers. Josie was on her tiptoes, trying to get a better look at her sister.

"Do you want to say something to her?" His eyes spilled tears, but his voice was clear.

She nodded, and he set a folding chair next to the elevated casket. She wasn't crying as he lifted her to stand in the seat. The look on her face was peaceful, at ease with the world. She looked down on her twin sister.

"What do I tell her, Daddy?"

His Adam's apple bobbed, and he swallowed the lump. "Well, I guess you can tell her anything you want. You're sisters."

Her hand slipped out and wrapped around Caroline's. She slid her thumb over the cool skin. "She's cold."

He tried but couldn't hold back. It was too much. Even in front of Josie, he had no strength left. She had just broken his wall, and the tears came rolling. He shook with sobs, crying the helpless cry of a man out of options. Sarah was there, and he drew into her. This was his time, and he needed to hear it would be okay.

Josie held on to Caroline's hand. It was just the two of them. The way they had begun. Out of the blue, she smiled.

"You look pretty, sissy. Grandma says Jesus will take good care of you." She went on her tiptoes and did something she and Caroline had always done. "I love you," she said, and kissed her sister on the lips.

Josie stepped down from the chair and looked at the sad faces of all the grownups. "It's time to go." With that, she walked toward the Suburban.

Somehow, it was the perfect thing to say. They couldn't stay there forever. It was time to go.

Chapter Eleven

Shiny blonde hair reflected yellow rays of light drifting through the window. Josie sat in her bedroom. A child-sized table and teacups were placed before her.

Isaac came to the doorway and stopped. He observed as she poured make-believe tea into two cups, visiting with a presence only she saw. She had been caught several times over the last few days talking into thin air, like someone was there with her. She spoke to the ghost no differently than a real person.

Everyone took comfort in how well she was adjusting. After all, she was closest to Caroline. They were blood, confidants. They had begun as one egg, sharing the womb. Where two had always been, there was now only one.

To the average parent, the one-sided conversations would not have caused alarm. Isaac, however, was in a heightened state of concern. He feared it might be Caroline she was speaking with, and if so, that Josie was in denial about her sister's permanent absence. Death could be difficult to understand at eight years old. Neither of the girls had ever lost a loved one. Not even a family pet had passed away. And Isaac thought they should talk.

He leaned against the doorway. "Hey, you have room for one more?"

She was immersed in her serving. "Sure."

The delicately carved chair set was too fragile for his grown body. Instead, he sat on a stool used to retrieve things from the closet shelves.

"Is this cup for me?" He gestured toward the second place setting.

"No, that's my friend's." She never looked up. Her hands fetched additional dishes from a stack. She placed a new cup and saucer in front of him. "Here you go, Daddy. These are yours."

"Thank you. Who's your friend?"

She paused in thought.

* * *

His mother had warned him not to push. "She's just a normal little girl, having normal playtime and pretending someone is there. It's no fun to have tea parties alone." She looked deeply into her grown son's eyes, really trying to get into his thoughts. "Even if," she went on, "Josie's pretending Caroline *is* there, what does it matter? It's only been a few days, and it's probably not even real to her yet."

He was apprehensive to think that Josie imagining her sister was there could be healthy on any level.

Helen made her point. "Is it real to you? Is it honestly? You're a grown man who understands death perfectly. She's eight. Give it time."

* * *

Josie met his eyes for a moment and then resumed her work. "Umm, she doesn't really have a name. We're just having tea." It didn't seem to bother her one bit that she made conversation with someone utterly fake.

"Oh, I see." He took a sip of the imaginary liquid. "Mmm, mmm, mmm. This is delicious. May I have some more?" He acted enthusiastic and closed his eyes in a gesture of the savory blend. His mother was right.

"Yes," she replied politely. She looked across the table to the place setting her imaginary companion occupied. "Would you like some more, too?" There was a pause. "Okay. Do you want sugar?"

Isaac sat back and drank the second cup slowly. *Maybe this is good. If she can't use her imagination to play, what else is there? She's a smart girl and will eventually put the pieces together. One day, it will make sense.*

He slurped the last drop and stood up from the table. "Thank you, sweetheart. That was fun."

"You're welcome." Her voice was calm and sweet, that of an angel. She placed the dirty dishes in a separate pile from the clean ones and resumed her play.

He didn't know how he would ever explain the events that transpired that one terrible night. *How does a father tell his child that someone intends them perverse harm? How can I articulate that Caroline's death was not the worst-case scenario?* He wanted Josie to sleep peacefully through the nights, not scared that someone was after her. She would find out eventually. That was certain. But doing it the right way—a way that wouldn't haunt her dreams—was the hard part. But the truth was, she had every right to be afraid.

Chapter Twelve

On the outskirts of Hiawatha, Kansas, Ricky waited anxiously in his cargo van. His next move was only minutes away.

Three weeks had crawled by since his failed attempt to abduct Caroline and Josie. Under normal circumstances, he would not have chosen another victim so quickly. He preferred to savor his prize, reliving the sexual humiliation and pain he put her through. Video footage, horrendously graphic pictures, and memorized physical sensations were all exceedingly erotic. He typically spent weeks wallowing in the success. The selection of a new target was sacred. His prize couldn't just be anybody. He wanted someone who was somebody.

The attempt in Ruidoso and news of Caroline's death drove him mad. He needed stimulation and hadn't gotten it. His ravenous appetite had brought him to the precipice of gratification, only to have the bottom fall out at the last second. Now, angry with himself and his pent-up desires, he was thirsty. He needed a quickie, someone to soothe the burn, absorb his toxic current, and quench the thirst.

Well-manicured, spindly fingers stroked the soft fur of his new puppy. *Kansas.* He had decided to name the seven-week-old golden retriever mix in honor of the locale. *You'll do just perfectly.*

After several days of observation, he realized the need for a lure. Nothing came to mind until he saw a sign. "Free Puppies." He couldn't resist. It was perfect, and the little guy was so cute.

It was time to go over the plan. As was his custom, he had already been through it more than he could remember. He even did a dry run, but repetition never hurt. *Her mom drops her off from Little Dribbler practice at five thirty. She gets a snack and plays in the backyard while the babysitter sits at the computer. As soon as they're both in place, I'll go.*

He fired the engine and drove out of the Walmart parking lot. The white van was ordinary, common with an aluminum extension ladder tied to the top. He was just another handyman, plumber, painter, or electrician.

He went to the babysitter's street and parked a few houses down. *Any minute now. Any minute.* Right on cue, a tan Chevy Tahoe came around the corner and pulled into the driveway. Becky Davis left the engine running and walked her seven-year-old daughter, Bailey, to the front door.

From the van, he could only watch. It didn't matter. The routine was always the same. Bailey had her bag and went inside. Casey, the high school-aged babysitter, listened to a few words of instruction and nodded in agreement. A ponytail pulled high on her head bobbed up and down. Becky turned on her heels, walked back to the Tahoe, and drove away. She wouldn't return from the country club until ten o'clock.

"Perfect," he said aloud. Every detail was just as he knew it would be.

A half hour later, little Bailey appeared inside the chain-link fence of the backyard and began shooting hoops. She bounced around, dribbled, and juked to improve her skills. Waves of flaxen hair followed every motion, propelled by a tan body from afternoons at the city pool. A low basketball goal hung over a cement slab. She went back there every time and religiously played while Casey surfed the Net or clicked on her cell phone.

He drove into the alley behind the row of houses. One backyard down from where Bailey was, a telephone pole rose out of the ground next to a junction box. He stopped directly beside the electrical equipment, got out, and opened both backdoors. He set a tool belt full of screwdrivers, pliers, and wrenches on the bumper. The setup had to look real, just in case.

The sun was high, hot, and stifling. Shade from ancient oaks and maples smothered the alley and the backyards. They towered above the half-century houses. He thought of the old TV series, *Leave It to Beaver*. People here felt such security. It was a weakness. And like liquid over glass, he moved forward without a ripple.

A blue shirt complete with fake nametag, navy pants, and work boots made up his disguise. A white hard hat perched on his noggin topped it off. Only a few paces were between him and the doorway to destiny. He cradled the pup, Kansas, in his arms. It was time for the fur ball to earn his keep.

The neighborhood yards backed up to the alley. Shrubs planted along the inside of their fence lines gave residents privacy. A gate opened from each yard to access the trash dumpsters. They were the only spaces not blocked by hedges.

Hidden behind the bushes, right next to the gate entrance, he extracted a bottle of cayenne pepper and unscrewed the lid. He poured it onto Kansas's nose.

The puppy whimpered from the burn, not sure what it was. He licked it and yelped when the pain didn't go away. He squirmed and pawed at his face, trying to get rid of the unpleasant scorch. But the harder he fought, the worse it hurt. The liquid pepper spread to his eyes, and he cried over and over.

Ricky set him down outside the barrier and directly in Bailey's line of sight. Like any typical seven-year-old, she immediately noticed the racket and ran to help. Her intention was to open the latch, coddle the tiny butterball, and take it to see Casey. She wanted nothing more than to bestow innocent love on the unfortunate little beast. But when she opened the gate, her hands never made it.

He jerked Bailey into the alley and behind the row of shrubs. Her back was tucked against his belly, a ropy arm holding her still. He quickly placed a dampened handkerchief over her face, holding it tightly to keep her from screaming. She went limp, and he swung her around his shoulders and onto his back. He leaned forward to keep her from flopping back, and curled both of his arms beneath her thighs. To the casual observer, it would look as though she were getting a piggyback ride. At the van, he dumped her into the open cargo doors, calmly closed them, and walked around to the front. So far, all was quiet.

As he drove to the end of the alley, turned onto the street, and headed out of town, there was absolutely no visual reason for suspicion. It was nothing but a uniformed man driving a service vehicle with Kansas plates. They didn't match the inspection sticker, but no one ever looked that closely. As soon as he crossed into Missouri, he would drop them into the first river, put on his Colorado plates, and keep cruising. And above all else, every speed limit sign was strictly adhered to.

"Shit!" he blurted. He pulled his foot off the accelerator to think. "Oh, shit, shit, shit."

He didn't know what scared him worse—the fact that his mind was slipping enough to leave Kansas the puppy behind, or the fact that the dog was evidence. Messy criminals were incarcerated criminals. That was just how it worked.

The flashlight drop in Ruidoso and now this. It's sloppy. He coasted along the road for a second longer, and contemplated the potential fallout. *Is there any way they can track the pup back to me?*

The dog was from a lady giving them away in a convenience store parking lot. No names were exchanged. There were no registration papers for the mutt and no transactions of any kind. Pretty sure that Kansas wouldn't be useful to the police, he relaxed. It couldn't be taken back, and didn't seem devastating to his freedom anyways. He stepped on the gas.

In just a few hours, his efforts were finally going to pay off, and Bailey's waking nightmare would begin.

Chapter Thirteen

Just before midnight, Ricky pulled into a truck stop outside of Sioux Center, Iowa. He wasn't tired, and he didn't need a bathroom break. The location was the stage for his next crime.

He liked to be out of the public eye, as far from scrutiny as possible, but a few years back, he discovered how much privacy a truck stop could provide. Eighteen-wheelers and other road-weary travelers used the large lots to park, rest, and be undisturbed. Many Americans have jobs that keep them on the road for days at a time, and sleeping in their vehicles is cheaper than renting a motel room. Those seeking repose will leave their engines running, headlights off, and parking lights on. It signals that the vehicle is occupied and desires privacy. It's an unspoken code between travelers of America's roadways.

He found a suitable slot, turned on the parking lights, and locked the doors. Behind the two front bucket seats, he had constructed a wall to separate the cab from the cargo area. It was covered in gray carpet to match the interior and had a door in the middle. He bent low, stepped through, and latched it shut.

Bailey was lying on a small bed designed to fold up against the wall. She huddled to the back, quivering from fear at his entrance. He had made a pit stop earlier to gag her, and he bound her hands and feet. Since waking in the dark, groggy from the chloroform, she tried to scream for help, but all that came out were muted sobs. The only sensation she could remember was road vibration. Tears ran down both flushed cheeks as she looked at the man before her.

He let the innocent, frightened image of Bailey burn into his eyes as he pulled her toward him. She tried to fight, but fear and an aching head robbed her muscles of strength. He secured a length of rope to the coils on her wrists. The opposite end was fed through a floor ring. He pulled it snug with Bailey's hands now above her head and tied it off. Her feet were separated and bound to floor rings below each bottom corner of the bed. Several loops were snaked around each ankle and stretched tightly. He didn't want her to have any wiggle room. The placement of the rings was not coincidence. He installed them himself, the exact arrangement allowing him to hold his company in ideal positions.

From above, her body was in the shape of an upside down Y. Her legs were spread with both arms pulled straight back. For what he wanted, the position was most accommodating. There was no regard for discomfort. The rough fibers cruelly bit her skin.

Pain and terror combined, Bailey's sobs grew stronger, and her body shook. But little to no sound emanated from the desperate screams. The large diameter rope used for the gag was too thick and cut into the corners of her mouth. She had to breathe through her stuffy nose.

"Take it easy, honey," he said. "It's no use." He smiled wickedly and kept working.

This was when things were hardest. Alone in the presence of his lover, he was ready for action. He had lost control of himself once before and regretted it. He hadn't taken the proper time to set things up. When it was over, there was no video to watch, pictures to review, or words to read on lonely days.

He went to too much effort in kidnapping Bailey and wasn't about to make the same mistake again. He had to do things right the first time. The camcorder needed to be set up, the angle checked, and the tape rolling. A digital camera was put in place. He adjusted the timer to snap a photo every few seconds. Documentation was most precious. It enabled him to relive each event whenever and however many times he wanted. It was so much better than memory.

He set up the electronics at the foot of the bed and along the side. Each had its purpose. It was imperative that Bailey experience the moment as acutely as he was. The more animated her reactions, the better the thrill.

He jotted down a few words in his journal. The page was titled "Bailey Davis" and scrawled with numerous notes from the reconnaissance phase. He finished scribbling, checked the camera equipment once more, and shifted gears. Finally, after more than a month of failed plans, letdown, searching, and making new plans, he was going to have his pound of flesh.

Chapter Fourteen

Bailey's eyes were closed. She tried to block everything out, but nothing traumatic enough had happened yet to receive any disassociation from her brain. She was completely in the present.

The sound of a zipper caught her attention, and she opened her eyes. The man was hunched over with his pants undone. She kept a close watch. Something bad was about to happen, but she didn't know what. To want someone else's body for pleasure was foreign, impossible to comprehend.

"Ah, now you decide to look?" Ricky gazed down, his piercing eyes unblinking. "Just lay still, and I'll do all the work." He said each word with a creepy smile.

His shirt fell to the ground. Someone might have called him scrawny, but there was too much muscle definition for that. His physique resembled a person on the edge of anorexia with a protein shake addiction.

"What do you think? Hmmm? You like it, don't you?"

She looked away. It was her last defense. There was no way to run and hide, but she could deprive him the pleasure of flattery. Too scared to shut her eyes, the ceiling became the object of her focus. It was covered in the kind of foam her mom put under the sheets to make the bed soft. It felt like being inside an egg carton.

He didn't like that she looked away. Someone watching was someone interested. Interest was approval, attention, and validation. *Look at me*, his heart cried. *Look at me.*

He was completely naked. Every inch of him was slick. A cleanly cut, if not slightly longer than normal, head of sandy brown hair was the only place not shaved or waxed. He climbed on the bed and stuffed a pillow under her head, propping it as high as possible. It was to keep her faced forward. She cringed at the contact, an invasion of her personal space.

"There now."

He raised himself up to where his pelvis was only a foot from her watery eyes. The dream that things would ever be consensual was given up long ago. People who managed to pull that amount of trust from their victims had to work at it over a period of time. A next-door neighbor, a teacher, or a friend's brother were good examples. They were also the same people who got caught. Sooner or later, someone found out. That lifestyle did not appeal to him. He didn't care for lasting relationships, and he didn't care to go easy. He wanted to do what he wanted when he wanted and not worry about some little shit tattling.

The van was warm inside. He had the air on, but anticipation heated his body. It was glossy, slick to the touch. The moment was huge, built in his mind for days. He could not rush it. A fine wine is supposed to be savored, relished, and consumed in small, conscientious sips.

Both his hands settled on top of her clothes and slowly massaged. His skin constricted into goose bumps at the first touch. The euphoria was always greatest at commencement, slowly leaking endorphins into his system of sins.

Bailey couldn't speak, so she pled with her eyes. The orbs beckoned for mercy. The softest most innocent eyes there ever were, pure virtue muddied by scum. She couldn't understand why she deserved it.

He lifted the bottom of her shirt and rested his clammy hand on her warm tummy. It palpated rapidly, up and down with each breath. The skin-to-skin contact sent another rush of thrills through him. It was what he felt, loved, and craved enough to steal a child. One was too many, and a thousand was never enough. His thin fingers searched, seeking more. Ever since he was young, more was the answer.

Bailey tensed as he pulled a long, stainless steel hunting knife from a scabbard.

"Easy. I'm not going to hurt you. It's just to help."

He slid the knife under the hem of her jeans and cut upwards. The leg split from cuff to waistband. Stroke after razor-sharp stroke produced a little girl in nothing but cotton underwear.

"Be very, very still now."

Her stricken look was priceless. The knife was for intimidation and practicality. He could strip a victim bare while they remained tied. And that was exactly what he did.

One corner of his mouth pulled into a grin, cheek twitching. "Do you like red?"

There was no answer. She was too scared, embarrassed.

"Do you like red?" he asked again softly.

She nodded, afraid not to. The next thing she felt was beyond pain. She arched her back in shock and sucked in.

"Daddy!" she called. "Daddy! Daddy!"

She tried to scream and scream and scream. But her words were prisoners. She sputtered, gagging in an effort to breathe through her nose.

Tied and stretched, torn and raped, the sacredness of her vessel was gone. But her soul remained untouched and clean, a place even Ricky could never tarnish.

Chapter Fifteen

O n a stool, back against the dividing wall of the van, Ricky
wiped a bead of sweat from his brow. A weak sneer played
across his lips as he composed himself.

Bailey was still bound to the bed. Blood seeped from her
wrists and ankles. The fibers had broken her skin during the
struggle. Her hands and feet were swollen from the lack of
circulation, and her whole body trembled in shock.

Ricky rolled his neck around. He just sat there, staring,
reminiscing, and loving his power. "Was that an experience or
what?"

Bailey didn't respond.

"Speechless?" He used words to stroke his ego. "Well, most
of you are after something that fantastic. Your little brains don't
know quite what to make of it."

He turned to her page in the journal. The details needed to
be written down while fresh in his mind, and with each stroke
of the pen, his emotions changed. They always did. Lust and
excitement turned into disgust and hate. His smile faded into a
frown. That particular element was left out of the notes. It made
him feel out of control and he did not care to dwell on it.

He climbed back onto the bed and straddled Bailey. Most of
his weight was on his knees, but considerable pressure smashed

her body. Cleanup was the worst. He had taken what he wanted, and now came the disposition. *What a mess.*

She was worthless at this point. He watched a lone tear roll from her eye and then spat in her face. The back of his hand flew across her right cheek.

She grimaced and let a barely audible whimper escape. The backhanded slap hurt, but her senses were dulled. Finally, her mind shut off certain switches to her body in an effort to protect itself.

He stayed on top of Bailey and turned her once beautiful face into a bloody mess. She was helpless to defend herself, mercy or torment at his sole discretion. Finally, a mouth full of blood restricting her airway, she coughed. Red flecks spattered him across the torso.

Ricky held his arms out to either side in disgust. Cleanup just got harder. "Oh, you little *bitch*!" he complained and knocked her cold with one final blow.

He peeled his sweaty body from the bed, wiped off, and took his time dressing. The last thing he needed was a picture, and he preferred his victims to be awake with their eyes wide open. He cracked a smelling salt beneath her nose. She woke to the powerful scent of ammonia and turned her head to get away from the acrid odor.

"Hey, hey. Look here. I said, look here!" He shouted to gain her attention.

She peeked toward the foot of the bed. Tears, blood, and swollen flesh blurred her vision. There was a flash and then another.

Chapter Sixteen

Fully dressed, hair neatly combed and a look of casual confidence, Ricky stepped into the retail store of the truck stop. He felt exhausted and needed fuel for the work ahead. He walked around the aisles until he found his poison, Planters Trail Mix. The kind with the M&M candies was his favorite. From there, he went to the coffee machine. *Nothing like a sugar and caffeine high for a middle-of-the-night project.*

People moved about the store, all road-weary minds looking without seeing. *They could be just like me, and nobody would ever know.*

The convenience store was typical. It was a little grimy around the edges with a couple of peculiar-looking clerks behind the counter. The night shift always had the funny ones. Country music played in the background.

At the counter, he put down the coffee and trail mix, removed his wallet, and awaited the total.

A big woman stood behind the register, her frame burdened beneath a hundred pounds of excess weight and hair pulled into a tight bun. Her uniform was simple; a red and orange apron draped over jeans and a black T-shirt. The getup did not flatter her figure. She wore too much blue eye shadow, and her nails were painted bright red. *She looks way scarier than I do, but she's probably the salt of the earth. No reason for her to look innocent.* Her nametag read "Verna."

She gave him a gap-toothed grin. "How ya doin', honey?"

"Just fine, thank you. And yourself?" He returned the smile. *Verna. Big Verna.*

"Pretty good. Just waitin' 'til my shift's up."

"I see. What time do you get off?"

"Not 'til seven. Still got a few more hours." She took the trail mix and scanned it.

"Seven will be here before you know it."

"Just like every other night, honey. Nothin' to it but to do it. That's what I always say."

He'd heard it before, a good quote for perseverance. "So what do I owe you?"

"Five dollars and seventeen cents, honey." It was a name she called most male customers. She studied him for a moment. "Coffee says you're staying on the road for a while longer." It was a statement, not an observation.

"Yeah." He dug bills out of the wallet. "I have a few more miles to cover before daybreak. This should keep me going though."

"Well, you just be careful out there. Too many of these truckers don't rest and end up falling asleep at the wheel. Keep an eye out."

He handed six dollars cash across the counter to Big Verna.

"Oh, honey!" Her eyes were wide. "You've got blood on your hand." Her sausage finger and bright red nail pointed at a nearly dried blob on the base of his thumb.

No! How did I miss that? No time to think. He had to say something quick. As if it were the gospel truth, he said, "I sure do. I thought I washed it all off." He made a puzzled look. "Dang nosebleed. Thing made a mess everywhere. Must have missed a spot."

"Must have." She put the bills in the drawer and extracted change, completely satisfied with his explanation.

"No thanks," he said. "Keep it. It bothers me in my pocket anyway."

"You sure?"

"Yeah, keep it. It just gets in my way."

Big Verna dropped the change in the "Need a Penny" tray by the register. "All right then. You have a good night, honey. Be safe. And get that blood cleaned up before somebody thinks you killed someone." She winked at him.

"Thanks. You, too. I mean about having a good night."

An elderly gentleman came in and held the door open without a word. *Privacy in plain sight. Glad the blood was on my hand and not my fly.* He made a toothy smirk, all pearly whites and piercing eyes.

In the van, he situated himself, drove away from the parking lot, and headed further into the Iowa countryside. A half hour down the main road, he turned onto a smaller pavement. After several minutes, he took a farm-to-market blacktop. The remote, yellow-striped ribbon stretched for miles into rural farmland. Finally, a green sign marked his next turn.

He was now on a gravel-covered road that led into an ocean of cornfields. Every so often, a farmers' private turn row wound into the fields. He found the one he wanted, bounced along the rutted double track, and disappeared inside walls of stalks. Headlights showed the way to the back of the plot where woods pressed against the tilled edge. He parked and killed the engine.

Darkness consumed the world. Anything could have hidden within its murk. Trees surrounded their position. No houses were within two miles. He used Google Earth in advance to scout the area. It worked impeccably. Even though he had never been to that particular place before, the program gave him a sense of familiarity. He knew he was safe.

His foot made a slight crunching sound when it met the earth. The sun had dried the top quarter inch of soil. The weight of his step cracked the surface.

He opened the rear doors and removed a shovel. Several rows into the corn was a good spot to dig. The moist, cultivated topsoil moved with ease, and the cool, night air made his work pleasant. He dug until a hole lay two feet wide by four feet deep.

By the time I cover this, another rain comes along, the crop is harvested, and it sits idle for winter, the soil will have compacted so tightly around her body . . . she'll never be discovered. Way out here, no farmer will be suspicious. Why would he be?

At the van, he found Bailey awake. She tilted her head back and peered through her nearly swollen shut eyes and into the night. She could barely make out the shape of a man standing behind her.

"Hey there, little darling," he said with fake sympathy. "Don't worry. You're not going to hurt anymore."

He raised the shovel, swung it down like an axe, and smashed her over the head with the spade. Bailey Davis was no more. He was tired and ready to be through with her. He cut the ropes loose with the hunting knife and dropped everything into the hole. She was dumped on top of them, a bloody tangle of naked body and matted hair. He threw in her clothes, followed by the bed linens and cleanup towels. He soaked them with a liberal amount of lighter fluid and lit it all with a match. Ten minutes later, her skin was charred, covered in a layer of ash. The loose pile of dirt was scooped, tamped, and packed until firm. Any leftover was spread around evenly to leave as little sign as possible. Soon, her body would begin to decompose.

Ricky loaded the van without a second thought and drove out the way he had entered, a ghost in the night. *Good-bye, Bailey Davis.*

Chapter Seventeen

The first day of Isaac's return to work arrived. If he were ready, he wasn't sure. Two days shy of four weeks had passed since the tragic night, and he wondered when or if he would ever feel like going back. On the other hand, he craved a sense of normalcy, a means to get on with life and get outside the emotional walls of confinement. The sky was the one place that offered escape. Three or four days of flying was good medicine.

Their home, once a joyous sanctuary and now a beehive of police activity, was silent. All the yellow tape strung across the yard was gone, and thanks to a new unlisted telephone number, days would go by without reporters calling to request a statement. Even the FBI and state police had stopped calling. That particular detail was bittersweet. The case was cold, and the killer was loose. Justice hung in limbo. However, peace at the absence of a chaotic, exhaustive investigation was undeniable.

Aside from his personal desires to get away for a while, Sarah concerned him most. She was strong. She'd always had to be. But the brave face she wore in the days up to the funeral was gone. Now time seemed to get the better of her. Random mood swings occurred, along with obsessive-compulsive tendencies. It was a whirlwind of behaviors, one vanishing as suddenly as the next materialized, like a magnet whose polarity unexpectedly changed.

His heart hurt for her. He was the man, the rock, the foundation. In hard times, he was supposed to be immovable, the constant for his family to cling to. He tried. He tried every second of every day, but it was hard to feel successful when there was no positive response in return. Even the simple things escaped his efforts. They had not made love since it happened, not even close. Sarah couldn't compartmentalize her emotions. To let down the bridge for passion was to also let it down for sorrow. That was fine, expected even. But stacked on top of the distancing, her mood swings, and personal struggles of his own, he wondered when his breaking point would come. *Maybe I don't have one. Maybe I'll go numb before I break.*

He sat on the bench at the end of their bed and tied his shoes. His mind felt full, utterly crowded. Somehow though, there was room for wishful thoughts. He slipped into a world of days gone by and youthful intentions, days when he and Sarah were joyful, not wrecked by life's unfairness.

* * *

Isaac graduated college from the Air Force Academy in Colorado Springs, Colorado. From there, he began his career as a United States aviator. He was sharp, instinctive, and solid under pressure, everything the military required of pilots. He craved the physical challenges and the mental demands and lived for speed. Flying a jet was indescribable. The skies belonged to the few. His tour of duty took him many places around the world, but the majority of his active duty was in the Middle East.

He still had a year of commitment left to the air force when he met Sarah. He and a few buddies were on leave and stopped off at a local pub one evening in Washington DC. She was their waitress. Unlike the other servers who worked the crowd of thirsty customers, those with their boobs pushed out the tops of their skimpy shirts and jeans so low their ass cracks or thongs peeked out anytime they bent over a table, she didn't have to flaunt the goods for tips.

Sarah's father left when she was little without a note, phone call, or gesture of explanation. From that point on, money had to be earned the old-fashioned way, hard work. Her mother held two jobs and loved her daughter dearly, but that relationship was also cut short. Breast cancer took her before Sarah's high school graduation, and all the money they had went toward insurance deductibles and treatment.

In her early twenties and no stranger to financial tight spots, she pushed through community college and toward a teaching degree. Shifts at the pub were a way to cushion the debt of student loans. She could have earned a fortune stripping at any of the high-end nightclubs, but a sense of self-worth and uncompromised morals kept her straight. It was easier to stretch a dollar thinner than be ashamed of how she earned it.

The pub closed at two o'clock in the morning, and Isaac chose not to go back to the hotel with his flyboy buddies. Instead, he waited outside until after three thirty. He didn't approach the knockout cocktail waitress earlier because he would have appeared just like all the other guys who swallowed too much liquid courage, and that was creepy. All he wanted was a shot. At what, he couldn't say. His lifestyle was not, at that date and time, conducive to a relationship. But there he was. A giddiness inside held him fast. If he didn't stay and talk to her, he knew it could be one of those pivotal moments in time, passed up and forever regretted.

He was leaned against a parallel-parked car when she stepped out the front door. She wore a formfitting black T-shirt, slim, black pants, and Rockport shoes. She had pulled her blonde hair high into a twisted ponytail. An untied apron was draped over her shoulder. Sarah recognized him immediately and unintentionally gave a coy smile, having no idea he was there to see her.

He blushed, suddenly embarrassed about his conspicuous service dress uniform. He had been at the Pentagon earlier and arrived at the bar without changing.

"Hello, I'm Isaac." He offered his right hand.

She held her polite smile but did not offer her hand in return.

"I was at one of your tables tonight," he explained.

Again, she didn't answer but cocked her head playfully to one side. It was an offering to go on.

"I didn't want to bother you at work, so I thought I should wait out here."

"We've been closed for an hour and a half." She raised her eyebrows and looked around the street. No one else had ever waited outside. If they didn't approach her while working, they usually wrote their number on a napkin with some corny line. *Call me, Candy Pants. Holler, Sweet Thang.* They were always so ridiculous.

"Yeah, I guess it has. Well, I waited because I was at one of your tables."

She let out a short giggle. "You said that already."

He joined her in laughter, feeling foolish as a schoolboy. "I did, didn't I? I've been thinking so much about what to say, and now I can't remember any of it."

She didn't know what she liked about him, but something was different. Perhaps it was because he came across genuine and confident, not calculated and cocky. Finally, she reached out with her hand. "I'm Sarah."

He didn't realize it, but a grin stretched across his face from ear to ear. "Nice to meet you, Sarah. I'm Isaac."

Again, she laughed. "Yeah, you said that, too."

His heart pounded. *This is going well, but why do I keep repeating myself? What is it about her that makes me babble like a buffoon?* He decided to keep it moving. "You probably already know, but there's a diner around the corner. I thought, since you get off work late, you might like a coffee or something to eat."

"We just met, and you're asking me on a date?"

He shrugged. It was sudden, but his window of opportunity was short.

"Don't you have to be at work or . . ." She studied his uniform. "Report for duty in a few hours?"

"Actually, I do have a plane to catch in a couple hours, so I only have about . . ." He looked at his watch. "Thirty minutes."

Sarah let her guard down another notch. *If he really has to leave in thirty minutes, he's not looking for a quick piece of ass. He must really be interested in me.* Indeed, she was tired, a little hungry, and wanted to get off her feet.

"Okay. We walking?"

"Considering I have no car, yes, we're walking."

They strolled down the sidewalk, side by side, close but not uncomfortably so. They sat across from each other in a red booth with a stainless steel table and ordered coffee. She was hungry but considered his time frame and declined anything to eat. If she filled her mouth with food, it would limit the conversation.

Time passed quickly, and Isaac had to say good-bye. He didn't leave without her phone number and email address. A year later, he finished his commitment to the air force, came back to the coast, and asked for Sarah's hand in marriage. They rented a little place in DC and began their life together.

When she gave birth to the twins, they decided it was time for a change. The city was fun but felt more and more claustrophobic with the new additions, and there was no family close by. They both loved Ruidoso, and Isaac began applying for jobs. With a little digging, the forest fire patrol position came available. Everything fell into place, almost like it was predestined. For years, life marched on as perfectly as could be. Then Caroline.

*   *   *

Still seated on the bench in the bedroom, lost in thought and hands on his knees, Isaac snapped back into the present. Someone was screaming.

He jumped to his feet and ran down the hallway toward the noise. It came from Josie's room. He entered and found her seated at the little table. Sarah was on her feet, stricken. A Polaroid picture, which Isaac could not make out from the doorway, lay on the floor beside a white piece of paper. Sarah's hands were pulled back to her shoulders. It looked as though someone had given her a present, and instead of a gift, she'd found a snake inside.

Chapter Eighteen

Judging by Sarah's posture, Isaac knew her scream was no joke. She wasn't the type of person to flip out. Whatever she had seen, it was bad.

He picked up the picture first and instantly knew why she reacted. A little girl was bound to a bed, stretched tightly. Her hands and feet were grossly swollen from a lack of circulation. Her face was lacerated in several places, disfigured, and bloody. It was not difficult to decipher the events that transpired. She had been brutally raped. On the bottom of the Polaroid was a name, Bailey Davis.

Tom and Helen had joined the commotion by this time. Isaac was not prepared to show anyone else the picture. He wanted to defuse the situation and protect Josie from any shock.

"Mom, will you stay in here with Josie?"

Helen had fear in her eyes. "What's wrong?"

He was not reluctant to withhold the perverse image from his mother. He was *dead set* on it. "Just stay in here, will you?" he snapped. The tone was not mean but serious.

She got the drift. "Sure, we'll stay in here and play," she said with enthusiasm.

"Honey," Isaac said toward Sarah, "Dad, come with me."

They followed him into the kitchen where he picked up the phone and called Charlie.

"Hello," Charlie's jolly voice sounded on the other end.

"Charlie," he hesitated, unsure of how to proceed, "I think you should come over. We've . . . gotten something . . . in the mail. It's pretty bad."

He never called Charlie "Charlie." He always referred to him as "Buddy," and it didn't go unnoticed. "Is it anything I should be worried about?"

"No, no need to bring backup or anything. Just drop what you're doing and get over here."

"Well, what is it?" he pried. He at least wanted to know the nature of his visit. One doesn't become the chief of police without asking questions along the way. "What do you have?"

He didn't want to describe it. "It's a picture and a letter that came in the mail."

"I'm on my way, but can you tell me what the picture is of?"

"I'd rather you just see it. I can't explain."

"Fine. What about the letter? What does it say?"

"Haven't read it yet. Don't really want to."

"Okay, okay, Buddy. I'll be right over."

He hung up the phone and turned to see Sarah with her face buried in Tom's chest. She was shaken badly.

"What is it, son?" Tom's look was anxious.

Reluctantly, he handed it over.

In all his life, Isaac had never before seen the expression on his father's face. Tom's gentle gray eyes turned to stone, and his naturally peaceful appearance hardened. Isaac wished he could have kept it from him, but there was no way around it.

Tom placed the picture facedown on the kitchen table. He used both arms to wrap around Sarah, like she was his own daughter.

Isaac chose not to read the letter until Charlie arrived. He wished he could burn it, eliminate all traces of its existence, and thereby erase the person who sent it from their lives. If the words on the page were even close to the vileness of the picture, there would be no way to forget it after reading it. But out of concern for evidence and the chance it might have pertinent information to the killer, he kept it folded and placed it beside the Polaroid.

His imagination spiraled out of control. He didn't have to read the letter to know that the sender was probably the same man who had escaped and killed Caroline. As he had, day in and day out, he saw the man in black standing in the bedroom. He could see his menacing stance, the shock in his eyes, and the fluid motion with which he jumped out the window. Although time had gone into slow motion, the prowess the man had to size up the situation, react as swiftly as a shadow, and fly the coop was commendable. Obviously, it was not his first rodeo. Now he was back, taunting them from beyond.

Worse than Caroline's death, Isaac had a visual image of what could have happened to his little princesses. All at once, he felt disgusted and, for the first time since she passed, grateful. If it truly were her time to go, at least it was not in the same fashion as Bailey Davis. He mourned for Caroline, and now he mourned for Bailey.

Audible only to himself, he prayed, "Wherever Bailey is, if she's alive, let her be found quickly. Please, God, don't let her suffer anymore."

The knowledge of what she must have endured made his stomach turn. The horrible things done to her by a grown man, an adult, whom children should be able to trust, was too much for him to bear.

"Okay, what's going on?" Charlie stood in the kitchen, hands on his hips, looking from one to the other. He had entered without notice and startled them from their thoughts.

Isaac wondered, *How long have we been standing here?* But he dismissed the lapse in time as unimportant and gestured toward the two items on the table.

Charlie chose the picture first and flipped it over. "Oh! Son of a bitch!" He was disgusted, then mad. He quickly set the picture down, face-up. "Why didn't you tell me? That's evidence, and now my prints are on it." He gave Isaac a hard look. "Who else has touched this?"

"We didn't know what it was," he explained with an apologetic expression. "It came in the mail."

"When did you get it?" He took a moment to gain a professional perspective and studied the picture.

Sarah said, "It was addressed to Josie. She just opened it a few minutes ago."

Charlie's eyes widened. "Has she seen this?"

She answered a little defensively. "It was addressed to her. Sometimes she gets letters from friends, and I had no reason not to give it to her."

"Where's the envelope?"

She handed over the standard-sized white envelope. Nothing about it was unusual. The hands of an eight-year-old had sloppily opened it. A regular first-class stamp filled the upper right-hand corner. The attention line was handwritten to Miss Josephine Snow.

"So, she did see the picture?"

Sarah nodded and began to cry. She felt ashamed that Josie had seen the graphic image. "When she opened it, she said, 'Mommy, why is this little girl naked?'" Again, she ducked her head into Tom's chest. With no living parents of her own, and a sorry excuse for a dad when he was around, Tom had become more of an adopted father than a father-in-law.

Isaac was about to ask Charlie to take it easy but didn't have to.

"I'm sorry, Sarah." He lowered his voice. "It's just . . . well . . ." Like the rest of them, words escaped him. "Have any of you read the letter?"

Tom shook his head.

"I think we better then. It was addressed here, but if you don't want to listen, I can read it silently and take it with me."

"We want to," Sarah said, a serious, composed air about her now.

This was the first lead they had in a month, and despite the horrific nature, she hoped that maybe the bastard would give something away about himself, if even by accident.

"We need to know what it says. It can't be worse than the picture."

The letter was sent anonymously, along with the Polaroid of Bailey Davis. Despite what they thought, the words hit closer to home than they dreamed possible.

> *My Dearest Josephine, I'm terribly sorry to have left in such a hurry the other night. I realize that you are without a sister, and I greatly regret the way things turned out. Had your father not come into the room and interrupted my visit, I can promise that you and Caroline would still be together. But since I was denied the pleasure of your company, I turned my attention to sweet Bailey Davis. As you can see, a flattering picture of her is included. What a special little girl she was, tasty, but I am over her and still hungry. No doubt Mommy and Daddy will be keeping an eye on you rather closely, but I relish the opportunity to spend time with you. Until we meet again, stay well.*
>
> *Thinking of you,*
> *XOXO*
> *P.S. Do you like red?*

Chapter Nineteen

A wall clock ticked in the background, each strike echoing with precision.

Ricky leaned back in his office chair and stretched both arms above his head. It was a quirk he had when in thought or battling boredom, which was often. He wondered how everyone back in Ruidoso had reacted to the letter. He imagined the shock in their eyes at the Polaroid and the fear they must have felt after reading the note. *I'll bet they're outside their minds.*

The day he dropped it in the mail, he didn't fully understand the depth to his actions. But now, days later, his brain stuck on one track, clarity came. He sent correspondence to Josie because he was completely and utterly infatuated.

It was still too soon to go back and try to take her again. No matter how much he wanted it, not enough time had passed. Instead, he tried to focus on his career. A paycheck provided a necessary distraction from extracurricular activities. But a lack of income didn't stress him in the least. He was a saver, not a spender, and planned for lean stretches. A frugal lifestyle was a worthwhile sacrifice because it allowed him time to come and go on a whim. And now, time had become the enemy. What he wanted, he could not have. His video collection from past victims quickly became monotonous, mildly amusing, at best. He wanted what was out of reach, Josie.

The sexual cravings grew, and he needed to do something. *Someone else. I need to find someone else.* It was that simple. Warm, live flesh was the only cure to his summertime blues. *Who will it be?*

He reached for a *New York Times* newspaper on the desk, and the search began. It was always the same, done with one and on to the next. Even from the time he was a boy, he always worried about what would come next. And two decades later, only one thing had changed, his capability. A boy's inclinations evolved into a man's skill.

*   *   *

The house he grew up in was, in all aspects, normal. It was a traditional three-bedroom, two-bathroom, fifties-style ranch home in a Florida suburb. It sat amongst a neighborhood with hundreds of other homes, basically identical in outward appearances. Middle-income, working people were the inhabitants.

His parents occupied the master bedroom of the home, and Ricky had one of the remaining two bedrooms to himself. Being the only child was easy. Both his parents worked, and he was free to do as he wished. Too much free time made way for idle hands. The family next door had two daughters, each a few years older than Ricky. He used to think of ingenious little ways to peep, finding them changing or bathing. Even as a child, when he would catch a lucky break and see them naked, a weird sensation ran through his body. It was mysterious and pleasing, a secret he felt but knew not to share. In those early days, desire awoke inside his heart and could never be undone, innocence unveiled.

He spent hours in his bedroom, strategizing a likely time for it to happen again. Even normal childhood activities were avoided in preparation for when his next chance might be. If it came along, he didn't want to be sidetracked.

*   *   *

He was grown now with years of experience under his belt. As he flipped through the newspaper, suddenly, as if ripped from a world of despair, hope burst into reality. A black-and-white picture of a beautiful little girl stared back at him. The face was young, innocent, and perfect. Enamored, he quickly browsed the article and made up his mind. *Yes. This is her.*

All the information was there. Her name and general location were more than enough to go on. He gently folded the page so that nothing except her pretty little face showed. He pulled up a program used to find people on the computer, and his fingers scurried across the keys.

In West Virginia, Lindsay Watson and her extraordinary gift waited. She was worthy of his attention.

Chapter Twenty

On Saturday evening, same as always, Isaac came home and parked his old Chevy in the detached garage. He had not wanted to leave after the arrival of the letter, but with encouragement and reassurance from Tom and Charlie, he let go of his fear, the instinct to stay, protect, and control, and returned to the job. It took a while for the anxiety to fade. Reason told him that worry did nothing to change the circumstances. Sarah and Josie were in capable hands, and he had to relinquish the negative thoughts and move on with life. And just like he had hoped, the second day of work was easier than the first, and the third was easier than the second. Nerves settled, and the world expanded again.

Inside the kitchen door, Josie came running. She jumped into her father's arms and squeezed. "You're back!"

"Did you miss me?" Their faces were less than a foot apart, and her hands were on his cheeks.

"I always miss you."

I always miss you. The answer was so simple yet different. There was a maturity to it, one that had not been there before, like the last four days had aged her.

"I missed you, too." He kissed her and put her down.

She's growing up right before my eyes.

Sarah wrapped her arms around his waist and hugged. "How was work?"

"Good. It was . . . good."

"Yeah?" She looked up to him, knowing how hard it was for him to leave after the surprise on Wednesday morning.

"Yeah." He searched for the words. "Liberating, I guess. How were things here?"

She tiptoed and kissed his curvy lips. There was a brightness in her eyes that had been gone for too long. "Good. We actually had some fun." She shrugged. "Is that weird?"

It was a little strange to hear they had fun. *But at the same time, what else were they supposed to do?* The comment did, however, catch him off guard. And it wasn't just her but also Josie. The whole energy of the house was different. It was better, like a shadow was lifted.

"Not weird, just . . . different."

The arrival of the letter had sent Sarah into near hysterics. Fear, not just sorrow, stacked on top of Caroline's death, and the burden was too much to bear. Then after a sleepless night, a switch flipped. The situation was no less painful, but she granted forgiveness to the unfairness of life, and gave up hope that the past could have been different. Pining for Caroline did nothing to protect Josie. And just like that, her outlook shifted.

Tom came in the kitchen and leaned against the counter. "Well, where'd you go?"

"Hey, Dad." He released Sarah and hung his flannel shirt on the coat rack. "I stayed up north the whole time."

"No fires?"

"Nope. All that rain has things pretty settled."

Helen came in from the hallway and set a glass of iced tea on the table. "Good to have you back." She hugged him.

"It's good to be back."

"You went over Taos?"

"Mmm hmm."

"Did you see the house?"

"You know, that reminds me." He scratched his stubble and cocked an eyebrow. "A moving truck was parked in the driveway."

"Good," Tom chimed. "I hired a guy to take away that old sofa your mother refuses to get rid of. I can't do it while she's around and thought this would be a good opportunity." He chuckled at the inside joke.

"That sofa," Helen informed, "belonged to my mother, her mother, and her mother's mother."

"So that would make it . . . what? Your great-great grandmother's?"

"That's right, buster. It would."

"All I'm saying is, just because it's sentimental, doesn't mean it's useful."

"Well, if old means useless, you'd better be glad I'm sentimental, or I'd throw you out with the couch."

Tom looked around with his eyebrows raised and a smirk on his face. "I guess I should be thankful she keeps me around. What do you think, Josie?"

She was smiling too. "I don't think you're useless, Pa Paw."

"There. You see, honey," he said. "Josie doesn't think I'm useless."

"Josie, I don't really think your grandpa is useless. He's just a nag about that couch, and I don't care what he thinks. It has history."

"Nobody else knows the history, nor do they care to. To them, it looks like a piece of wood covered with soiled canvas."

"My great-great grandfather made that sofa from the scrap wood of an old wagon, and my great-great grandmother covered it with fabric from flour sacks. Nobody thought anything of it back then, except for 'Hey, that's creative.'" Helen's Italian passion showed through. The enthusiasm was contagious and put everyone in a good mood. "Folks were poor and admired her craftsmanship. The frame's been repaired since, and I've had the fabric cleaned."

Isaac looked from one to the other like a spectator at a high-tempo tennis match. The topic was old, and the argument repetitive, but the spirit was great. It meant something. This restored, positive atmosphere was not a product of his imagination. It was real, and it was relief, the beginning of a new normal.

Chapter Twenty-One

T he next morning, after breakfast and coffee, Tom and Helen drove back to Taos. They longed for home after being away for four weeks, but the good-byes were not easy. Isaac stood in the front yard with Josie and Sarah, waving until his parents were out of sight. It was just the three of them. Their life was never going to be the same.

"We should probably get ready," Sarah said. "Anna's doing this meeting for us, and it would be nice to get there early."

"Are you sure you're up to it?"

"It won't be easy. Nothing with this is. But if it means keeping our family safe, I'll do whatever it takes."

At the Smith's house, Isaac helped Anna's husband, Riley, set up for the meeting. They pushed all the living room furniture aside and made rows with folding chairs. Sarah was in the kitchen with Anna. An assortment of veggie trays, fruit platters, and finger foods were prepared while they visited. It had the look of a party but not the feel.

Josie went upstairs with Jason with strict instructions to not let him do anything unsafe. She promised, and they went to play.

At twelve o'clock, the guests began to trickle in. All of them lived in or around the neighborhood. In attendance were the elderly, newly retired, empty nesters, and other young couples with kids. Despite the age range, everyone shared the common goal of keeping the street safe.

They were in their seats, munching on snacks, when Anna stepped to the front and called their attention. "Thank you for coming. As I explained in the letter you received, we are here to discuss the safety of our neighborhood. This isn't just for Isaac and Sarah. It's for all of us. We all have or know kids who run around without supervision." She scanned the room. "Because of recent events, I've asked someone to speak who can help us keep things, as much as possible, like they were and teach us what to be more aware of. I think everyone knows our chief of police, Charlie Biddle." She raised her arm, palm up, toward the back of the room.

Charlie? Isaac had no idea he was there or that he was coming. He turned to look for his best friend and found him at the food table with a half-covered plate of snacks.

Clearly, Charlie was not ready, and the look on his face was that of a kid caught with his hand in the cookie jar. He quickly straightened up, set the plate down, and swallowed the last of his punch.

He squared himself at the front of the living room and tugged on the heavy gun belt riding below his belly. "Folks, it's real simple. Anna asked me to give a lesson on safety, and regardless of where you are or what you're doing, these rules apply." He cleared his throat. "Rule number one. If it looks funny, report it. If you see or hear something and the thought crosses your mind, 'I wonder if I should mention this to somebody?' do it. We're not so busy at the station that we can't handle the calls. In fact, we want them. Citizens are our best sources for crime prevention. In town alone, we have several thousand citizens and only a few police officers. And by things, I mean suspicious vehicles, persons, or something out of place. Just call it in, and we'll check it out. Then you won't have to wonder anymore."

He looked around to see if there were any questions. No one raised a hand. "Now more specifically, I believe Anna's letter explained the current situation next door with Isaac and Sarah." He drew a long breath and pulled his lips in tightly, figuring on how best to proceed. "When the intruder broke into their home, it was the middle of the night. The abduction in Kansas—admittedly done by the same man—happened in the late afternoon. A little girl was taken in broad daylight. According to the letter he sent, there are implications that he may come back this way. That threat could be empty, or it could be true. It might be never, but it might also be tomorrow, next week, or next year. Please know I don't tell you this to suggest that he will, but to make you aware of the possibility. Reaching out like that is a serious action. Hopefully, he will be caught sooner rather than later. In the meantime, we need to keep a watch out, and it's up to you to help make this neighborhood safe."

Isaac held Sarah's hand. This was what a small town is all about, and despite the uncomfortable topic, he knew it was the best thing that could happen, especially for Josie.

"You all know the ins and outs around here. You know each other's cars, vehicles that visit frequently and park on the street, and who walks around the streets. If someone you don't know or have never seen is prowling around, give us a call. If they belong, they won't mind a few questions from us. If you see a company car or any company vehicle that is unusual or has an unfamiliar logo, give us a call."

Isaac was impressed with the way Charlie presented the material. He didn't see this side of him often. It was direct and straightforward. Through his chubby appearance and good-ol-boy façade, there was a professional. By the looks on the guests' faces, they too were surprised. They didn't know him like Isaac, but opinions were opinions. Charlie was not a washed-up city cop who couldn't hack it. He simply wanted a different lifestyle, and that was why he returned to the scenic mountain village.

When it was over, Josie came down from playing with Jason. Her facial expression was one of pure exasperation. That was how everyone felt after an hour with the energetic little boy.

Outside on the lawn, the day was bright. It was the first time in a while that Isaac felt productive. Like any road to recovery, though, two steps forward eventually means one step back.

Chapter Twenty-Two

A double vision of wavy blonde hair, fair, smooth complexions, and deep green eyes seductively stared at Ricky in his daydream. He smiled, and his cheek twitched. The world was perfect, the best he could imagine.

"Caroline . . . Josie," he whispered. A false anticipation of events heightened his demented, mental stimulation.

He was in Shepherdstown, West Virginia, waiting for nine-year-old Lindsay Watson to finish her music lesson. When she was through—just like every other Monday, Wednesday, and Friday—she walked to the corner, turned off the main street, and made the one block trek home. She lived less than two hundred yards behind the historic row of main street offices where she took violin lessons.

The streets in Shepherdstown are classic, old-town style and have no end to their charm. Since the late 1700s, business fronts have lined the sidewalks where pedestrians and cyclists move about. The atmosphere is friendly, college liberal, and eclectic. An artsy, quaint atmosphere is ideal for all walks of life, and Ricky relished the unsuspecting nature of the citizens.

On that warm, July afternoon, Lindsay stepped outside, violin case in hand, and walked to the corner. She turned right and stayed on the sidewalk between the street and the two-hundred-year-old brick wall. The building opposite her side of the street was the same, a two-story, windowless wall where shopkeepers once lived above their stores. Beyond the shadowy stretch, commercial zoning turned to residential, and she could see her next-door neighbor's backyard. The white van parked by the curb did not look out of place, no different than dozens of other delivery vehicles in and out of the alley.

The violin case swung at her side, and she skipped merrily along. But as she approached the passenger side, a man in a wheelchair fumbled with the sliding door.

"Hi," Ricky said. He wore jeans, a North Face T-shirt, and a ball cap with the local college logo.

"Hi," she politely responded and continued down the sidewalk.

The street angled slightly uphill toward the neighborhood. After ten more paces, she would cross the entrance to the alley and officially enter her little village of old, refurbished houses.

Ricky fumbled with the latch and made a clumsy show. "Excuse me," he called to her. "Would you help me out? I can't get the door open."

Lindsay stared, unsuspectingly for the moment, and sized up the situation.

"I'm sorry to bother you, sweetheart," he went on. "But when I try to open it . . ." He reached with his hand and let the wheelchair roll backward. "My chair won't stay still. Whoa!" He smiled and acted helpless. "If you could just pull the handle, I have a lift that helps me in." He flashed his pearly whites and played on his handicap to draw out her tenderness.

Her parents taught her to be wary of strangers and especially to never get into vehicles with them. They also taught her to be kind and courteous and to assist the less fortunate. She didn't think anyone in a wheelchair would hurt her.

"Yes, sir." She came closer. There was so much life in her movement, so much innocent joy. Good manners kept her from staring, and she reached for the handle.

"Thank you so much! You're an angel." False gratitude emanated from every pore of his being. His eyes averted to one end of the street and then the other. So far, he had not broken any laws, even if someone were watching. But all was clear, and he tensed, a compressed spring energized for release. "I don't know what I would do without you."

She swept the handle up and had no more said "There you go" when Ricky peeled the door open with one hand, wrapped his other hand over her mouth, jumped into the back, and slid it shut. The action happened so fast that she never had time to scream. He placed a moist handkerchief over her face as she kicked, swung, and squirmed to get away. The chemical took effect within seconds.

He put her on the bed, bent through the little door into the cab, and glanced at the mirrors. The street remained empty. *You're mine now.*

Chapter Twenty-Three

Deep into the country, no stops planned until they were faraway, the van rolled on. In the seconds, minutes, and hours after a kidnapping, distance was Ricky's best friend. But travel was the toughest part. Once he touched a child, placed his hands on her flesh and she was in his possession, the wait was near unbearable. Only self-preservation pushed him on.

Lindsay was in the back, knocked out from a second dose of chloroform. She would have a splitting headache when she woke, but he didn't care about that. Her comfort was not a concern.

She reminded him of his childhood neighbor, the younger of the two sisters he used to peep on. Their appearances were undeniably similar, and he recalled the original feel of obsession awoken within him all those years ago. The girl's young, female form dominated his thoughts. He wanted to be with her, around her, to touch her.

*   *   *

On a few occasions, he and his parents went over for dinner. This was his favorite. He was in the same house, close to the girls and able to brush against them while they played. The sisters included Ricky in their games with an elaborate Barbie collection. Even then, he realized the importance of appearance. If anyone watched, he played nicely with the dolls. He dressed Ken in masculine clothes, careful to go with the flow. But when no one was looking, things changed.

He stripped the Barbies and examined them methodically. He ran his fingers over them—much the same as he did Lindsay Watson's newspaper photo—and sniffed their spore. It was real to him, more than a wild imagination. His heart raced as sweat glands clammed his skin.

He dreamed of doing obscene and vulgar things with the dolls. Sex was an unexplained mystery, but the compromising positions pleased his mind. At first, it was enough to excite him. Eventually, however, one doll always became violent toward the other, one dominant and one submissive.

*   *   *

Now, traveling down the dark road with cargo far more precious than a Barbie, Ricky recalled the unmentionable things he did to those poor pieces of plastic. The progression of his actions was plain to see: dolls, peeping, and, finally, finding a way to actually caress real human flesh. He wondered if things would have escalated to their current status had he ever been caught.

Could I have gotten therapy? Was I . . . curable?

But like cancer, no cure existed, and he knew it. This cancer wasn't in his body. It was in his mind, a deep-rooted, mutating growth, out of control, undetected, and unchallenged. Satisfaction was the only real treatment, and only temporary at best. A drink of poison could merely quench the thirst.

"Turn left in five hundred feet."

A female, computerized voice emanated from the portable GPS and pulled him from thought. He was close. They were close.

Chapter Twenty-Four

Everything felt fuzzy. Lindsay thought her eyes were open, but it made no difference. Wherever she lay, darkness was complete. Something bit her ankle. Then she felt the same bite on her other ankle. Neither leg would move. She tried to sit up, reach down, and scratch. Suddenly, grogginess faded, and her senses sharpened. *I'm tied up.*

"Hello?" she shouted. A gag stifled the call into a guttural, throaty noise. She hadn't noticed it before.

Now panic gripped her, and she writhed. Her gusto faded with the sting of rope fibers. The road vibrated beneath her. She could feel it and hear it, the hum of tires on pavement. A bump, the sway of a turn, and its pull on her body were decipherable. She tried to think and remember how she had gotten there. Pain prevented a clear picture. Her head, ankles, and wrist hurt badly. She squirmed again and rebelled against the impossible restraints. *I have to get loose. I have to get help.*

Her teeth clenched down on the gag, defiant. She fought to exhaustion. It seemed hopeless, but the road noise had stopped.

Then someone spoke. "Hi, there. Do you remember me?"

A man was with her now. The only light came through a small crack of an open door behind him. It wasn't much, dusky and barely enough to see him hunched over. *Who is he?*

"It's okay. You can nod your head if you don't want to talk." He latched the door and flicked a toggle. A yellowish glow illuminated everything.

Memory hit her like a slap to the face. The man with the wheelchair was no longer in a wheelchair. *I'm in the van.* A lump in her throat grew, and her tummy bounced with a sob. She knew this was bad.

He moved steadily and deliberately. She watched him like a hawk while he took things off the shelves, set up camera equipment, and wrote in a book. She should have been glad he left her alone, but even at nine years old, it was plain to see he had something big in mind.

The only naked male she had ever seen was in a museum. Hardly any of the stone statues had clothes. But those men weren't real. This one was. When the bad man took everything off, she didn't know what to think. It was certainly different from the statues. *Wrong somehow.*

He boasted like a little kid with a show-and-tell trinket. He bragged, struck different poses, flexed his muscles, and came closer. On the side of the bed, his naked hip pressed against her ribs as he sat down. She wanted to scoot away, but the tight ropes and tiny space left nowhere to go.

He placed his hands on her chest, worked them up and down in circles, and closed his eyes.

Tears of anger, fear, and embarrassment welled up in Lindsay, and she screamed at him. "Stop it," she commanded. "Stop it right now." Her face was livid and strong, but the muted orders were indecipherable.

"A spunky one, I see." He open-hand smacked her on the cheek, enough to aggravate but not hurt. "I like spice. That's something girls your age are in short supply of."

Lindsay's body had started to mature earlier than most. He looked down at her. A devious smile played across his lips. She kicked to get loose.

"Whoa! Now we're talking."

Her resistance excited him. He was finished being gentle and immediately ripped off her shirt. The fabric held tightly enough to bruise her skin before pulling away. Silvery and cold, his hunting knife sliced until she was down to skin.

Crystal tears of torment ran down her cheeks, and she crooned in agony. She tried to get enough air through her runny nose and tears to fight the feeling of suffocation. She coughed and sputtered, struggling to gain a rhythm. Her heart and mind were strong, resilient to the stress. Unfortunately, it warded off shock, and she felt everything.

His hands prodded and molested, and she retracted at his vile touch.

He bent down to her ear. Gently, with his blue eyes in a penetrating stare, he smoothly said, "Sugar, do you like red?"

Lindsay couldn't gain a full breath. Mucus ran down her throat, and she retched. A cough would clear her windpipe, but the gag was in the way. Asphyxiation was now scarier than the man was.

"Do you like red?" he repeated.

She tried to answer, but her throat caught, and her face bulged with blood as she gagged.

"Oh, fine." He slipped the knife between her cheek and the rope. "No one can hear you scream out here anyway." After a harsh flick of his wrist, the rope popped loose. The back of the blade lacerated her cheek, and a bead of blood mixed with tears.

Lindsay sucked in. She inhaled one, two, and three deep breaths. She looked up, and despite the circumstances, was grateful for her captor's mercy.

The man was on his knees, between her legs. He leaned over and used his arms to hover above her. "Now." His voice was edgier this time. "Do . . . you . . . like . . . red? Hmmm?"

Instinct told her to answer and hope for the best. "Yes," she whispered, relieved at the ability to breathe again.

Yes. She likes red. And with that, he began and watched the anguish spread across her face. She had no choice but to suffer through the humility, the ultimate stripping away of decency.

Chapter Twenty-Five

"Hey . . . Hey . . ." Lindsay heard the man calling and felt a stick whack her across the tummy.

"Would you like to play for me?" he asked.

He had removed a black case from under the bed and opened the latches. Inside was her elegant violin. He put it to his shoulder and pulled the bow across the strings. It hissed, and Lindsay turned to look. Her body was in bad shape, but her mind was far from broken. A strong mental fortitude had allowed her to master the instrument, harness its music like few others her age. She froze the wiry man in her glare without blinking.

"Well, that got your attention, didn't it?" He was seated on a stool, bouncing up and down like he was playing a jig. With sweat-laced blood slathered across his naked body, he brought a jumble of screeches to a crescendo and bowed like a stage actor who'd just completed a masterful performance. "Thank you . . . Thank you." Again, he swatted Lindsay with the bow, this time on a swollen foot. "That's the last time you'll ever hear music, baby. I can promise you that."

Music had been such a joy in her life. Now it was used to mock and provoke. She didn't care though. She just wanted to go home.

He put the violin back in its case and took a second to change his focus. Lindsay sensed a pivotal shift. The man straddled her and came to rest on her chest. One hundred and seventy pounds pressed down on her tiring lungs.

She looked directly into her captor's eyes and silently begged for mercy. Life was a precious gift she hoped to keep. She didn't want to die. She wanted to live and see her parents again.

This feeling of solitude and helplessness was not fun, and she pled, "Please." It came out faintly more than a whisper. "Please don't hurt me anymore."

His knuckles made a smacking sound as they flew across her cheekbone. The contact broke the skin, and water filled her eyes. She shied away, but he hit the other side. There was nowhere to go. Her hands and feet felt like balloons from the cutoff circulation. She lost count of how many times he wailed on her, but then it stopped.

He pulled out the hunting knife. Its silver blade glowed in the yellow light. It slashed across her chest and made a laceration six inches long and an eighth of an inch wide. Her accelerated heart rate pumped more blood from the wound than it normally would have. Another slash seared from the menacing sickle. The man was mad now, unstoppable. Her skin turned to ribbons beneath the torture, and blood ran down her sides. Precious little energy was left, but she managed to scream one last time before passing out.

Chapter Twenty-Six

Not even a Pentecostal preacher's wife would have suspected Ricky of anything other than being a well-groomed gentleman. He had cleaned himself up and behaved like a world-class citizen.

Lindsay remained unconscious, and he dressed while waiting for her to come around. It aggravated him that she wouldn't wake up. The beating and cutting had exhilarated him, but none of it was worthwhile if she couldn't open her eyes for the final picture. It gave so much more effect if he could coax his victims to look into the camera. He checked her weak pulse several times and made sure she was still breathing.

He was parked at the back of an abandoned rock quarry. When he had first arrived, a padlock was on the old but still effective gate. A set of bolt cutters solved the problem. Appearances were everything, and after pulling through and closing the gate, he put the rusty chain and padlock back to give the notion of security. Still, he didn't think it would matter. The property had been out of commission for years and looked like it would stay that way for many more to come.

His chosen spot was so far into the bowels of the quarry that the entrance was way out of sight. Even if someone did come to prowl around, it would have been near impossible to find his van tucked into a tiny alcove under the black, country night. The surrounding walls were light gray and branched off into a myriad of sub-quarries. Not only was it the perfect place to do his dark deed, it could not have been better for body disposal.

He stepped outside, opened the back doors, wrapped a thick wad of Lindsay's hair around his hand, and jerked. She didn't twitch. The blood from her face had run onto her scalp and glued her hair into maroon clumps. One giant glob clung to his hand, and he shook it off.

A first aid kit hung on the wall just inside the back doors. Smelling salts were one of many useful items he kept there. He was resolute on taking the final picture of Lindsay with her eyes open. The hard packet popped and became saturated with pungent liquid, and he held it against the bottom of her nose. She immediately awoke with eyes wide.

He climbed back into the van and sat on the stool beside the bed. Worse than the smell of ammonia, urine and feces hit his sinuses. He looked at the bed between Lindsay's legs and turned his face away in disgust. She had lost continence. A pile of brown mush was partially smeared on the sheets and on her inner thighs. Urine had pooled, and a large yellow stain was visible. The combination, mixed with the blood and smelling salts, was sickening. He knew it was his own fault, but that didn't make cleaning the mess any more appealing. *No matter. I'll make sure and get it in the picture . . . for effect.*

He worked his way to the foot of the bed and tried to breathe through his mouth, but the humid, Kentucky air held the scent closely. "Oh, you nasty, little bitch! You stink! Oh . . ." He continued to degrade her, wondering if she heard him. When he finally took the Polaroid camera from its place, he clapped his hands and then whistled. She moved her eyes in his direction, and he snapped the capture button. Again, he whistled and clicked.

She was barely cognizant, and he felt no remorse when he popped her over the head with a ball-peen hammer. Eerily, her eyes didn't close.

Ricky cut her loose, drug her body out the back, along with the ropes, sheets, and clothes, and pulled her to the base of a rock wall. He couldn't tolerate the smell any longer and soaked the pile of fabric and flesh with a whole bottle of lighter fluid. A match lit the heap, and he listened to the "woosh" of air as the fire consumed the surrounding oxygen and shot ten feet high. While she burned, the van doors closed, and he drove up a path to the top of the wall. Back outside, the smell of cooking flesh carried up in the rising heat. Soon, the flames died out, and all that remained was a smoking, black mound.

The location of her body was not random. Twenty feet above, next to where he stood, a massive hill of small stones awaited use. They ranged in size from pebbles to tennis balls. With a little coaxing by his shovel, they began to roll over the edge and bury everything below. Finally, a rockslide started, and several tons poured down at once, encasing Lindsay into a deep, stone tomb.

Chapter Twenty-Seven

C ream-colored paint shone gray in the breaking daylight as Isaac peered up at the ceiling. There was no breeze outside to rustle the windows, nor did the air-conditioner blow through any vents. A rhythmic hum from the overhead fan made the only noise.

He continued to gaze through the semi-darkness, saying a silent prayer that today would go smoothly. The past few days, to his delight, had been closer to the way things were before. Josie was going full tilt with her friends and showed fewer signs of sadness every sunrise. Sarah, however, had made the biggest change. Since the arrival of the letter, she settled back into a more solid state of mind. Purpose and Josie's future well-being abruptly became more important than the past.

He moved his legs from under the covers and searched the hardwood floor for his house shoes. When he found the warm, shearling-lined moccasins, he went to the window and opened the shutters. The room brightened as he observed a thick fog set over the forested landscape.

Sarah stirred in the bed. He loved every ounce of her body and mind. But something was lost between them, and it saddened him. Time, he hoped, would be the cure.

"Honey, it's time to get up," he said.

"Mmmm," came a sound from the bed. "What are you doing?"

"Rise and shine."

Sarah yawned. Her eyes were still shut. "What time is it?"

"Six forty-five. I'll get Josie up." Sarah was not a morning person and never would be. "Coffee will be ready in the kitchen."

"Okay." She rolled over.

"Honey, are you awake?"

She pulled the covers over her head in response, completely vanishing beneath the duvet.

"I mean it. I have work, and both of you have hair appointments."

"Okay, okay, okay . . . I'm up. I'm up. I'll be there in a minute." She still didn't budge, and the linens muffled her voice.

"Coffee," he reminded as an incentive.

He silently strolled down the hallway, opened the door to Josie's room, and found an empty bed. The covers were neatly pulled up, not a pillow disturbed. Neither he nor Sarah had the heart to change Caroline's side of the bedroom. They felt like she belonged to them, still, in their house.

He sat beside Josie, his hip against her side, and stroked her hair. It was messy and beautiful. "Pumpkin, it's time to get up."

She stretched, needing only one call to wake. "Am I going with Mom today?" she asked through a yawn and squinty eyes.

"Yes, ma'am."

"I couldn't remember."

"It's because you're so busy playing with friends. Summers seem shorter than when I was a kid."

She nodded. "I had good dreams."

"What were they?"

"I dreamed of breakfast burritos."

"Burritos?"

"Yeah. Can we have some?"

Isaac looked to the clock on the nightstand. It was six fifty. If she and Sarah were going to make their hair appointments in Las Cruces, they needed to leave in an hour or less.

"You are a strange little thing," he said, referring to her dream, "but it's your lucky day, kiddo. I have to fly, so I need a good breakfast, too. If you can get all the way ready first, that will give me time to cook. What do you think?"

Josie vigorously nodded. "Deal!"

"Okay then. Go get your mom out of bed. Chop, chop," he teased and tickled her.

In the kitchen, he made coffee, thawed out some sausage, scrambled a few eggs, shredded cheese, and, to Josie's liking, added green chilies. He also pan-seared potatoes. "Let's eat!"

Josie dashed into the kitchen, all cute and dressed for town. "They're ready?"

"Yes, ma'am. Breakfast burritos à la Josie."

"Potatoes!" she said with great surprise.

Sarah also came into the kitchen and sipped her coffee. She still didn't look very happy to be up so early in the summer. "What's the occasion?"

Isaac pointed to Josie. She had an overstuffed tortilla in her small hands, slowly chewing a far-too-large bite for her mouth.

"I see." It put a smile on her placid expression. "What time are you leaving?"

"Just after you guys."

She nodded and sighed. "Be careful, will you?"

"I always am. Just another walk in the park."

"You say that every time, but it's still dangerous."

"Nah, the ground crews do the sketchy stuff. I only spot the danger. Then the real workers get sent in. I'm the eye in the sky, watching, waiting, and watching some more. It's slower than a jet, but at least I can take in the view."

Sarah had heard it all a million times. She always thought the world would be a better place if everyone, like Isaac, was blessed enough to enjoy his or her job. "All right, Mr. 'Eye in the Sky.' Don't eat too much fast food either."

"I didn't tell you?"

"Tell me what?"

"I'm staying with Mom and Dad. Taos is my dispatch point. No fast food for me."

Isaac used Ruidoso Municipal Airport for his personal base. He flew from there to wherever his patrol base was set to be. Depending on the scouting area, different towns in the New Mexico Rockies could be his home away from home. Any other town but Taos, and he had to stay in a hotel or hangar apartment and eat fast food. Of course, all of this was on the state's dollar, but it was his least favorite part of the job.

"Good. Then I won't have to feel bad about you eating crap every night."

"Nope. You'll just have to worry about Mom stuffing food down my throat."

"True."

When everyone finished, he hugged his girls at the door, watched as they walked across the lawn to the garage, and pulled away in Sarah's navy blue Jeep Grand Cherokee.

Fifteen minutes later, the kitchen spic 'n span, Isaac was halfway out the door when the telephone rang. He answered, thinking maybe Sarah had forgotten to tell him something.

"Hello?"

"Hey, it's Charlie."

"Hey, man. What's going on?"

"I wanted to catch you before you left." He paused. "I think you should know. There's been another abduction . . . in West Virginia."

Chapter Twenty-Eight

Isaac sat at the kitchen table and listened as Charlie relayed the details. He wished he could have left without answering the phone, without a new burden pressing on his shoulders. To stay informed was the best way to protect Josie, but that didn't make it easy. If the same man who killed Caroline did this new abduction, he wanted to know everything. No one else should have to endure what Bailey Davis must have gone through. But until the demon responsible left a large enough clue to be tracked down, more innocent little girls might go missing.

"Hey, you still there?"

"Yeah, I'm here. Just thinking that . . . I don't know what to think."

Charlie thought it best to sum up his intent rather than leave his friend hanging on the report. "Look, I didn't call so you would go off and worry. I promised to keep you in the loop, and that's what I'm doing. The FBI informed me, and I didn't want you to have any more surprises."

Isaac tried to relax and think positively. "I would rather know. I just . . . hoped the next piece of news might be that they caught him. I'm ready to pull my hair out here."

"I know. That's what we were all hoping."

"What makes the FBI so sure it's the same guy anyway?"

"I'm not clued in on everything. Not even close. And I don't pretend to be. But it does feel the same. This little gal just disappeared. She was last seen walking home from her music lesson."

"Yeah, but it's in West Virginia. Why there?"

"Why not? The last one was in Kansas. We're in New Mexico. He obviously has reasons. One may be as likely as another, but it's my guess that he wants to spread things out. And it's working. There's no way to know where he might live as long as he keeps things scattered across the country like this."

Isaac leaned over the table. His thumb and pointer finger massaged the pressure points on his nose. "Come on, Charlie. There's got to be more to it. Just because this guy was in New Mexico and Kansas, why do they think he's in West Virginia? You said it yourself. 'These things are rarely, if ever, random.'"

"Well, for starters, the missing little girl fits the profile. Also, a wheelchair from a grocery store was found in the area where she was last seen. The parking lot surveillance tapes were reviewed from that particular store, and it turns out a man in a white cargo van took it. The video is grainy, at best, and they can't get a close-up to see any details, but the basics are there. Lastly, there have been no other recent abductions in the area."

He heard everything, but Charlie's first sentence stuck. "And what profile is that?"

"The lead agent on the case says your girls, the one in Kansas and the girl in West Virginia, have similar physical descriptions. In fact, they're darn near identical."

"So what's the description?"

Charlie didn't want to explain what these children looked like. Painting a picture made the whole thing very realistic. He, too, loved Caroline, and the idea of someone targeting her because of a physical appearance sickened him. But facts were facts, and Isaac needed to know.

"They're all blonde, light-eyed, and middle to upper middle class. And they all live in relatively small towns."

"Yeah? What's it mean though?"

"Mean?"

What does he mean, "What's it mean?"

"It means," he said pointedly, "they're pretty. They're good-looking girls with good families and live in towns where people feel safe. This prick isn't some random asshole taking kids. He has a picture in his head, a picture of what he wants. There's something about these little kids that he's after."

"And their ages?"

"About the same. Seven to nine."

"What about the van?"

"According to the footage, a Ford is the best guess. Again, the tape is too grainy to see clearly. That's why this guy always gets in and out so quietly and, seemingly, without anyone noticing him. What's so out of place about a white cargo van, you know?"

"And that's it?" Isaac's tone prodded for more.

"No, there is one other thing." Charlie tried to calm his friend. "It's not anything that matters on our end, but . . ." He cleared his throat. "After they found the wheelchair in West Virginia, the FBI is pretty certain he is luring his victims. They went back over the Kansas abduction and followed up another lead. Again, it doesn't matter since he confessed in the letter, but he left a puppy in the alley where he took Bailey Davis."

"How'd they figure that one out?"

"Old-fashioned cop work. An agent found someone who recognized the pup. This person said that a friend of hers had set up in front of a local gas station and given them away to anyone willing to take them. When the agent questioned the lady who had the litter, she said she remembered a man with a white van taking that particular dog. Unfortunately, she can't remember exactly what he looked like or where the plates on the van were from."

"Just like that? This lady didn't see where the van was registered, and now we don't know anything more about him or his whereabouts than before?"

"Look, I don't like it any more than you do. This is a slick operator, and even his mistakes seem benign. I've never seen or heard of anyone like him. He's all over the map."

Isaac stayed silent. Too many thoughts sloshed around for words.

"I promise," Charlie assured, "this is all I know. The West Virginia kidnapping happened on Friday evening. Technically, it takes twenty-four hours before someone can be called a missing person. The FBI got involved on Monday and found similarities worth noting over the next day or two. Now here I am calling you after they called me. To them, I'm just a podunk policeman who's half a world away. My conversation was blunt and brief."

Isaac stayed quiet for a moment, thankful that Charlie had reached out. He didn't want to receive another gruesome picture of a little girl, no matter how much of a clue it could be. Even more, he didn't want anyone else to suffer pain and indignation.

"What's her name?"

"Lindsay," Charlie solemnly said. "Her name is Lindsay Watson from Shepherdstown, West Virginia."

Lindsay Watson. God help you, baby girl.

Chapter Twenty-Nine

The next morning in Taos, Isaac awoke to the sound of rain dancing off the Spanish tile roof above his bedroom. His head peeked from under the covers. A grin spread across his face as he realized the inclement weather would most likely ground him for the day. He reached for his cell phone on the nightstand and found a text from his patrol dispatch that confirmed his assumption. A thick line of storms had moved in during the night and stopped directly above half the Rocky Mountain range.

He threw on a long-sleeved T-shirt over blue jeans and walked across the terra-cotta floor to the kitchen. His parents' home had that Santa Fe, Western New Mexico, feel to it, like so many others in the area. It wasn't as much of a decorating style as it was a lifestyle or culture. The American Indians greatly contributed to the local population, and their influence was everywhere. Tom and Helen's house was fully modern but filled with Pueblo charm.

On the kitchen counter, he found a fresh pot of coffee with a handwritten note laid across the top of an empty mug.

Good morning! Mom has gone to work out and run
a few errands in town. I'm in the shop. Come on out
when you're up.

Dad

He looked out the bay window that surrounded three sides of a breakfast nook. It gave a panoramic view across the wrought iron fenced lawn, valley, and mountains beyond. But today, the rain obscured anything past the fence.

Tom's woodshop sat at the back of the driveway, barely out of sight through the haze. Isaac stepped under the porch overhang, slipped on his boots, and popped open an umbrella. After a few paces down the sidewalk, the little barn came into view. It didn't look like much from the outside, a standard tin structure. The inside, however, boasted a layer of creativity and craftsmanship far grander than the humble exterior.

The building had insulation. It allowed Tom to work comfortably, regardless of the temperature, weather, or season. The main floor, and by far the largest area of the shop, housed work tables, saws, planers, routers, jointers, lathes, and a myriad of other woodworking equipment necessary for the noble art. In one corner, an enclosed office with a large picture window looked into the shop. In the other, a staining room with ventilation fans provided a dust-free environment for wood finishing.

When Isaac was a little boy, Tom had his woodshop in his detached garage—the one behind Isaac and Sarah's house in Ruidoso—and built much of the furniture for their home. But like most working people, time had parameters, and he was unable to dedicate himself to the hobby as much as he would have liked. Now in the golden years of retirement, the parameters were gone.

In the middle of the floor, on one of the working tables, Isaac spotted a beautiful cedar chest. The rectangular cube consisted of solid walnut raised panels, spiraled corners, and inlaid corbels to support a half-moon, intricately hand-carved lid. Natural wood grain swirled and burst into random patterns of shapes and shades. A coat of lacquer would soon turn the flat sheen into pure radiance.

Tongue-and-groove cedar planks lined the shell, each precisely cut and seated into the next with seamless touch. It, unlike the walnut outside, would remain unfinished and raw to better protect its precious contents from moths and the slow decay of age.

Tom blotted a rag with lacquer thinner and guided it over the chest. It had to be clean, spotless from dust, before varnished.

"Dad, this is fantastic." Isaac let his hand slide along the edges. They were sanded to a smoothness rivaling a baby's bottom. "How long did it take?" He kept his eyes on the wood.

"I've been at it every day since we got back. Isn't the color of this black walnut great?"

Isaac took up another rag, dampened it with lacquer thinner, and went to work on the opposite side of the chest. He knew what to do and how to do it. Ever since he was big enough, Tom showed him how to shape something plain into a thing of beauty. "There's so much contrast and definition. This is higher quality material than most you get. Where'd it come from?"

"It's special order. I've never gotten this high of grade in this quantity."

"That must have set you back." The steady motion of gliding across the wood felt mysteriously relaxing.

"Nah, it wasn't too bad. The cedar lining is top grade, too." Tom looked over the open lid and pointed. "See, not a knothole in one piece."

Isaac took a break from his rag to peek over. "Was that special order, too?"

"Son, everything on this baby was special order. Lumber stores don't keep wood like this lying around."

"Does Mom know about it? I mean, is it a present for her, or did she ask you to do it?"

Tom stopped cleaning, and hung his head with a thoughtful expression. "Yes, she knows about it. And no, it's not for her."

"Then whose is it?"

He stood tall. His long, thin frame squared as he looked with watery eyes at his son. "It's for you and Sarah."

"Dad, this is too much." He inspected the handcrafted chest with admiration. Every square inch was completely original, designed from scratch by a master's hand. There was no other in the world like it and never would be. Bewildered, knowing how much money and effort must have painstakingly been poured into it, he said, "Did Sarah ask you to do it?"

Sarah frequently asked Tom for little things here and there. She knew it made him feel good to build things for the family. He had hand-carved the child-sized table and chairs in the twins' bedroom from large chunks of pine. When Caroline and Josie were babies, he also made their bassinets and cribs. Anytime he needed another project, Sarah was the first person he asked.

"No. This was your mother's idea. She thought that . . . because of . . ." The last thing he wanted to do was bring up bad memories. They were having a great time together, but there was no way around it. "Your mother thought that, because of what happened, you, and especially Sarah, need something nice to keep all your memories in. Caroline's memories. This is for her things."

Isaac held his father's gaze. The lump in his throat rendered him speechless. He could feel tears welling up, ready to spill from the corners of his eyes. If he spoke, his composure would slip. Silence protected what little strength he had.

"We thought it would mean more if I built it instead of buying one. It's supposed to be a happy gift, not sad."

Isaac had no more space for the tears. They dripped down his face and stuck to his dark, unshaven beard.

"I tried to have it finished. But since they canceled your shift this morning, we get a chance to work on it together. Maybe you'll like having a hand in it."

Tears came harder and faster, and he let go. It was too much to hold back. He hadn't felt this helpless since the funeral.

Tom stepped around the table and pulled him into a hug. Like any father who loved their son, he wished he could take up the mantle and bear all the pain himself. He wished, as Isaac did, that he could protect his family from all harm and danger.

They held each other until drained. Red-faced and puffy-eyed, they picked up their rags and continued to work. Without a word, stroke by stroke, they prepared a place for Caroline's material memories to rest.

Chapter Thirty

Video footage of Lindsay Watson played on a flat-screen television. Ricky stared, rapt from the comfort of his living room recliner. The intensity heated him, inside out, as he relived the gratifying event. Images of little girls fed endorphins to his body like flesh to a starving dog. The cravings were insatiable. The beast needed fed, regardless of whom it hurt. Still, in times after his addictive nature had been satisfied, deep down in a hidden part of his mind, he could see all the way back to the beginning.

He wondered if life could be different or if everything were predetermined and people only have the illusion of free will. He imagined himself in a parallel universe, one where a different Ricky made different choices, but the point was mute. Maybe there was another Ricky, and maybe there was not. Either way, he was this Ricky and on his own path. Life is what it is, not what it could be.

*   *   *

At the young age when he peeped on his neighbors and molested their Barbie collection, he still didn't know what sex was. But that did nothing to quell the natural instincts in his mind, and vivid fantasies ran rampant. He pretended that the sisters knew he watched them and that they liked it. Conversely, and to his disappointment, it soon became old.

Ricky began slipping out at night to peep through other windows. He learned which houses had attractive women or girls living in them and which rooms belonged to them. Darkness also gave him a sense of security. Through illuminated windows, he could see his subjects, but they could not see him.

Occasionally, he lucked out and found ladies changing, bathing, relaxing in the nude before they dressed, and thinking they were alone. He particularly liked to catch neighbors tanning topless or fully naked by their swimming pools. His neighborhood did not have any two-story homes, and the backyards were relatively private, especially the ones surrounded by high fences or hedges. Florida sunshine provided almost year-round warm weather, and it didn't take him long to make a schedule of who sunbathed on what days and the time on the clock when they did it.

There were no windows between him and the sunbathers. Only air separated him from their bodies. He wanted so badly to walk up, touch them, and rub the shimmering oil all over their glistening skin. On numerous occasions, he tried to talk himself into it, but knew he had no chance. The only way to keep enjoying the ride was to do so in private. If he were to make himself known, it would surely end.

One evening after spying on a lady, he walked down the alley behind his house. A stack of magazines on the ground by an overflowing dumpster caught his eye. The top cover had a voluptuous brunette posed seductively, a strand of ribbon veiled the tips of her bosom, and her legs were crossed to conceal the obvious. He looked around, decided the coast was clear, flipped the magazine open, and discovered a dream come true. Naked ladies gazed directly into his eyes, smiling, posed with bedroom expressions and yearning lips. They begged him to look, lust, and burn for their supple, gratifying flesh.

"Yes," they called to him. "Yes, you can have me whenever you want, however you want, because I want you, too. Turn the page. I'm here for your pleasure."

The pile of magazines was too large to carry, and he shuffled through them, hurriedly selecting the covers that looked most satisfying. He stuffed them in the front and back of his shorts and pulled his shirttail over the top. When he went inside, his mom and dad weren't there to ask him where he'd been, how his day was, or what he was up to. He sat in his room, alone, and pored over the pages of each issue. His fire burnt hotter than ever.

For weeks, he obsessed over the magazines in the comfort and privacy of his bedroom. He conversed on a first-name basis with many of the adult models. Dirty words, the kind he heard older boys use at school, started working their way into his one-sided conversations. It became another way to push the limit, expand his horizons, and keep it fresh.

The dumpster in the alley ingrained itself in his mind as a means. He checked it daily for new material. It didn't matter where they were coming from—maybe some guy with a flavor for nudie entertainment constantly refreshing his collection—but occasionally there were more. They replaced all but a favorite edition or two he prized too much to trash. This went on until puberty and hormones aggressively mutated his compulsion for the images. The magazines were great, but no longer as exciting as they once were. Every issue had differences, but they were all the same, one girl on the beach or another on a velvet couch with fine fabrics or hides lying here and there. There was an issue for the blonde lovers, brunettes, or redheads. Exotic bodies with dark skin, hair, and naturally voluptuous curves hit the pages one after another.

As chance had it, a cure presented itself. On a walk home from the beach, a street bum approached and asked for money. Without intention, a bold plan blossomed, and Ricky acted. It happened without even trying.

The newsstand on the boardwalk sold gum, candy, a few pairs of cheap sunglasses, newspapers, and magazines. Blacked-out shelves obscured a certain section of the magazines, only revealing the top one-third of the cover. It left little to the imagination, but enough to entice buyers with a taste for more. Ricky tried to buy several different issues with titles like *Hustler*, *Penthouse*, and, more obscure yet obvious, *Juggs*. The foreign man in charge of the cart refused him unless he had a valid ID. Short of stealing, another means of attainment never crossed his mind until lightning struck.

"Look." Ricky snatched a ten-dollar bill from his pocket, waved it in front of the homeless man, and motioned toward the magazine stand. "If you'll go back there and get me a *Penthouse*, you can keep the change and . . ." He patted his pocket. "I'll give you ten more."

He couldn't believe the words that just shot out of his mouth, but they had. He felt scared and thought about running. When the grungy beggar didn't say no, though, he held his ground.

The man scratched an inch-long beard with a set of fingernails that looked like they hadn't been washed for a year. "*Penthouse*, you say?"

"That's right, *Penthouse*. You keep the change, and I'll give you ten more bucks." Ricky's heart thumped from adrenaline, and his hands shook. His ears turned red, and he searched over both shoulders for anyone eavesdropping.

"You've got the money?" the homeless man asked.

"Yes."

"Let me see it." The bum raised his eyebrows in anticipation. Ricky pulled another ten-dollar bill from his pocket.

"How do I know you're not a cop?"

Ricky thought for a second. "Do I look like a cop?"

"No, I guess you ain't old enough. Suppose you tell someone where you got it?"

"I'm not telling anyone." He tried to think of the right things to say. "Not if you don't."

"All right. I guess it don't hurt none. Where you want me to bring it to ya, sonny?"

Ricky looked around for an ideal spot. He pointed across the road. "How about over there by those trees?"

The man looked toward the trees and nodded. "*Penthouse*?"

Ricky nodded in return and handed him one of the tens.

Five minutes later, he jogged home with a new magazine wrapped in his beach towel. In his room of an empty house, he slammed the door and ripped off the plastic cover. He sat down on the bed, opened the crisp pages, and, for the first time in his short life, learned from an erotic image the meaning of sex. The pictures soaked into his mind, a dry sponge willing to absorb the first wet thing to come along, and stained his psyche. With an illustrated guide to follow, his first physical experiment began.

Ricky established a rapport with the homeless man near the beach. Every so often, he scouted the newsstand for what he wanted, found the man, and paid him the same way. He always based his selections on the pursuit of nastier, riskier magazines. Once, he came to buy another magazine and was instead presented with a videotape and asked what he was willing to pay. The urge grew irresistible, and he bought it with extra spending money his mom had given him.

He sat on the couch in his parents' living room and watched the live, vocal action right before his eyes. He was only fourteen and had the house to himself. In the privacy of neglect, another layer was added to his lustful addiction.

He started requesting increasingly graphic films and eventually developed a taste for violent sex. A year later, he met the bum at their usual spot near the beach. Ricky burned through a video a week and found himself bored with each film more quickly than the one before. He waited in earnest to see what new material the guy would have for him.

"What's going on?" Ricky said when he arrived.

"Got something a little different for ya today." He made a gesture toward his backpack but made no motion to retrieve it.

"All right. What is it?"

The bum eyed him suspiciously. He bored a hole right into Ricky and said nothing.

"Well?" Ricky pushed him.

"You're always asking for something new. That right?"

"Yeah." No matter how many times they did this, it felt awkward to engage in conversation, like it made it more wrong. It was easiest when they did the exchange and went their separate ways.

"You got to promise not to tell." The man had a serious look on his face, like Ricky might not like what he had.

"I promise. I don't want to get caught any more than you do."

"Yeah, I suppose you're right." He let out a long breath and kept his face down. "Listen here, sonny, if you get caught with this . . . you don't know me, ya hear?"

"I hear," Ricky said. He felt hesitancy in his voice. *What the hell?* He couldn't imagine what all the cloak-and-dagger shit was about.

The sooty salesman extracted a VHS from his backpack. It was in a black case, not like the commercially sold videos he usually brought. He handed it over.

Ricky turned the case over, but the back was also blank. "What is it?"

The man looked off into space. "It's . . . young girls."

"Cool! Like college girls?" His grin ran the width of his face. He locked his eyes on the little plastic box.

"Look, they're just . . . younger."

"Okay." He liked the thought of it. "How much?"

The man shook his head and pulled up his cheeks in a grimace to make his eyes wrinkle around the edges. "Just take it home and see if you like it. If you don't, throw it away. If you do, I can probably get more, but you'll have to pay next time. This is a . . . sample."

Ricky took the tape home and put it in the VCR. The undisclosed mystery that shrouded its contents held him in suspense, and his fingers busily fumbled with buttons and the remote. The screen came up. The image on display was not what he expected. There was no music, only a solitaire little girl in a room filled with toys. She sat on a daybed with white linens and pillows. She was pretty, a sundress and strawberry blonde hair in a braid, and couldn't have been more than five years old. The scene did not look authentic. Rather, it was like a stage.

He watched in silence for the next thirty minutes, too tense, shocked, and deeply infatuated to move. A man who never showed his face entered the picture, molested, raped, and violated the little girl in more ways than Ricky could fathom. The girl screamed and cried as she was used. Without question, it was the highest of all highs, the thrill Ricky spent each subsequent day of his life in pursuit of. Children were no longer safe in his company. They were his ultimate drug.

*   *   *

Still in the recliner at his cabin, thoughts moving from the past to present, he couldn't shake the feeling of dissatisfaction. Regardless of the glory of his last success, Lindsay Watson was no Josie Snow. Somehow, someway, he had to have her.

Chapter Thirty-One

The remainder of Isaac's patrol went by without incident. The weather cleared, and the sky shone bright. He thought it peculiar how life has a way of sustenance. When a soul needs fed, the cosmos delivers. When he left Ruidoso, there were no expectations beyond flying a patrol and spending the short evenings in between with his parents. What he never saw coming, or even realize he needed, was for things to go exactly the way they had. Inside, he still had broken pieces yet to mend. One rainy day, a cancelled flight, and a morning with Tom in the shop worked a small miracle and led one step further down the road to wholeness. He didn't even know he needed it until it happened. Letting go of his strength and allowing himself to crumble, submit to the weakness of sorrow in his heart, renewed his spirit and made him stronger.

He turned his classic Chevy pickup onto their street on the mountain above Ruidoso and saw the little house he called home. He missed his girls and could hardly wait to see them. He wanted to walk up the back steps and receive the same "welcome home" greeting he did every Saturday evening. Now more than ever, such a small thing seemed so big. Everything he and his family were forced to endure was awful. But it did stir a new awareness and appreciation for life, an awareness that he knew would last until the end of his days. He was blessed. Truly blessed. It was impossible to walk this earth without attaining scars along the way. They remind us to hold life in perspective and not forsake the richness of each moment.

Josie came running to the sound of the back screen door. She leapt into his arms and squeezed him tight. "Did you see MaMaw and Pa Paw?"

"I sure did, kiddo, and they said to do this." Isaac nuzzled his nose and mouth into the crook of her shoulder and began kissing her cheek and neck.

She squealed and squirmed to get away from the ticklish whiskers. "That tickles!"

"It's from them, not me." He set her down. If they had done this once, they had done it a thousand times. Somehow, it felt new. "Did you and your mom have a good time?"

"Yeah." Josie put a hand on her hip, turned her face to the side, and tossed her hair. "Do you like my hair?"

Her new cut was shorter than the last one, just long enough to cover the back of her neck and put into a ponytail. It flowed, soft, smooth, and light. In that moment, Isaac was the most important man in her life, and she cared what he thought, more than any other. Soon, he knew it would not be that way. In the blink of an eye, she would blossom into a woman and turn the heads of boys who thought they were men. Hopefully, like her mother, a strong sense of self-worth and good morals would keep her on a track of healthy relationships and in the company of people with her best interests at heart. Not much longer, important life choices would begin falling into her lap. Isaac could only watch and pray that he had prepared her for the long, arduous, and rewarding journey we are fortunate enough to travel.

"I love it!" he proclaimed. He squatted to her level, squared her shoulders with his large hands, and looked into her eyes. "You are just as pretty as your mother."

"Thanks." The sparkle in her eye said that she felt pretty. "I helped Mom make supper, too."

"What else have you done while I was away?"

She shrugged. "Everything. Mom showed me how to make cherry cobbler."

"Oooh." He looked around the kitchen. "Where is it?"

Josie pointed to the utility room where it was cooling.

"Think we should try some?" He stood back up.

"I wouldn't. It just came out of the oven, and unless you want to burn your taste buds off, you'll have to wait." Sarah stood in the double doorway open to the living room. She came forward and kissed him on the lips. "You had a good trip?"

"Yep. Rain had me grounded at Mom and Dad's the first morning."

"At least you were at your parents and not a hotel. Did you and your dad get to hang out?"

"Yeah." He decided not to tell her about the chest. He wanted it to be a surprise when Tom finished it. "How was your week?"

She looked at the floor. "Fine. You know, just did stuff around the house, showed Josie how to cook, and went to the Smith's one night for dinner."

He knew she had something she didn't want to say. It wasn't difficult to see. A personality without pretension, she was an open book. "Anything else?"

"Josie, if you want to help put supper on the table, go wash your hands and face."

She brightened and ran from the room. Isaac gave his wife a puzzled look.

"A letter came in the mail today," she said. "I haven't opened it. I don't know. Maybe I'm paranoid, but it seems out of place."

His heart sank, and he recalled the conversation with Charlie on Wednesday morning before he left. Other than that, there was no reason to assume the worst.

She shrugged. "I didn't want to be alone. It's gross. What if there's something bad in it?"

He knew exactly what she meant. For hours, he had laid awake at night, seeking to understand what corrupted some creep's mind to send gruesome pictures and sick letters to children. Isaac loved life and the world, but he also understood that evil people shared it. And one of them was after his family.

"Where is it?"

"In your desk box. I didn't want Josie to see it."

He went into the living room and stepped through a set of French doors that separated his office. Stacked on top of a book sat a plain, white envelope with a handwritten address. If it were from the killer, more than a letter was inside. He could feel an object approximately a quarter-inch thick.

"I think something is in it," Sarah noted.

He nodded.

"Should we open it?"

He inhaled and let out the long breath with a reserved sigh. "I think we have to." He gestured toward the doors. "Close those, will you?"

Sarah leaned her head out. "Josie, after you wash your hands, set the table, please."

"Okay," came a reply from the hallway bathroom.

He put the blade of his pocketknife to the envelope and went to cut it.

"Wait!" Sarah scolded. "Charlie said not to open anything suspicious. We could contaminate evidence. Call him and tell him we might have another letter."

Isaac didn't want to. He wanted to open it right there and find out what was inside. If there were another threat against his little girl, he wanted to know about it immediately. But Sarah was right, and he had to make the call. If he messed up anything by opening it, he would never forgive himself. He picked up the handset and dialed.

"Charlie Biddle," he heard after the second ring.

"Hey, it's me." His tone was grave and emotionless. "I think we have another letter."

Charlie's voice grew serious. "Are you sure?"

"No, I'm not sure, but it's suspicious. There's no return address, and the handwriting looks like the other one."

"Is anything else in it?"

"Yeah, there is, but I don't know what. It's right here on my desk." Isaac tried to remain calm. He hadn't been home for more than ten minutes, and the situation grew more agitating by the second. "I don't know what to do with it."

"That's fine," Charlie reassured. "Don't touch it anymore. I'm coming right over. Just . . . leave it where it is."

Chapter Thirty-Two

C harlie leaned over the desk in Isaac's study and analyzed the standard white, slightly bulging envelope. He removed his cap, frowned, and tucked a jowly chin to his chest. The longer he scrutinized the handwritten address, the more his balding scalp shined.

"What do you think?" Isaac asked from the opposite side with his arms crossed. He looked at Charlie, then to Sarah, and back at Charlie.

"I think." He let out a huff. The creases on his forehead and between his brows grew deeper by the second. "I think I don't like this. At all."

Sarah scooted away from the built-in bookshelf she leaned against and moved closer to the desk. "It's from him, isn't it?" She eased up to Isaac. The side of her arm touched his as a subconscious fear leeched into her heart.

"Well . . ." Charlie continued to ponder the evidence. "Maybe. There's no return address, like the last one. The handwriting is definitely not a child's." He squinted. "And it looks similar, if not identical to the first letter, but without having them side by side, I can't say for sure."

"So what now?" Isaac rocked back on his heels.

Charlie stood up straight and made eye contact. "The usual. Investigate. I take this down to the station, open it, and take a look. That's the only way to know for sure."

"Can you do it here?" Sarah asked.

"I suppose," he said uncertainly. "It arrived in your mailbox, and that means you have a right to see it. But, if it is from him, are you sure you want to?"

"Dammit, Charlie." Her expression was now stern. "You don't have to tiptoe around me." The fear that had previously been in her voice vanished. "I've already read one letter and seen the picture with it. This can't be any worse." She lowered her voice so Josie couldn't hear from the kitchen. "If it's idle threats, then so be it. But if it's not—if it has anything to do with when he might come back—then I have to know. This shithead's pushed me way beyond niceties." She jabbed at the letter with her pointer finger. "Let's get on with it."

Charlie relinquished with a slightly shocked, slightly somber expression. Sarah's directness was new to him, different from her usual mild way. He didn't know if it had always been a part of her personality, the current circumstances revealing a dormant persona, or if she was hardening in a way that she never previously had need of. Whichever, he couldn't blame her. "Okay, then."

From a bag of forensics and evidence collection supplies, he put on a pair of latex gloves and draped a thin piece of painter's tarp over the desk. He set the envelope in the middle and, holding it down gently with one hand, slipped a scalpel under the flap. The sound of metal slicing through paper scraped against the anxious silence in the little room.

Isaac wrapped his arm around Sarah and pulled her close.

After Charlie slit the paper across the top, he inserted his thumb and pointer finger, pinching the contents between them. A plain sheet of neutral stationary, twice folded, came out. He opened the folds and held the corners down.

Dear Josephine, This being my second letter, I hope it reaches your hands. My recent attention has been on Lindsay Watson in West Virginia. I noticed this little music prodigy and immediately wanted to see how special she really was. My time with her may have been brief, but what we missed out on in quantity, she more than made up for in enthusiasm. I, however, am amazed that miles and variety fail to curb my hunger, my hunger for you, the one who slipped away. I do hope you are adjusting well to life as it is. I think about you and Caroline every day. Until we meet again . . .

Thinking of you,
XOXO
P.S. Do you like red?

Isaac flared with anger. How anyone could want to hurt little kids, Josie, evaded comprehension. "I'm going to kill him," he said flatly. He looked into Charlie's eyes. "I'm going to hurt him, bad, and then I'm going to kill him."

"Isaac?"

"You can say whatever you want, Charlie. But if it comes down to it, if I ever get lucky enough to be alone with him, I will kill him slowly. Some people on this earth need killing, and he's one of them."

Charlie didn't look away. He locked eyes with his best friend, his childhood pal, and nodded his head. He knew there was no talking him out of it. And honestly, he couldn't blame him. *I hope you never have to.*

"Before you kill anyone," Sarah chimed, "shouldn't we see what else is in the envelope?"

A month ago, she lived on the border of reason and hysterics. Now the reality that Josie remained a target for a demonic pedophile made her more centered in terms of behavior and logic. Caroline no longer needed their protection; Josie did.

Charlie refocused on the task at hand without comment. Reaching back inside, he pulled out two more items. They quickly passed around a Polaroid picture—held between a Kleenex—of Lindsay Watson. The image would have previously been just cause for nausea, but they had seen the like with Bailey Davis, and their faces remained emotionless.

No mother should ever see her child like this, Sarah thought.

The second item, a plastic baggie with something bloody inside, Charlie held up to the light and squinted his eyes. He wanted nothing more than to throw everything away and never look at any of it again, but his job was to detect information from the evidence at hand, no matter how unpleasant. Finally, he set it aside and wiped his brow with a handkerchief from his hip pocket. The meal in his stomach felt like it might crawl back up his esophagus and make a second appearance. He closed his eyes and inhaled.

"What is it?" Sarah asked.

He picked up the Polaroid and laid it directly beside the baggie. "I think . . ." He looked back and forth, studying them closely. "I think it's . . . her nipple."

Chapter Thirty-Three

"I want to talk about this before I leave tonight," Charlie started. He closed the lid on the forensics kit and hesitated. "Knowing more about this pervert probably won't make life easier, but it will help both of you to better understand him."

"Understand?" Isaac asked scathingly. "I think it's pretty cut-and-dry, don't you?"

"Not necessarily, no. I don't think it's cut-and-dry." He hardened his face, arched his eyebrows, and looked serious. "I'm not talking about physical pleasure, the seemingly obvious motive. What I'm talking about is: Why does he really do what he does? What is the very basis for his behavior, the true core of why he is the way he is? Absolute motive?"

"Don't give me that," Isaac held up fingers in quotations, "he's probably got Mommy or Daddy issues line of crap. It shouldn't matter why. It *doesn't* matter why. The fact is, he does. End of story!" He looked at Sarah for confirmation.

"I'm not saying that both of you don't have the right to feel the way you do. But from an investigative point of view, it matters a great deal."

Sarah paced to the corner and turned around. "Why? Why can't the all-powerful FBI just catch him already?" Her frustration emanated, and she threw one hand in the air. "Why do we have to get to know him?"

"Because, in case you haven't noticed, he implies he *will* come back for Josie. If he does, don't you want to know as much about him as possible?"

Neither answered. They knew Charlie was right. To know their enemy better could turn out to be the only means of protecting Josie.

"He wants us to know who he is, guys," Charlie continued. "Not personally, but with his identity as a child predator. Otherwise, there is no reason on this earth that he would send letters to someone he wants. He's waving a flag saying, 'Look at me! Look at me!'"

"All right then." Isaac shifted his weight to one foot. "What about postmarks? Where is he?"

Charlie shook his head. "The first was from Nebraska, and this one is from Ohio. He's mailing them on the road. However, I think he lives somewhere in the western half of the country."

"What makes you think that?"

"Both letters were processed by the Postal Service west of where he made the previous abductions. If he's mailing them on the drive home, then he lives west of Hiawatha, Kansas."

Sarah wanted clarification. "So just west?"

"That's right. Just west. Without a name or state where the vehicle is registered, that's all we've got."

She paced four more steps to the opposite corner and turned again. "Back to the motive. Isaac told me the FBI is working on a profile. What do you think he's after?"

Charlie rubbed a hand over his shiny head, a nervous tick when thinking. "In the past three abductions—this is beyond the physical resemblance of the girls—there is a recurring thread. Maybe it's a coincidence, but I don't think so."

Sarah stood akimbo. "And?"

"Within one month prior to every kidnapping, each of the girls, Josie and Caroline included, have been recognized for an outstanding quality or action."

Realization popped into Isaac's head. "You mean catching Jason with the tablecloth when he jumped off the roof?"

Charlie nodded once. "And Bailey Davis from Kansas. She raised over two thousand dollars for a local food drive with a lemonade stand." He shook his head. "Can you imagine? Two thousand dollars with lemonade? The local paper covered her, and so did a Kansas City paper." Charlie zipped his bag and let it rest on the desk. "Lindsay Watson has also made the papers recently."

"What did she do?" Isaac asked with new interest.

"Lindsay plays," he stopped short. "Lindsay *played* the violin. She was scheduled to make a guest appearance with the New York Symphony Orchestra. Once a year, a select group of musically gifted kids is chosen. The *Times* printed an article about her a couple weeks before she disappeared."

Sarah's hands were over her mouth. Shock was in her eyes. Before all of this, she didn't have her mind wrapped around the idea that the killer's motives went beyond the physical weakness of lust. Now that changed. "You're saying he only goes after kids who have done something special?"

As soon as she said the word, a sentence from the letter flashed in her memory. *I noticed this little music prodigy and immediately wanted to see how special she really was.*

Again, Charlie's hand passed over his chubby, balding head. "I'm not saying that as an absolute," he clarified. "Only, as I see it, there is a high probability that public recognition is part of his selection process."

Sarah's eyes began to tear, and she sat down on the couch. Bad things were not supposed to happen to good people, especially kids. But all over the world, they do. The fact that the good deeds themselves—good deeds that her little girls did—were the cause for all this hurt and chaos felt unbearable. *When Josie is old enough and we tell her that a man tried to take her and Caroline to do bad things with them, how will I explain it was because they saved Jason's life? I can't tell her to stop doing good for others. I won't.*

"If that *is* why he chooses them, why mention it?" Isaac wanted to know. It didn't make sense to him. *Maybe it takes one to know one.*

Charlie pulled up his utility belt and put the other hand to his mouth. He put one finger across his upper lip like a mustache. "I want to clarify that all of this is unofficial and just my opinion. The Bureau may have a similar one, but if they do, they haven't shared it with me. I think our man is trying to level the playing field. For himself, I mean. Maybe he has a particular taste, like some men prefer blondes to brunettes. If that's the case though, why not simply go after the most convenient, pretty blonde girl he can find? Why drive halfway across the country to take someone who looks like the girl next door? Why New Mexico? Why Kansas? Why West Virginia? I think *destination* is coincidence and *selection* is calculated."

"Do people really do that?" Sarah asked, incredulous.

"Sure. Everybody wants something out of life. Just because you want nice, common things for yourself doesn't mean everyone else does. This guy wants little girls, particular ones. Why? I don't know. But I'd bet my life that it has something to do with the way it makes him feel on the inside, not the outside. It could be a misgiving from childhood, and these girls' accomplishments help him feel more important. The old saying, "You're known by the company you keep," applies to criminals more often than most care to know. Maybe he feels like he's never amounted to much and fulfills that desire by feeding off the achievements of others. Sure, it's a sick way of doing it, but it is possible. He picks rare victims and then gets off by rubbing it in everyone's faces. It's a roundabout way of making oneself feel important, but if he were like the rest of us—"

"What could possibly be in his past to justify his actions?" Sarah shook her head. "Even to himself?"

"Who knows? Maybe something terrible, perhaps a traumatic event or traumatic several years made him this way. Most of us experience times in our lives we wish differently. In odd ways, we even try to return there and fix it. And since we never can go back in time, we spend our future trying to balance the scales." He shrugged. "And maybe nothing at all happened to make him this way. Lots of people do bad things because, simply, it makes them feel good. Whatever it is, though, all people—I don't care who they are, where they're from, or how they go about it—have the same desire."

Charlie looked them in the eye and paused to make sure they digested this little piece of clairvoyant gold. "We all want to be seen. We all want to be heard. We all want validation."

After a silent moment of contemplation, Isaac asked, "In every letter he asks, 'Do you like red?' What does that mean?"

Charlie let out a long sigh. "No idea."

Chapter Thirty-Four

The abode sat beneath towering fir trees, tucked a hundred yards off a remote, forest road. Ricky's fifteen-hundred-square-foot log home was his pride and joy. It took him a year of hard searching to find the secluded gem outside the suburbs of Denver. The wait, however, was little consequence to the reward of total privacy. A national forest bordered his two-acre spread on three sides.

The allure of Rocky Mountain weather was his original attraction to Colorado, as it is to thousands of college graduates looking to make their way in life. A sales job for a big-box electronics retailer came easy enough, and he went to work. There was definitely something special about life in the mountains. Something fresh, new, and invigorating. But before long, he grew bored with the daily grind. Answering to a boss, day in and day out, put a damper on extracurricular activity. He needed out.

A skilled hand with electronics could easily find work on a private, per job basis. He started soliciting home stereo, surround sound, movie room installations, computer, and car stereo jobs to customers at a fraction of the price the store charged. As a store employee, he also had the benefit of purchasing discounted equipment and selling to customers for a markup, a win-win for everyone. The customer saved, and he made money. In a few months, Ricky had enough business through word of mouth to quit the day job. He lived frugally, controlled his work schedule, and finally had time to pursue other more exciting interests.

Now, several years later and in the middle of the most intense summer of his life, Ricky still wanted more. If he couldn't have Josie, another had to take her place. *Someone pretty. Someone special.*

Of course, Josie remained the ultimate goal, and he couldn't stop himself from sending the letters to inform the most important person in his life what he was up to. But even the quest for her would eventually come to an end like so many before. At this moment in the infinite span of time, though, she was his huckleberry, his luscious little peach, ripe for the taking. He wanted her more than he knew how to handle. The buildup felt like nothing else before, not since the first time he actually placed his hands on live, warm flesh. If he sat still and concentrated on the memory in enough detail, sensations of her fresh-out-of-the-sun skin stimulated the corpuscles of his hungry fingers once again. Her sun-bleached hair tickled the bottom of his nostrils. The taste of salty hair from the seawater lingered on his lips. He thought of the clamminess of her damp skin beneath the elastic fabric of her swimsuit as he greedily searched her body with his spindly paws.

*   *   *

He found her at the local beach on a memorably hot day, not far from where the homeless man used to buy the dirty magazines for him. Over time, pictures and even video lost their luster. The monotony of watching slowly festered into a rancid poison in his mind and bred the desire for a new corruption, touch.

The target-rich environment of a local snow cone stand made an ideal place to stalk his prey. And after all these years, he could see the girl like it was yesterday. She had her hands wrapped around a white, Styrofoam cup, a towering dome of blue coconut shaved ice on top.

From twenty yards away, he ran his eyes over every inch of her elementary body. Another girl, a few years older, approached and stood with the younger one amongst a scattered floor of picnic tables. He instantly knew the newcomer was his target's older sister.

"Olivia, I'm walking back to the house," she said. "Are you ready to go?"

Olivia, he mused with satisfaction. A name made it much more personal.

"I'll be there in a minute," Olivia replied without looking away from her treat. She took a bite off the top of her monstrous snow cone. "It's too big to walk right now."

The older sister let out a huff and put a hand on her hip. "Fine." She rolled her eyes. "Just don't take long. I'm not supposed to leave you."

Little Olivia nodded her eight—to nine-year-old head. Her lips were already stained blue. The older one walked away.

Five minutes later, the snow cone chewed down to a manageable mass, Olivia went in the same direction as her sister. She walked, only paying attention to her rapidly melting ice. Ricky followed at a distance until he discovered her destination, a row of bungalows along the beach about a quarter-mile up a deserted sidewalk. The houses were popular with families who spent summer vacations on the beach.

As he followed along the palm tree-shaded path, halfway between him and the houses, a landscaped bed of overgrown bushes and shrubs caught his attention. The sidewalk passed directly beside it. And in the middle of the blistering afternoon heat, not a soul was in sight. Everyone around was either in the water, laying out, or relaxing in an air-conditioned space.

Ricky sped to a jog and ran past Olivia like any teenage boy in a hurry. He sniffed as he passed, trying to catch a whiff of her sunscreen lotion. When he reached the flowerbed, he looked back and saw her spooning out slush from the cup. He quickly ducked into the bushes and hid.

Her yellow bikini grew brighter in the shade of the palms as she came nearer. She hummed a sweet tune, some song stuck in her head, not a care in the world. Then, at precisely the right instant, a hand slipped over her mouth and an arm around her tummy before she could react.

Ricky's spontaneous plan succeeded, but the reality of it felt very different from how he imagined it might. Wild, perverse fantasies that previously occupied his thoughts swirled into fear as seconds on the clock ticked away. He decided to get down to business and get the hell out.

With one hand still clasped over her mouth, pulling Olivia's head tightly against his chest, he used his free hand to explore her body. His sweaty palm roved over her suit in a medley of rushed motions. Time went into overdrive.

She squirmed, not sure what had just happened and no idea who had her. What was left of her blue coconut snow cone pooled on the cement. A few dribbles ran down her bare legs. She reached with both hands to the one clamped over her mouth and pulled at it. A barely audible scream escaped. It wasn't enough to alert anyone, but one of the strange, bony fingers slid between her teeth. She seized the opportunity, bit down hard, and held it.

Ricky's fantasy abruptly ended as pain shot into his finger. Reflexes took over, and his hand flew away from her face. An ear-busting scream pierced the air before he could regain control. As suddenly as he had taken her, it ended. He leapt from the bushes in a mad panic and ran for his life, a throbbing, bloody finger clenched tightly in a fist.

It had taken so long to catch his breath after running away, even after sitting on his bed at home for fifteen minutes. He remembered the palpating thump of his heart sending blood to his shaking limbs. But it had been worth it. Olivia had been worth it. From that point on, society at large—at least the young, female population—was at his disposal, food for his sick addiction, minor obsessions. He put a Band-Aid over the bloody teeth marks where Olivia broke the skin on his finger and abstained from washing his hands for a week.

*   *   *

That was so long ago, almost two decades since his shortsighted youthfulness, but the desire remained strong. He needed someone again. The computer screen at his desk glowed with life from a touch of the mouse, and the hunt began. News station websites were good places to start.

Chapter Thirty-Five

Unlike Ruidoso, Hiawatha, and Shepherdstown, he did not have to go far this time to stalk his prize. Ricky sat leisurely but aware in his van. A gentle Colorado breeze sifted through the open window and into cab. The drive to Woodland Park had taken less than two hours from his home-in-the-woods hideout.

Once a small, alpine town outside of Colorado Springs, the neighborhoods of Woodland Park were only accessible by jeep trail. Now paved roads lead very near the peaks of granite spires. The town is picturesque, full of residents who seek serenity and an outdoor lifestyle. People who live there love it, and people who visit wish they lived there.

The gorgeous mountain summers inspire local residents to do one thing above all else, enjoy an array of outdoor activities. Mindy Kessler and her mom were no different.

Each day after lunch, they would pack a snack basket, walk from their house to the park, and lay for an hour on the green, outfield grass of the softball field. Mindy's mom liked to roll up the sleeves of her T-shirt and tan while her daughter played with other kids. They had done this three days in a row now, and Ricky followed each time. Their simplistic routine obvious, he devised a plan that might work famously. But if he didn't get lucky today, no skin came off his back. He was guilt-free until the actual second that he grabbed her.

Once again, he watched from down the block as Karen, Mindy's mom, strolled along the sidewalk toward the park. Mindy skipped happily beside her. When they turned the corner and disappeared, Ricky circled around to enter the park from a different street.

Dozens of people were scattered about the recreational area. A few junior high and high school kids shot hoops on the ball courts. A handful of elementary-aged kids played on the swing sets and monkey bars. Another group kicked a soccer ball back and forth. Even with all the people, the conditions were perfect. Sounds of life and action were ideal camouflage to hide a stalker in plain sight. Besides, the noisier the atmosphere, the longer Mindy's mother would take to realize the sound of her own daughter was missing.

Parked in the lot next to where the walking trail connected with the parking area, Ricky stepped out of his white utility van. He wore a set of thin, navy blue coveralls with "Joe" written in block letters on a white nametag. On top, a grungy, neon orange vest, the bright ones seen on road workers or city maintenance crews, hung over the bogus uniform. A dirty, old cap and a pair of soiled leather gloves completed the disguise.

As he strode into the park to find Mindy, he pulled a rolling trashcan behind him. The container was the same type used by professional janitors, a big, industrial gray, cylindrical tub on wheels. An extendable grabber hung from his other hand to give the appearance of a cleanup worker. Inside the container, several candy wrappers, empty soda cans, crumpled papers, and plastic bottles partly filled a black liner. It had to look authentic. Not to mention, a certain satisfaction over cleaning the environment made him feel good. He hated how people littered, filthy people who drank from disposable water bottles and discarded them after one use. It had taken him less than ten minutes to gather two fistfuls of candy wrappers from a highway median. It pissed him off how so many cared so little about the health of nature. And the irony of cleaning the earth while hunting was not lost. A smirk crossed his lips as he reached out with the grabber and disposed of another piece of loose trash.

He found Mindy running pell-mell with a group of kids, an energetic game of freeze tag in session. He watched her play, certain to keep busy with his service duties and avoid notice. Every so often, he fidgeted with a trash receptacle, not actually doing anything to it, picked up a stray cup, and never ventured far from the public bathroom facilities. All little kids had to pee after playing. It was only a matter of time until Mindy had to go. Time passed in slow motion, but finally the words came.

"Mom," Mindy shouted toward Karen lying in the middle of the huge lawn. "I have to go the bathroom."

Karen didn't even look. She simply raised an arm off the blanket and waved in acknowledgement. The only people in the neighborhood park were local residents. In their secluded little village, there had never been a threat of insecurity. And that was exactly why Ricky had come.

That's it, Momma. Don't even look. Just keep on cookin' in that sunshine.

The restrooms were forty to fifty yards away, positioned at the edge of the grass, mere steps from the trailhead entrance. Ricky was closer and beat Mindy there. The ladies' room had no door, only a cinderblock wall that doubled back to create a privacy barrier.

He peeked his head in. "Cleaning crew." He paused for an answer. "Anyone in here?"

The room returned silence in answer.

He stepped behind the bend and flattened himself against the interior wall. Five seconds later, Mindy screeched around the corner and never had time to scream before a set of arms wrapped around her. A wet cloth pressed tightly against her face stifled any cries for help. She squirmed, but to no avail. Her eyelids fell shut seconds later, and her knees buckled.

Ricky snatched the partly filled liner out of the rolling trash container and immediately slung Mindy over the edge. She plunked to the barrel bottom, and the black liner went right back on top of her limp body. If anyone were to look inside the bin, all they would see was a bag full of garbage. The whole process took less than twenty-five seconds.

He came out of the bathroom, wheeling the trashcan out in front as he walked. Everything seemed just as it had been a moment ago. A basketball bounced. The pitter-patter of feet running across a drawbridge echoed. Laughter and sounds of nature filled the air. He dared a quick glance toward Karen. She had not budged.

At the back of his inconspicuous white van, he opened the rear doors and lifted the tub inside without a hitch. Just then, another mother-and-daughter pair walked behind him and entered the park.

As he turned to leave, the little girl tugged on her mom's arm. "Are they here yet? Is Mindy here?"

Chapter Thirty-Six

Ricky made his way home with Mindy still drugged in the bottom of the trash can. The back of the van would not host the events he had in store. She was going inside his house, the guest of honor at their private party.

The idea of sharing his real bed excited him beyond measure. Never before had he brought a lover home. But the monotony of his previous two episodes grated on his personal satisfaction. Bailey and Lindsay were had in similar fashion, submission by force, not choice. This time, he wanted to mix it up and change the pace.

Like a good conservationist, Ricky tried not to overhunt his local area. Wary prey and suspicious eyes were not conducive to his actions. Instead, he ventured far and wide, taking victims from scattered locations, and leaving no pattern or links for the authorities to connect until now. Now he actually took the time to fess up to the abductions through letters to Josephine Snow. There was an undeniable thrill to pushing the envelope, but he also needed to be more cautious than ever. Police and citizens alike would be on the lookout for Mindy as soon as the Amber Alert hit the waves. And this time, Ricky's whereabouts were directly inside the soon-to-be search radius.

He steered the van around a curve and saw his plain, galvanized mailbox on the roadside up ahead. His pulse quickened as he drove down the twisting, spruce-lined driveway, and backed into the garage. Despite an undeniable relief, his cheeks flushed with heat. No matter how many times he did it, stealing a kid made him feel vulnerable, alive.

This was it. Time for gratification had come again. He opened the back doors and hauled the trash can onto the cold, cement floor. It thumped on impact, and a groan came from inside. His hands slipped under Mindy's armpits, pulling her up and out. Her head rested on his shoulder, like a father carrying his sleeping child.

"It's okay," he reassured in a whisper and patted her back. The other hand slid under her bottom to support her weight. "I've got you. We're going inside." He patted again. "You're okay."

He laid Mindy's limp body on a couch in the surprisingly cozy—for a child abductor, murderer, and rapist—living room. On his bed in the master suite, he stripped the linens and spread a plastic tarp over the mattress, then put the sheets and comforter back on. If this turned out to be another blood bath, like Lindsay, he wanted to be prepared. He smoothed the cotton fabric with soft-skinned hands and made sure they were straight. Everything needed to look nice for the pictures. The back of the van was not conducive to elaborate photography, but here at the house, he could take his time and get as creative and imaginative as possible. This being a new way of doing things, he wanted to make sure and document it extensively.

With the bed prepared, he brought Mindy in. His little lover looked so sweet, soft, and tantalizing. In the comfort of his own home, Ricky's mind began to play tricks. He started to believe that she might feel the same way about him as he did her. *Somebody out there cares about me.*

Giddiness fell in with hatred, twisted love, anxiety, lust, and the other quagmire of warped feelings he harbored in his hardened heart and blackened mind.

He prepared the camera, video, and audio equipment, his mood further brightening as Mindy opened her eyes. Her brow furrowed in confusion, and her eyes squinted to filter the brightly lit room. He watched as she ran through her senses—smell, sight, and sound—to detect anything familiar.

He sat on the bedside and leaned over her as he had with so many before. "Welcome back." The words came out softly, genuinely.

She was only seven, confused and unable to remember how she had gotten there. She tried to speak, but her dry throat stuck.

"Would you like some water?"

She nodded.

Ricky handed her a glass of water from the nightstand. He kept his hand cupped underneath while she sipped. Intentions of violence were far from his mind. After a few swallows, she looked at him expectantly, searching for an explanation.

"I'm not going to hurt you, baby." He put the glass down and stroked a loose strand of hair over her delicate ear. "I need you to trust me. Can you do that? Will you trust me?"

A willingness to cooperate from his victims was new to Ricky. Not that he hadn't coaxed cooperation from them before, just not without threats or punishment. If he could keep Mindy operating of her own free will, fantasies he had conjured up over the years were finally within reach. *Easy, Ricky. Play nice.*

He scooted her toward the headboard, sat her up, and favored her with a charming smile. "You really don't have to be scared." His hand gently squeezed hers, and she didn't pull away. Instead, she looked around, trying to make sense of it all.

"I need you to do a favor for me." From a small, pink sack, he pulled out a size double zero lacy outfit. "It may be a tiny bit big," he said and held it up. "But I bet you'll look beautiful. I got it for the fun pictures we're going to take."

Mindy scrutinized the outfit. While she didn't understand that it had deeper meaning than just being pretty, she had seen similar pieces before, mostly on her parents' bedroom floor. She was an only child. At her young age, the "birds and bees" were simply that, birds and bees. Her mom and dad could be somewhat careless with their love life and still get away with it.

"Tell you what, gorgeous. I'll turn around, and you can change. Okay?"

Ricky left the lingerie on the bed and took a couple steps away. He turned his back. "Go ahead." He waited.

He heard her shirt slip from over her head, and then the snap button on her shorts popped loose. When Mindy slid the zipper down, the sound carried to Ricky's ears. He gave her a minute until he could wait no longer.

When he turned, she sat with her legs hanging over the side, head looking down at a pair of dangling feet. Her arms were wrapped around her body, chill bumps covering her skin. She looked like a child playing dress-up in her mother's clothes.

"You . . . look . . . stunning!" He continued to dote with each step toward her. His pointer finger ran down her arm. The hand that was capable of killing so coldly felt warm to the touch.

Mindy did not flinch; nor did she look up. She just sat there, devoid of reaction. Ricky convinced himself that her lack of enthusiasm came from nerves, not disapproval. *She loves me and wants me.*

From the time he was a little boy, he had just needed someone to care, but no one did. At least not in the right way. He didn't need more spending allowance. He didn't need more free time, video games, or satellite channels to be a happy kid. He simply needed attention from the people who gave it to him least. He needed quality time with his busy parents.

Ricky knew Mindy had never been involved with a man before. He made up his mind to show her how love worked. He would make her feel pretty, wanted, and special. He would do that for her, and she would love him in return.

First, he made her pose in numerous positions on the bed. He snapped and clicked with a digital camera, each shot striving to capture the sensual nature of her body, the kind only a creep can find in a child. He instructed her on how to make seductive faces and where to put her hands, saying that was what big girls did. With a smile and kind words, Ricky squeezed every ounce of modesty from her.

No matter what she did, though, her purity remained unmarred. She felt nothing of a sexual nature in any of it. Even his best efforts could not spoil her innocence. Children have places even the vilest of monsters cannot touch, not even in the personal porno he forced her to star in.

A message on the camera screen stopped him. "I have to get another memory card." *Damn.* "Don't you move now. I'll be right back."

He stepped from the bedroom, through the living room, and into the kitchen. Extra camera supplies were in the top drawer below the bar.

He fumbled through the cords, disks, and flash drives and found a new memory card. He removed the full one from the camera, labeled it with a post-it note, and put it in a plastic baggie. Already, he couldn't wait to download it and look through the pictures. The new card inserted flawlessly, and he checked the settings to make sure they were the way he liked. All set, he hurried to get back to the main event in the bedroom.

A door from the kitchen entered the cushy living space. What he found there shattered his world of imagination and sent him back into the reality where he was a violent kidnapper and Mindy was the kid. The fantasy he had dreamed of for so long popped like a soap bubble in the sun.

Chapter Thirty-Seven

Mindy stood on a cushion, the black, lace teddy sagging on her tiny body. She was in the foyer off the living room with one arm stretched as high as she could reach. The safety chain at the top of the front door jingled against her fingertips. She had already unlocked the deadbolt. It took every ounce of her concentration and nerve to do it quietly and overcome her quivering hands. Just ten more seconds was all she needed to slide the chain free and open the door. She could almost hear freedom knocking on the other side of the knotted pine barrier.

While taking pictures on the bed, she had managed to hold her tears at bay and fight the paralysis of fear. There were things her mom had told her to do if anyone ever took her.

"If somebody grabs you, scream as loud as you can. Don't stop screaming until you get help." But it was too late to scream. There was no one to hear.

"If you can't get help," her mom went on, "do exactly what they tell you to do. Make them be nice to you. Just keep doing whatever they want. And if you get the chance, you run. You run as far as you can and don't stop. Find a house, a store, a town, someplace with people. Use a phone to call nine one one and tell them what happened."

That was exactly what she tried to do. The man went away and gave her an opening to escape. There was no phone in sight. Instead, she found the door and undid the lock, but she had to tiptoe because the safety chain was too high. She tried once, twice, three times. It was still too high. She only needed an inch more to reach it. Heavy furniture was all she could see in the room to stand on. There was no time to move it to the door, and besides, it would make too much noise. No, she needed something quiet and used a throw pillow from the couch. If only the latch were lower, she could be out the door and free. Without something to stand on, though, it was impossible. She set the pillow down and stretched with fingers touching the chain. That was when she heard it. Footsteps came into the living room and stopped.

Ricky froze in his tracks, utterly shocked. He had hoped that Mindy wanted to be there with him, alone together. Ultimately, whether she did or not, the outcome would be the same. He was the butcher, and she was the lamb he meant to slaughter. The walls of insecurity, denial, and rage crumbled.

The look on his face spoke volumes. She was in big trouble. Like a scolded child, she ran back into the bedroom, evidence of terror and panic in her quivering wails.

Ricky came into the master suite and found her back on the bed. She had drawn into the pillows at the headboard, one pulled tightly to her chest. Before, he acted kind and gentle. Now, his consensual fantasy over, he made no show of happiness or kindness. The shift in his mood must have been palpable because terror filled Mindy's cries.

In the middle of the bedroom, Ricky removed each item of his clothing with no show of emotion or decency. From this point forward, the night was only about his personal fulfillment. He let his anger escalate with each passing second until he was stark naked. In slow, purposeful strides, he walked to the bed, toes curled against the cold, wooden floor, and grabbed her ankle.

When she struggled, a hand shot out quicker than a striking snake and clamped her throat.

Mindy jerked and squealed at the violation. Ricky's upper lip twitched in sinister satisfaction before he released her neck and open-hand slapped her across the face. *If she won't cooperate, I'll beat her into submission.*

He ripped at the teddy. Lace burned her soft skin with each vicious tug. When it broke loose, he fell forward and smothered her beneath the full weight of his lank body.

"Do you like red?" he demanded.

She bucked in defiance.

"I said," he growled and held her wrists above her head firmly to the mattress, "do . . . you . . . like . . . red?"

Again, Mindy bucked. This time, she let loose a shriek, and her face turned cherry.

He didn't ask again. She was not likely to give him the desired reply. That was how the night was setting up. She tried to escape while he had given her the chance to play along, and now she screamed and fought instead of answering his question. Like always, he would have to take what he wanted.

A grown man and a seven-year-old girl were never intended to be together in intimate ways. Mindy felt the brutality in the mismatched experience, and her wails for mercy caught in her throat as shock filled her eyes. A look of pain flashed through them that she previously never could have imagined possible.

Chapter Thirty-Eight

Hell hath no fury compared to what Mindy endured. With her heart still beating, her breaths came slow and shallow. The worst part was that she remained alive, suffering beyond help and on the cusp of death. She continued to stare with lifeless eyes into some far-off place, unseen by the living.

Behind his secluded home, Ricky kept a tree stump for chopping firewood. It stood two feet off the ground and three feet in diameter, perfect for long hours of swinging the axe in preparation for winter. He carried Mindy's naked body to it, her skin puckering in reaction to the cold, night air. Otherwise, she stayed sheltered within her state of shock. *I wonder if she'll feel this.*

He hefted an axe, its blade embedded two inches deep into the stump for temporary storage, and eyed her body up and down. It briefly crossed his mind that she might scream, but he dismissed the thought. That was a perk to living in the country, surrounded by forest. If she did cry out, there was no one around to hear. Besides, the trees would mute the sound before it traveled far. The real conundrum he faced was where to begin working on her. Rage from her attempted escape still smoldered inside. She had hurt his feelings, and she was not finished paying.

Piece by piece, he decided.

The axe arced high over his head and followed the same path down. The blade connected with her left arm, just below the elbow. Mindy's breathing accelerated, but she showed no other signs of pain. Strangely, the blow made almost no sound, not like the loud clack of splitting wood. Her flesh dampened the blows to dull thuds. Ricky found it amusing that, in the night, her blood spilled black. Black like shadows. Black like his heart.

Steadily and rhythmically, he swung and swung and swung, methodically hacking her to pieces.

The last thing Mindy saw was fireflies, thousands and thousands of fireflies in the dark sky above. Suddenly, she felt her body rising, and the lights were all around her. Warm, beautiful lights.

Chapter Thirty-Nine

A heavy mountain drizzle settled onto the green lawn, millions of tiny water beads clinging to each blade of lush grass. As Charlie ambled up the sidewalk, his mood mirrored the weather.

No matter how much he wished it, Caroline's killer remained on the loose, and a sunny forecast was nowhere in sight. He held his head down, climbed the few steps up the porch, and knocked on the door. This investigation needed a rainbow. His friends needed a rainbow. But to get a pot of gold, one must first see the light.

Sarah came to the door and welcomed him in.

"Hey!" she beamed and stepped to the side. She looked out the open door at the damp day and closed it before the unseasonably cool air came in. "This is a nice Monday morning surprise."

Charlie stopped on the rug, not bothering to stomp the water off his boots.

Sarah reached for his wet raincoat. "Let me take that for you."

"No, that's okay. I can't stay long. Just out running a few errands and thought I'd stop by."

"You won't stay for a cup of tea? I have a pot almost ready."

"I really can't, but thanks. It sounds good." He still didn't move.

Sounds of cartoons came from the kitchen television. Josie was in there, no doubt, soaking up the summertime pleasures of leisure and late breakfast.

"Maybe next time." Her face changed from one of a chipper greeting to business. "So if you can't stay, what's up?" She knew Charlie did not make a habit of simply stopping by just to say hi. If he weren't staying, something was up.

"Where's Isaac?"

A screen door shut in the kitchen and answered his question. They heard a pair of boots stomp on the floor and then come walking into the living room.

"I heard a car pull up and a door slam," Isaac said. He gestured behind him, back toward the detached garage workshop where he had come from. "Looked out the window and saw it was you."

The fact that Charlie was an open book to his friends was one of the reasons they loved him. The sorrow in his eyes, despite his best effort to smile, was unmistakable. It was unnatural for a man with such a jolly appearance to be so gloomy.

"Something's happened, hasn't it?" Isaac stood next to Sarah. "He's done it again, hasn't he?"

"That's the way it looks." He shook his head and clucked his tongue. "Of course, there's no way to know for sure yet, but a little girl just up and disappeared."

Isaac looked from Charlie to Sarah and then back. No one spoke. No one knew what to say, but Charlie knew the questions they both wanted answers to.

"Woodland Park, Colorado," he confirmed. "Mindy Kessler. Seven years old. Good family. Safe part of town. So safe, in fact, it's like Mayberry, if you ask me." He shook his head again and let out a long, frustrated sigh. His meaty hand clasped the back of his neck and rubbed. "I don't know. Maybe it's not him, but the similarities are undeniable."

"The profile, you mean?" Sarah looked for confirmation. "The profile of the victims you told us about?"

He nodded.

"Just because it's been him the last two times," Isaac started, "doesn't necessarily mean it's him this time, right? Don't abductions, kidnappings, and missing children take place all the time?"

"Sure. More than any parent cares to know actually. I'd say, total, close to eight hundred thousand in the United States alone."

"Eight hundred thousand?" Sarah sounded exasperated. "You're saying eight hundred thousand kids go missing every year?"

"Something like that, yeah. I don't remember the exact number, but it's in the ballpark."

"That is absolutely insane, Charlie. Do you know how many a day that is?"

"The vast majority of those are noncustodial kidnappings," he clarified. "A parent without custody breaks the rules and picks up the kid from school without informing the other parent. Or occasionally, they never bring the child home after a visitation. Stuff like that." He kicked the toe of his boot on the rug. "Then you have family abductions. A grandparent takes the minor from the parents because he or she doesn't agree with how the child is being raised. An aunt, uncle, or cousin takes a kid to get even. You wouldn't believe what families will do when they get pissed at each other."

"And the rest?" Isaac asked.

"A small portion of kids are taken by people they don't know. Say, around sixty thousand a year. Again, this is ballpark, but it's real close. This is when somebody takes a child, does what he wants, decides it's a bad idea, and turns him or her loose. They're found in a grocery store parking lot or abandoned on the side of a road. Sometimes they're okay." He shrugged his rounded shoulders. "Sometimes not."

He took a second and changed the beat. "Now our guy is different. He's a member of a much more elite club. Out of all the United States, an estimated one hundred kids, maybe a few more, are taken by what's called stereotypical kidnappings. That means that they are abducted by someone they don't know and/or held overnight, transported more than fifty miles, used for ransom, killed, or intended to be kept permanently. *That*," Charlie held up his finger, "is our guy."

"And you're pretty sure this . . ." Sarah trailed off.

"Mindy Kessler."

"Mindy Kessler. You're sure he did it?"

"I can't make any promises, but yeah, I'm pretty sure."

Isaac crossed his arms. "What does the FBI think? What do they have to say about it?"

"They're tight-lipped, as usual, when someone out of their jurisdiction asks questions. But without jumping to conclusions, they feel the same."

"Why Mindy, Charlie? What did she do? If it is him, why her?" Sarah's eyes had tears in them. Somebody's little girl was missing. That little girl's parents, Mindy's parents, were surely scared and brokenhearted at this very moment.

"The *Denver Post* and several other newspapers across the state recognized her for academics. She won the state championship spelling bee last year. Her face is still on several websites. Accomplishments, looks, and age range, all the same. Each new girl is a cookie-cutter of the last."

Isaac looked at the floor. This was not what he wanted out of life. He could have stayed in the Middle East and had all the conflict and heartbreak he wanted. That was why he had come home. That was why he had married a sweet soul like Sarah. That was why he had moved his family to Ruidoso. All he wanted was his little slice of heaven, away from pain and suffering. He had no desire to be on the cover of a magazine, write great music, or star in a movie. He just wanted peace.

"When was it? How'd it happen?"

"Four days ago. She disappeared from a neighborhood park. She and her mom went there almost every afternoon during the week. The whole place is really set up so kids can come and go freely. She told her mom she was going to the bathroom, and that was the last she was seen or heard."

"Anything else?" Sarah encouraged him to go on.

"The funny thing is, no one ever saw her come out. There were several locals around that day, and not one of them saw her leave the bathroom. It's like she vanished. I can't figure that one. People see her go in . . ." He paused. "But not out. Not *one*." He shook his head and rubbed his neck harder. "I don't know."

Isaac asked, "Any chance she's still alive?"

"I doubt it. I really doubt it. With predators like him, victims have about three hours. Beyond that . . . well . . . it's not good."

"What do we do then?" Sarah shifted her weight from one leg to the other and blew a strand of hair out of her face. "We can't keep doing this, Charlie. We can't keep sitting and waiting for something, nothing, anything to happen. We have to make a change."

Charlie pursed his lips. He had been dreading this part of the conversation. "If it is him, and I think it is, we all know what to expect. I hope this lunatic has long forgotten about Josie, but I'd bet my meager municipal salary that he'll send another letter."

Chapter Forty

The following day, Isaac watched from the window of the garage as the postman deposited a stack of mail into their box on the curb. He didn't expect the killer's letter to arrive this quickly, but since the news, neither he nor Sarah had been able to turn off the thought.

Did he take Mindy? Will he send another letter? Will it be like the others, another threat against Josie?

Neither knew for certain if anything would happen, nor if Mindy Kessler was even the victim of the same man, but waiting, sitting in limbo, and watching the storm felt worse than nothing actually happening. The old adage, "Shit or get off the pot," kept coming to mind. Good or bad, they didn't want to live their lives in constant fear.

So far, since the horrid night when they lost Caroline, a nightmarish pattern had consumed them whole. The killer was on the prowl. He did terrible things to innocent little girls. Despite this, he couldn't get Josie out of his head. He wasn't ready to come back for her, but he wanted to. Instead, he picked another victim. And round and round it went. The pattern was steady and, worst of all, usually ended in their mailbox.

Isaac walked to the street, collected the envelopes, coupon circulars, and advertisement cards from the box, placed them in the crook of his arm, and went to the kitchen. Everything seemed normal, except the manila bubble envelope tucked into the middle of the stack. It was addressed to Miss Josephine Snow and sent off more than a warning or two. It had no return address in the top, left corner. It was different from the previous two letters—both arriving in a standard, white envelope—and looked innocent enough. Isaac's subconscious did backflips. *Please be from a friend. Please.*

The letter opener slid through the adhesive flap. With little resistance, he opened the envelope and removed a piece of bloody, black lace, and immediately he knew he should have called Charlie. But he couldn't bear the anticipation. He had to know.

Lace in hand, his mind soaked up the unpleasant reality, just like the fabric had soaked up Mindy's blood. He didn't need to read a piece of paper to know who it was from and whose life had been spilled on the pretty material. His heart ached and raged at the same time. Letters, for this guy, were not enough. He obviously felt compelled to send sick treasures.

The dried blood on the lace made it feel stiff and crusty. Isaac wiped his hand across his jeans in reaction. He was white as a ghost and felt as thin as one, too. His heart pounded loudly, like it wanted to escape. Everything centered on the rhythm of its beat, the anger welling within.

A neatly folded paper remained inside the bubble wrap. The note was handwritten.

> *Dear Josephine, Mindy was good. Real good. But not good enough. There is simply no one else that will do. I'll be seeing you. Soon.*
>
> *XOXO*
> *P.S. Do you like red?*

Part Two

When in Rome, do as the Romans do.

St. Ambrose, 387 A.D.

Chapter Forty-One

A shadow box of arrowheads hung on the wall. In the polished glass surface, Ricky could see a reflection of the dining room behind him. He sat in a corner booth, slowly chewing a bite of burger without revealing his face. The last thing he wanted was to be caught staring. And in a room full of people, he feared the slightest mistake might draw unwanted attention.

Jack's Café sat off the beaten path, away from the tourist restaurants that lined the main drag in Ruidoso. The old lumberjack's kitchen served a steady stream of locals, hungry for a hearty lunch on weekdays. On both of the previous Tuesdays, Isaac, Sarah, and Josie had gone there for lunch. Going on a hunch that they would go a third time, Ricky arrived early, found an ideal seat at the self-seating establishment, and patiently nibbled at his meal. Coming back to where it had all gone wrong three months earlier felt like jumping into the fire. But then again, no one had seen his face at the scene of Caroline's death, and he was certain he could go unrecognized.

Bells rattled on the front door. He looked up from his plate and into the reflection on the shadow box. His heart skipped a beat as Isaac stepped inside.

Ricky had thought of this many times over the summer. He knew he and Isaac would meet again, someway, somehow. Now the moment was upon him. Certain the reunion would stir something inside, he never imagined fear to be the overwhelming sensation. Sitting a mere fifteen feet away from the protector of his most treasured target, Josie, was not like watching through a set of binoculars while hidden in the woods a hundred yards away. This felt much more intense, unnerving. The tall, athletic man had a confidence about him, an essence of capability. Ricky had seen it firsthand, barely escaping Isaac on a dark, rainy night through a lucky turn of events. Ricky had no doubt that, if Isaac had gotten his hands around him in the girls' bedroom or out on the lawn, he would be dead or in prison.

He watched Isaac casually glance around the room and turn back to hold the door open. To anyone who knew him, Isaac probably seemed like a kind friend and loving family man. Ricky, though, had seen a different side of the ex-airman, a dangerous, unflappable side with menace and determination in his black eyes. He truly hoped this was the closest he would ever have to get to Isaac again.

Then Josie came inside. Ricky stopped chewing, his jaw freezing in place as the little ray of light filled his putrid mind with heat. Only his eyes moved as her reflection floated across the glass in front of him. She shone like a double exposure, only a half reflection, but enough to make Ricky's mouth water. Fresh saliva pooled on his tongue with a craving more ominous than food could quench. He let the liquid slide around his mouth, moistening his cheeks and lips before swallowing it down. It took every ounce of willpower not to turn around, drink her in, fall on his knees, and caress her tender skin. An image of him grabbing her and running away flashed in his thoughts.

Finally, Sarah came inside the restaurant and placed both her hands on Josie's shoulders. Ricky felt a tinge of jealousy. She was allowed to touch Josie. He was not.

Sarah pointed to a table in the middle of the room and nudged Josie forward. Two men were seated at one end of an eight-top and smiled as the Snows pulled up chairs alongside them.

"What have you two scoundrels been up to?" Ricky heard Isaac ask.

"Fishing and golf," one of the retired men replied with mock sarcasm. He had the look of a sun worshiper, tanned skin, deeply grooved lines around his eyes, and a decently fit body for his age.

A skittering sound echoed around the square dining room as Isaac slid his chair legs across the ancient linoleum floor.

"Yeah?" Isaac studied the man for a moment. He wore a short-sleeved, plaid, button-down shirt, and, despite the warm weather, a sweater vest and khakis. A pair of golf shoes was still on his feet. "And how'd you shoot this morning?"

Both old men chuckled. "Humph. Too high to brag about." The first elbowed the second. "But we sure gave it hell, didn't we, Ed?"

This started another round of chuckling. The old friends were clearly enjoying the fruits of long years and hard work. The most stressful part of their day was fretting over a stroke or two on their golf score.

Ricky steadied himself and remembered to look casual. He drank a swallow of iced tea and had another bite of burger. It all felt so trivial, but details made for good spy craft. He needed to appear as one with the setting, whatever it may be. He focused on slowing his heart. His blood pressure and temperature were certainly up, evidence of tiny sweat droplets showing on his upper lip and forehead. Caroline was gone. That couldn't be changed. He knew her death was his responsibility. There was no one else to blame. He could still feel the glass crushing around them as their bodies flew out the window and into the rain-drenched lawn. Even though he didn't know it at the time, he wasn't surprised to learn that a piece of glass had sliced into her little body and drained her of life. His junior mistake, followed by a poor reaction, had killed her. Now Josie was all he had left. And if he messed this up, he would fail completely. The pressure weighed heavily on his mind.

Ricky wondered if anyone might see through his disguise. He looked down at himself. A heavily worn pearl snap shirt, faded jeans, and work boots fit the setting perfectly. A baseball-style cap with an industrial equipment emblem sat on his head. He looked like any other guy who earned a paycheck with his hands. He even had a shallow story concocted, just in case he was forced to engage in brief conversation. A ski mask covered his face when last Isaac saw him. And anyone else in town—anyone who had seen him at the hotel where he stayed—had no reason to remember him. He remained a perfect stranger.

Secure in his confidence of anonymity, he felt the unsuspected squeeze of a hand on his shoulder. Startled more from his previous train of thought, he jerked slightly before looking up into a pair of eyes intent on his attention.

"I'm sorry," he said. "Did you say something?"

The pregnant waitress held up a pitcher. "Would you like some more tea?" She nodded toward his glass across the table. It was just out of reach with her distended belly.

He lifted the red, plastic cup for a refill. "Please."

As she shuffled away, he tuned his ears back to the table where Josie sat. They were in the middle of a conversation, and he could hear them clearly.

"That's right, Paul," Isaac confirmed. "Just me and Josie."

"Sarah, you're not going with them?"

"Part of the way," she said. "They'll fly me to Albuquerque on Thursday and go on from there. I have a three-day cancer walk Friday through Sunday."

Ricky perked up his ears. His mind was bent on every morsel of information as Sarah continued. He knew there was no realistic way he would find to kidnap Josie around Ruidoso again. At least he didn't think so. She was watched closer than ever, and he felt too vulnerable to work where his luck had turned sour. The place felt like bad voodoo. He wished he could catch Josie somewhere out of town, someplace where her parents' guard was down.

"I started doing them in college," Sarah explained, "and decided to keep it up. I've done one every year since my mother passed away from breast cancer."

"This weekend?" Paul, the retiree, shook his head. "It's gonna be a hot one. Isaac, you're not doing it with her?"

"Are you kidding me? Sixty miles in three days. I'm not so sure I'm tough enough. Besides, it gives Josie a chance to see her grandparents in Taos before school starts."

The same waitress who served Ricky arrived with their food. The two retired codgers were finished and stood to excuse themselves. The same one who had done all the talking, Paul, said, "Good luck, Sarah." He put his hat on and gave a casual salute to Isaac. "Say hi to your folks for me."

Ricky's mind ran with the potential. It was impossible to form a plan yet, but Josie was headed out of town, and he knew right where she would be. If they were flying to Taos, there was one obvious place to intercept them, Taos Regional Airport. Luckily, it was the only airfield in town and the only place for them to land. As sure as the sun rose in the East, he would be there waiting.

He stood, put ten dollars on the table, and made for the door. Outside on the pine needle-covered parking lot, he opened the door to his newly acquired Chevrolet pickup truck. Bringing the van back to Ruidoso was entirely too risky. The truck fit the bill nicely, and he had to admit that it made a good change from the cumbersome van. He stayed with a white paint job to keep a low profile. Four doors with a backseat provided a good amount of extra room. Not like the van, but enough. He also bought it with four-wheel drive. It would more than pay for itself in the Rocky Mountain winters.

In the bed of the pickup, he stored a shovel and a chainsaw with a few scraps of wood. And no working man's vehicle was complete without a ball attached to the trailer hitch. With his newfound information and disguise in place, he had to lay down some miles. He didn't know exactly how Josie would come to him, but she would. He wouldn't stop until she did.

Chapter Forty-Two

August heat waves lifted off the candy apple red hood of Isaac's classic pickup. He parked outside a row of rental hangars at the Sierra Blanca Regional Airport. Josie and Sarah waited in the cab to enjoy the air-conditioner while he prepped their airplane.

Inside the sliding metal doors, he attached a tow bar to the front wheel and pulled. Sunshine glinted off the brilliant white paint as it nosed out of shadow and into light. A welcome breeze felt cool on Isaac's glossy skin in contrast to the stagnant air inside the tin structure. When he cleared the doorway, Sarah pulled forward and stopped the truck where the plane had just sat. They would keep it there, locked away for the weekend.

While Isaac went about the pre-flight checklist, Josie helped Sarah transfer the luggage from the bed of the pickup to the storage compartment of the Cessna 172.

A few minutes later, Isaac declared, "She's good to go. Let's load up."

Josie needed help climbing into the backseat, and Isaac lifted her in. He playfully popped her on the bottom as she ducked her head and went to sit. Flying was his favorite pastime in the world. Combine it with the company of his family, and life didn't get any better. The wounds of an unfriendly summer still itched, and their party of three always felt incomplete. He had gone over it numerous times during the last few weeks. Time away, separation from all the little reminders that Caroline was gone, felt exactly like what they needed, a last-minute hoorah before Josie went back to school.

Sarah took the copilot's seat on the right, and Isaac crawled in on the left. She had stated concern at the onset of their relationship regarding small planes. Isaac assured her that her reservations were based on the same thing that holds most people back in life, fear of the unknown. And he was right. He took her up a few times, showed her the ropes, and explained how safe private aviation can be. Slowly, after a fair share of coaxing, she began to enjoy it and set aside her unfounded apprehension.

Isaac called, "Clear prop," and engaged the ignition.

The propeller buzzed to life, a steady wash of air now flowing through the open cabin windows. He taxied out of the row of hangars and stopped before hitting the taxiway. A run-up on the gauges confirmed that everything was good to go.

"Cessna zero-zero-niner, requesting permission for takeoff," he called over the headset.

"Roger that, zero-zero-niner," a voice came back. "Proceed two-four. Hold short."

"Two-four, hold short," he repeated.

At the start of runway two-four, Isaac stopped short of the airstrip. In the distance, a glimmer of an aircraft came closer and closer. They waited until the Beechcraft Bonanza V-tail passed and finally settled to the asphalt. As it slowed and turned off the runway, the air traffic controller came back on.

"Zero-zero-niner, clear for takeoff."

"Zero-zero-niner, clear for takeoff," Isaac repeated.

He turned onto the runway and throttled up. The air speed indicator passed ten knots, twenty, thirty, forty, fifty, sixty, and finally sixty-four KIAS, or knots indicated air speed. Easing the yoke back, the Cessna rose at the nose, and the rear wheels quickly followed. They were off, reaching for the heavens, the skies belonging to the few.

"Up, up, and away!" he proclaimed.

Josie and Sarah were both glued to the windows. He adjusted their course to the north northwest and slowly gained altitude.

When they arrived in Albuquerque, Sarah said her good-byes and got in a yellow taxicab. Isaac hated to see her go alone, but wouldn't have it any different. The weekend was her way of remembering her mother.

The second leg of the trip went by faster than the first. The scenery below began to make more drastic changes. Mountains grew larger, and the desert in the west drew nearer. Isaac knew every square inch of it. Out of habit, he broke the landscape into grids and searched them for signs of smoke. Even though he was off duty, it never hurt to go the extra mile in the hot, dry months like August.

Down below, the ground looked like it could use a drink. Moisture from the early summer rains was gone. Here and there, small clouds of dirt drifted off rural roads leading across ranches and National Forestry lands. Powdery logging roads plunged into the alpine-covered slopes of hardened granite and winding streams.

Josie noticed the change. "Are we there yet?"

"Almost. Are you ready?"

She leaned forward, riding in the front seat since leaving Sarah behind, and made a look of exasperation. "I've been ready since forever."

Isaac laughed at her small display of drama. *Me, too, kiddo.*

Summer was at its end, and he couldn't say he was sorry. But despite the change of seasons, desperation continued to stalk him, desperation like he had never known.

Chapter Forty-Three

Ricky sat in the reclined front seat of his pickup and waited for Josie and Isaac to arrive. He had backed into a parking spot at the Taos Regional Airport with his windows rolled down. Warm, high desert air filtered through the cab while he dozed and listened for the buzz of an inbound aircraft. He had waited since early morning and didn't know what time to expect them, but by the conversation he overheard a couple of days prior at Jack's Café, today was the day. He ran his tongue between his top teeth and inside of his upper lip. Josie played in his head. A quiver crawled up his body with the incredibly detailed fantasy.

The remote landing strip stretched across the sage-littered valley floor. On that late Thursday afternoon, the airport was virtually uninhabited. The only other forms of life were an older gentleman tinkering on a fuel truck in front of a closed hangar and a person inside an office attached to the same building. The tiny, uncontrolled field had no need for security measures as the only flights in and out had nothing to do with commercial air travel. This, like so much of rural New Mexico, Ricky liked very much.

On the drive up from Ruidoso, he had nothing but his thoughts and an infinite expanse of scenery to keep him company. The landscape stretched out forever, an inland ocean of sand, rocks, grasses, and cedar trees. Combinations of browns and greens monopolized his eyes. The only splash of color came at a railroad crossing. A pair of candy cane gates dropped in front of him to make way for a passing train. A mile-long string of cars went by in smooth, thunkedy-thunk motion. Vivid splashes of graffiti adorned the sides. He couldn't make out many of the signs or words, but all had taken talent to achieve desired looks. He knew the culprits, misguided teens or youngsters with a real gift for art.

At the airfield, and for the first time in more than three hours, someone in a vehicle drove onto the grounds. He looked toward the entrance and watched a late-model, charcoal gray GMC pickup come his way. Instead of lying back in the seat or exposing his whole face to the newcomers, he lifted a newspaper and used it to block the lower portion of his face while peering over the top. But as the vehicle passed in front of him, the older couple inside didn't look his way. They drove on until stopping in front of the administrative office.

Ricky wondered if the new arrivals were Isaac's parents. He had a pretty good idea they were. Neither of them got out of the truck after backing between two white stripes. They just sat there and looked out the windshield to the south, like they were there to meet someone.

As he pondered the situation, his attention was drawn to an approaching drone. He set the newspaper aside and grabbed his high-dollar binoculars off the dash. It didn't take but a second to find a glimmer in the distance, the setting sun reflecting off a shiny surface. He used his right pointer finger to adjust the focus dial in between the lenses and clear the visual until a crisp image of an airplane appeared. It circled to the north and lined up for a southwesterly landing, directly into the light breeze.

His heart quickened. *It's them. It has to be.* What were the odds of someone else flying into the tiny airport, in a single-engine aircraft, to be picked up by a retirement age couple? He intently held the binoculars to his eyes and watched the little Cessna come closer.

Some jobs required more planning than others did. Kidnapping Josie was not going to be easy. And although Ricky wondered what type of scheme he would have to hash out to do it, he felt quite pleased with how the current events were unfolding. Just like in Ruidoso at the beginning of summer, when he had hidden in the woods and posed as a jogger, there was nothing suspicious about his current disguise. He was there to airplane watch.

The plane glided lower until it touched down. A slight screech sounded as rubber tires met pavement and began to roll. He could discern a man in the captain's seat and a shorter person, small enough to be a child, in the passenger seat. *This has to be them.*

The pilot slowed to taxi speed and made his way to a tie-down area on the tarmac. Metal rings were bolted into the pavement with lengths of rope coiled neatly on the ground. The airplane came to rest in the middle of a three-ringed triangle and the propeller blades fell silent.

Ricky had to control himself from bobbing up and down in his seat at the near unbearable anxiety of who could be inside. Really, he already knew, but he wanted to see her so badly and refused to let the binoculars leave his eyes.

As if a dream come true, the passenger door opened, and out she came. In his mind, Josie shined brighter than the sunset painted across the wild background behind her. She was there, ripe and ready to be plucked by his hungry hand.

Chapter Forty-Four

"Young lady," Isaac instructed over the mike, "do not open that door until the propeller stops spinning."

"I won't," Josie agreed without looking at him. She focused out her window, enthusiastically waving at her grandparents.

Isaac used the foot pedals to maneuver the Cessna into a tie-down space. As he idled the throttle, Josie's hand already rested on the door latch. When the engine turned completely off, she sprang from the cockpit and ran the ten yards to Tom and Helen. Tom bent down, gave her a hug and kiss on the cheek, and left her with Helen.

Isaac took a moment to stuff their headsets and flight plan into his bag. Removing the key from the ignition, he stepped out into the final minutes of daylight and found Tom waiting under the wing.

"Y'all are early." His father grinned.

Isaac set his flight bag on the ground. "Albuquerque was a quick stop, and we had a nice tailwind to push us."

They wrapped each other in a tight embrace.

"Sarah's all squared away?"

"Yeah, she's ready to go."

"We're glad she's excited about it, but we sure wish she could have made it up here, too."

Isaac walked out to the end of the wing and lifted a coil of rope attached to a tie-down ring. He fed it through a brace and tied it off. Tom went to the other side and did the same while Isaac secured a third rope to the tail. With all three ropes pulled snug, it would keep for the weekend.

"How was your flight?" Helen greeted him at the pickup. She wrapped both arms around his neck, and he pulled her into a tight hug.

"Good. Fast." He looked down at his mom, a head shorter. "How are you?"

"Excited that you're here. Let's head to the house, and we can talk on the way. Supper's almost ready." She turned and started to get in the backseat with Josie.

Isaac slung the bags into the bed. "I'll ride in the back, Mom."

"Nonsense," she said with a flick of her hand. "I'm getting back here with Josie. You ride in front with Dad."

As the door closed, he heard Josie ask if she could help cook.

"I hoped you might," Helen assured her. They settled into girl chat, Josie happily answering all the questions her grandmother asked.

He looked out the window, out across the expansive valley floor to the western horizon. The change in scenery worked its magic, slowly leeching into his system. At home, he felt vulnerable, exposed to the predator who threatened to come back and visit his mayhem on them. But away from Ruidoso, he had no worries, no anxiety over a bogeyman hiding in the shadows. A casual smile parted his lips.

The sunset cast the village in radiant light, a glow that happened for only a few minutes each day. Headed up the mountain, he took in the whole picture—the desert valley, all the Pueblo-style houses scattered across the landscape, and, in the distance, the Rio Grande Gorge running south with its white water churning in the depths. He absorbed it all, all except the vehicle that followed at a discreet distance. That, he thought nothing of.

Chapter Forty-Five

Every few minutes, a hiker or biker went by on the nature trail's dirt path. It led to a clear water streambed where giant cottonwoods and poplars rose from the wet soil. Not only did Ricky find the location ideal for observation, he also appreciated the serenity and ease with which he blended into a steady flow of outdoor lovers.

One meandering road accessed Tom and Helen's house where Josie stayed. From his vantage point at the bottom of a hill and seated on a split-log bench, if she or Isaac left, he would see it. All he had to do was jump in his truck and follow.

A fueling station with two gas pumps and a convenience store sat just across the road from the trailhead. He could buy snacks when hungry and keep watch through the front glass. Instead of going into the public restroom to take a leak, he ducked behind trees for relief. Taking his eyes off the road, a potential window to miss Josie leaving the house, was unacceptable.

Friday rolled by with no activity from his target. He spent the better part of Saturday bored and perplexed. Like all creative thought, a plan had to sprout from an idea. As of yet, he had none. Plenty of made-up scenarios tumbled through his mind, but nothing realistic. Another break-in—a strategy he used the first time to go after Josie—made no sense, especially with Tom and Isaac inside the house. He had no wish to relive an event similar to the one in Ruidoso ever again.

He viewed Josie and the rest of her family like a herd of cattle. If he could somehow corral them, steer her to a destination, and hem her in, he might have a chance. The problem of how and, more importantly, where could not be solved without movement. They had to leave the house at some point. But until they did, he had only one option, sit and wait.

As the sun sank in the sky and approached the end of another day, it finally happened, and his boredom turned to anxious hope. He looked at his watch. It was almost six o'clock.

Tom's pickup, the same one from the airport, wound its way down the twisted blacktop and headed for town. Ricky's lip curled into a lopsided, menacing grin. When it passed the trailhead, he saw Isaac and Josie inside. *Where are you two going?*

He sprang into his newly acquired work truck and followed. They drove into the village, passed through several traffic lights, and pulled into an adobe façade shopping center. Isaac parked in the scarcely occupied lot and walked into a small grocery market. Josie skipped in pace, holding her father's hand.

At the far end of the center, Ricky found a row of empty spaces along the outer wall of the grocery store. He couldn't see the front of the shops, but kept their vehicle in his line of sight. The alley was mere steps away.

Josie was so close yet so far away. He fidgeted restlessly. His normally calm demeanor betrayed his desire as he evaluated the situation. He had already made his move by coming to Taos. Now Josie was on the move. The ball was back in his hands. *Do something or keep waiting*. He felt the short weekend slipping away.

Chapter Forty-Six

Isaac stood in a grocery store aisle with an array of brown sugar options before him. Josie waited in silence as her father debated over which kind he should get, dark or light. He held the dark bag in his left hand and the light in his right, eyes roaming back and forth.

"Is there anything I can help you with, sir?" a voice came from behind.

Isaac looked over his shoulder and found a youngish guy in a green store apron. "I'm not sure." He held up the two bags of sugar for the clerk to see. Strong fingers gripped around the soft granules of sweetness. "Which kind do most women buy?"

The clerk tilted his head and was about to say something when Isaac looked down to a tapping on his leg.

Josie politely poked him on the thigh with her finger. She looked up with her bright eyes. "Mom gets the dark."

"She does?" He didn't know why he hadn't thought to ask her before. She loved to go shopping with her mom, and Sarah had taught her to cook for a couple years now. "Is this what MaMaw likes?"

Josie shrugged her little shoulders. "I don't know. Mom says the dark has more flavor and keeps the food moist."

"There you have it," the clerk said, somewhat surprised.

Isaac, also surprised at how much Josie knew, raised his eyebrows and confirmed, "And there you have it."

Sometimes he forgot how smart she was, how many things she knew despite her stature. It was one of those moments as a parent that reminded him how quickly children change. Sometimes he had to be taken off guard to realize it.

Isaac put the light sugar back and turned to leave when the store employee asked, "You guys aren't from here, are you?" He made a gesture toward them with his hand. "I don't recall seeing you before."

Isaac looked the guy over. He had a five o'clock shadow, slightly greasy brown hair tussled in a million directions, and a laid-back demeanor. Isaac guessed him to be around the same age as himself.

He stuck out his hand. "I'm Derek."

Isaac returned the gesture, and they shook with firm grips. He smiled at the situation. Only in small towns did store employees formally introduce themselves to customers. It felt a lot like life in Ruidoso, wholesome, minus the bad memories that haunted them there. *Derek the tree hugger, ski bum, raft guide . . . grocery store worker to help pay the bills.*

So many guys Derek's age came to Taos—mountain towns all over New Mexico and Colorado were full of them—to be ski bums for a while. Some loved the life so much they never left. The purity of nature and slower pace never lost their appeal. He completely understood why it beckoned to people. They could lose the madness, forget about what society says one must do to lead a full life and be considered successful. He had seen many guys and girls over the years, just like Derek, people who turned their backs on the status quo and beat to their own drum.

"I'm Isaac. And this . . ." He nodded his head down. "Is my daughter Josie. We're in town from Ruidoso to visit my folks."

"That's cool," Derek said. "Big plans while you're here? The river's flowin' pretty well for this time of year. It's a good time to hit the rapids."

"No, we'll have to take a rain check. We're leaving in the morning." He placed a hand on Josie's shoulder to include her in the conversation. "Isn't that right, kiddo?"

She nodded. "Daddy, can I have some candy?"

"Candy?" He didn't know where the question came from.

"Please," she begged with puppy dog eyes.

"Absolutely not." He held up the sugar. "MaMaw is making dessert."

"Just a little one," she stared up, eyelashes fluttering.

Where did she learn to do that? He knew she was working him, but it did the trick anyway. *What does it matter? We're on vacation.*

"Fine. Something small, and you're not allowed to eat the whole thing." She darted away around the end of the aisle and out of sight. "Small," he called loud enough to reach her ears.

"Well," Derek said, "is there anything else I can help you with?"

Isaac looked up and tried to glance over the top of the shelves. "Butter?"

Derek thumbed over his shoulder to the back of the cozy market. "In the cooler section."

"Excellent." Isaac stuck out his hand, and they shook again. "Thanks for your help, Derek."

"Anytime. You guys have a safe trip tomorrow."

Isaac retrieved a box of stick butter, then made his way across the back of the store to the candy aisle. When he turned, he found it empty. Bags of candy and sweet treats lined the shelves, but Josie was not there. It had only taken a minute or two to find the butter. She couldn't be far. He went back one aisle and looked down it. *Nothing.* He went to the aisle on the other side of the candy section. *No Josie.*

"Josie!" he called. "Where are you?"

He didn't feel anxious at this point, but he couldn't imagine where she had gone off to. He walked to the front and looked from side to side. Two teenage girls in store aprons worked separate registers. One customer walked out the door with a handful of plastic sacks held in her hands. Another customer counted out change from her purse. *Still no Josie.* The small-town market was little enough for his voice to carry throughout the whole store. He didn't want to shout, but the seed of fear slowly crept in. The most recent letter from the killer rang fresh in his memory. It plagued his mind, always present. *I'll be seeing you. Soon.*

"Josie!" he hollered. "Josie!" He stayed in one spot, turned in a circle, and waited for a response.

Finally, she poked her head around a checkout stand shelf covered in magazines and tabloids. "I'm right here."

He let out a breath without realizing he had held it. Fear receded, and he could feel his accelerated heart rate thump. "Where were you?" he demanded more out of desperation than anger. "Why weren't you in the candy aisle?"

She held up and rattled a yellow box of Milk Duds. "They were all big over there." She pointed to the place she had just come from by the vacant register. "The small ones were up here."

It wasn't fair to be mad at her. She had only done what he said and went to find the smaller servings. "Don't wander off like that, okay?"

Josie had no idea of the last two letters, and everyone had agreed not to tell her.

"Are you ready?"

She shook the box of candy again with a satisfied expression on her face. "Yep!"

A pretty high school girl at the checkout counter set down her jewel-covered cell phone. She scanned the sugar and butter without making eye contact. Isaac didn't think she looked old enough for the job, but it was encouraging to see young people at work. She tucked a strand of golden hair over her ear. Fingers with neon pink nail polish busily punched a series of keys on the computerized register.

"Did you find everything you need?" she politely asked.

"Yes, thank you." He held his wallet at the ready. "Derek helped us out."

She giggled and scanned Josie's candy. If Sarah had been there, she would have later told Isaac that the girl thought he was cute. Her nametag read "Ashley," and she hit a final button. "Your total is nine ninety-two."

Isaac handed over ten dollars. "Keep the change."

She put the sugar and butter into a sack and gave the Milk Duds directly to Josie, who accepted them with obvious excitement. "Have a nice day."

"You, too. Let's go, Jo," he said to Josie. "We don't want to keep MaMaw waiting."

Once they were clear of the front doors, Ashley turned around and spoke to the teenage girl at the other checkout stand. "Sam, will you cover for me? I'm gonna find Derek and take a break."

Sam glanced about the store. No other customers were in line on the slow Saturday evening. "Sure." She rolled her eyes. Ashley and Derek were tight and liked to have a smoke from time to time in the alley. "Is he working tonight?"

Ashley didn't answer. She was already gone, headed to the back in search of Derek. At this hour, he would be stocking an aisle or loading carts in the supply room. She liked Derek, a lot, even though he was two grades above her. He was so popular at school and athletic.

In the rear warehouse area, she flipped on the lights and looked around. No one stirred. A row of coat pegs lined the wall outside of the employee break room. Derek always hung his on the end. It was gone. She almost flipped off the light switch and went to find him on the aisles when it caught her eye. The exterior door, next to the loading dock bay entrance, sat slightly ajar. It let in just enough of the fading outdoor light to catch her attention. She grew giddy at what hung on the door handle, Derek's green apron.

A sparkle shone in her eye. *I bet he's outside having a smoke.* She went to the door and pushed out into the cement paved alley. *I could use a drag.*

Derek was only seventeen and, therefore, not supposed to have cigarettes. That was part of the reason Ashley liked him. He was a rebel, so mature.

She took off her apron so it wouldn't smell of smoke and hung it on the handle with his. Rickety metal steps wobbled as she stepped to the ground and walked past the dumpsters. No one was around.

"Derek?" she called.

Silence.

Chapter Forty-Seven

Ricky pulled over and leaned his head forward, rested it against the top of the steering wheel, and closed his eyes. His hands trembled, and beads of sweat dampened his upper lip. He couldn't believe what he had just done. Never before had he allowed himself to be so reckless. In truth, he had never wanted to be. Pushing the limits in privacy with his victims did not in any way represent how he comported himself in public. All of that, however, had just gone out the window.

When he went into the back door of the grocery market, he had done so with an open mind. Perhaps he might be able to find Josie alone, close enough to an exit to make a break with her. That was best-case scenario. Worst-case, he would get to spy on her from up close and personal. But when he found the rack of store aprons and hardly a soul in the place, Ricky decided to play cat and mouse. In his wildest dreams, he never imagined he would speak directly to Isaac, shake his hand, and pull off such an impromptu performance.

Now on the roadside with pulse pounding, he praised himself for such an audacious show of confidence and chastised himself for acting like an impulsive idiot. The events of his entire life had brought him to Josie. He would never forgive himself if he screwed up again.

"Shit, that was crazy." His body shivered to release the tension. "Get it together," he coached himself.

The grocery store event had provided valuable information. Ricky was certain that Isaac and Josie would not leave Taos until morning. They would stay at Tom and Helen's one more night, and he had no reason to follow. He now had enough freedom in his schedule to set an ingenious trap. The idea was basic but not entirely simple, and he needed supplies for ultimate effect. He put the truck in drive and turned deliberate thoughts into actions.

The hardware store was his first stop on the list. A few necessary items were in order to set the ball in motion.

He paid for them in cash and asked the clerk, "Does anyone in town sell fireworks?"

"All the Fourth of July shops are closed," the Native American-looking man explained. "This time of year, the only guy who might have some is on the edge of town. He sells Roman candles, bottle rockets, firecrackers, things like that. My kids love them."

"Thanks, friend. You mind writing down the name and directions for me?"

"Sure." He wrote the information on a yellow legal pad and tore it off. "Better hurry. Old Joe likes to close early on weekends. You might catch him if you get going."

"Will do." Bells rattled as he walked out the front door.

To have a real chance, he needed those fireworks. Certain details could not be overlooked, and this was one of them. Progress depended on Old Joe keeping his doors open for a few more minutes.

To Ricky's delight, an "Open" sign flashed in Joe's window. The little shop looked like it had once been a single-wide trailer that someone covered in tin. It sat off the road a few yards. Nothing but sage and desert surrounded it for miles and miles. The inside was just as ragtag as the exterior and happened to carry everything he needed. Again, he paid in cash.

Stocked up and back outside, he rejoiced in the early sunset of the Rocky Mountains. Darkness made everything easier, and the more hours of it he had, the sooner he could get things done.

Twenty minutes south of town, he turned off the pavement onto a nameless road marked on his GPS. A gravel and dirt lane led deep into the forest and far up a mountain. Time was of the essence. Tomorrow, his wits were a fundamental part of the trap. He had to prep everything and still have time to sleep.

Almost a half hour later and several thousand feet higher, Ricky found himself at his chosen destination. He had discovered it on Google Earth. The aerial computer program helped him find some of the best hiding places. Having boots on the ground, however, was still the best insurance policy.

The cabin looked better than he expected it to. All four log walls stood straight, and with the exception of a fallen pine on one corner of the roof, it appeared relatively whole. A sense of satisfaction enveloped him.

He quickly unloaded some gear and sensitive cargo. The inside wasn't exactly the Ritz. He guessed that elk and deer hunters still used the dilapidated shanty during the fall and winter. Some things were newer than the building itself. A table with a plywood top sat against one wall. Two rope bed frames were pushed against another. No one had been there for months. His feet disturbed a solid coating of dust on the wooden plank floor, and he felt confident his things would not be bothered after he left. The clock ticked.

He retraced his route down the dusty logging tracks, up the highway through Taos, and out to the airport road. A glance in the rearview mirror revealed solitude. He stopped, turned off the engine, pushed the emergency brake in one notch, and restarted the pickup. The adjustment allowed him to override the automatic headlights and control them manually.

Even though his front beams were out, if he tapped the brakes, his tail lights would still glow bright red. To eliminate the need to slow down, he entered the grounds at a turtle pace. The lethargy aggravated him. Quick in and outs were best. He reminded himself of the tortoise and the hare and hoped the fable held true.

Inside the entrance, he found the first hangar and parked against the opposite side from the watchman's office. Dressed in black, he stepped out and peeked around the corner. All was calm. At the far end of the buildings, a lone window glowed. The watchman was inside, no doubt bored and possibly snoozing on the job. Ricky felt sorry for the poor schmuck who had to be in a place night after night where nothing ever happened. But the scenario created a perfect working environment for himself.

Halfway between his hiding place and the office, the tie-down area had three airplanes tethered to the ground. *Excellent. Isaac won't feel singled out.*

He shouldered his black backpack full of supplies from the hardware store. One cautious foot stepped around the hangar and then the next. He crept at first, low and slow. Certain the coast was clear, he sped to a run, keeping close to the walls for cover. His catlike frame darted across the distance, and he took shelter behind the fuselage of the first airplane.

Come morning, this particular crime would only be one amongst a long line of tipping dominos, a smooth chain reaction designed to drop Josie directly into his lap. And for that reason, he went to work with a practiced steadiness and determined mind. If he botched anything, Isaac might suspect foul play and go on high alert.

From the backpack, he extracted a can of spray paint and shook it vigorously. The Cessna Corvallis before him had a shiny white body and a sticker price of over a half-million dollars. He snickered before pressing the button, then spelled out "Rich Dick" in big green letters along the entire side. He slipped around the tail, a silhouette in a dream. Again, he sprayed "Rich

Dick" from back to front. Fifty yards away, the light continued to glow inside the office window, but not a creature stirred.

Next, at a beautifully handcrafted kit plane, he changed to blue paint and altered the letters. The idea was to make it look like a group of punk kids had come through. On the sides, he wrote "Lucky Bastard" and sprayed a squiggly line up the vertical portion of the tail. Subtle differences would convince the police that more than one person had been involved.

Finally, the third object sat before him, Isaac's aircraft. Ricky couldn't resist and he grabbed a can of red paint. The little jab felt too good to pass up. He shook it and painted red Xs on the windows and windshield. Along the fuselage, he simply wrote "Suck It."

Once finished, he hunkered beside Isaac's Cessna and made sure all the paint cans were stowed with lids on. He had achieved the look he wanted. Now he needed to put the final, much more drastic touches to the job.

In the side pocket, he gripped the handle of an ice pick. "It's all for you, my Josephine," he said aloud and gouged the sharp spike into a tire.

He didn't stop there. Ricky shuffled to the front and punctured another. The third tire joined a chorus of hisses when he extracted the thin metal shaft from rubber. They deflated and went flat against the ground. He hunched under the wing and rammed the pick upward. Fuel dribbled from the tiny hole in the aluminum veneer as he yanked it out. Twice more, he stabbed until the overhead tank let loose a steady bleed.

He worked backwards and did the same to the kit plane. Its tires went flat, and its tanks emptied to the destruction of the pick. The first plane in the lineup also succumbed. As he stood back and studied his handiwork, Ricky sneered and nodded in approval. The smell of fuel burned heavily in his nose as he turned and ran away.

The illusion was set. The spectacle was planned. He had never fancied himself a magician, but tomorrow he would make Josie disappear.

Chapter Forty-Eight

At seven forty-five in the morning, Isaac rolled out of bed. He arched his back and looked at the shade-covered window where early rays of light filtered through the fabric. In fifteen minutes, Sarah would begin her third and final day of the cancer walk in Albuquerque. The thought of seeing her brightened his morning.

In the bathroom, he reached in the shower and turned on the hot water. When steam coated the glass door, he stripped off his boxers and stepped in. Both hands flat against the tile wall, he ducked beneath the spout. Warm water soaked his thick, black hair, cascaded over his broad shoulders, and coursed down his tan back. He bathed in the warmth, letting it invigorate his senses.

After drying off, he tucked a towel around his waist. A sharp razor knocked twenty-four hours worth of dense, dark stubble off his face. He dressed in olive cargo pants, a V-neck T-shirt, and lightweight hiking boots.

In the kitchen, he found Tom and Helen with piping mugs of coffee in the breakfast nook.

"Good morning," Helen greeted him.

"Good morning, Mom."

"Did you sleep well?"

"Like a rock." He took a mug from the cabinet. "I didn't want to get up."

"I know." Helen had a far-off, thoughtful look in her eyes. "I feel the same way when we go on vacation. On the last morning, I always think, if I don't get up, it won't be over."

Isaac took a sip of his coffee. He slurped because it was too hot. "Something like that."

Tom said, "Why don't you fly down and get Sarah? Bring her back here and stay another day or two."

"Believe me, I've thought about it. But she'll be tired. Josie starts school this week, and I have work."

"Sixty miles in three days," Helen shook her head. "I don't blame her. You know, I should do one with her sometime, but I don't want to intrude."

Isaac looked into his cup as if the ink-black liquid might hold all the answers. "I think going alone forces her to get involved and share her story with others. She's met some really great people over the years. The most amazing thing is that, no matter what day it is, how far anyone has walked, how many blisters they've rubbed, or how sore their muscles are, she has never heard one person complain. They are either tough enough to go on or hurt bad enough to stop. When you've seen someone die of cancer, I guess it puts your own discomfort into perspective."

Tom tapped his finger on the kitchen table. "It affects way too many. It's scary to think of really. I've known a lot of people who've died over the years . . ." He looked to Helen for confirmation. "And I'd say cancer was responsible for half or more."

She nodded in agreement. "We're not exactly spring chickens."

Tom had a smart comment halfway out of his mouth in reply to her age observation when the telephone rang. He answered it, "Hello." He listened in silence, a crease slowly forming between his eyebrows. "Yes, he is. Hold on, please." He pulled the handset away from his ear and handed it toward Isaac. "It's for you. Some doctor in Albuquerque."

Isaac made a puzzled expression and took the cordless set without a word. "This is Isaac," he spoke into the phone.

"Mr. Snow, my name is Dr. Ellison. I'm an ER doctor at Saint Mary's Hospital in Albuquerque," a professional voice on the other end informed. "Am I speaking with Isaac Snow, husband of Sarah Snow?"

The world froze. He did not like the way this sounded. "Yes, Sarah is my wife. May I ask what this is in regards to?"

"Mr. Snow, are you where I can speak with you for a moment?"

Isaac's heart fell to the pit of his stomach. He was scared. *Why is a doctor calling? Did she injure herself during the walk? If she did, why isn't she the one calling?* None of the questions gave him clarity.

"Yes," he said back. "I can speak now." His voice sounded slightly irritated.

"Mr. Snow, are you driving a vehicle or operating a piece of machinery?"

Isaac wanted an explanation, not questions. *I'm fine, dammit. Now tell me what the hell is going on.* He assumed whatever the doctor was about to say was bad news, and now he started to fear the worst. Something had happened to Sarah. He wished the doctor would just come out with it. *To hell with safety protocol.* He looked at his parents, and they both wore concerned faces.

"Doctor, I'm sitting down. Please get to the point," he added with force.

Dr. Ellison's voice came back. "Your wife has been in an accident."

He waited for more. *What kind of accident?*

"We're doing everything we can. She is alive but unconscious. We don't know the extent of the damage yet. The ER staff is assessing her now."

Isaac went as pale as milk. The lack of blood in his upper body almost caused him to drop the phone. He hung on but said nothing.

"Mr. Snow? Mr. Snow, are you still there?"

"I'm here." He had so much he wanted to ask, but he didn't know where to begin. The doctor's words, "She is alive," replayed in his mind. The "alive" part threw him for a loop. Panic was not in Isaac's nature, only a desire to comprehend.

"What happened, and how bad is she?" He needed to know what they were looking at. *Possible death? Brain damage? Paralysis? What type, if any, of recovery could she have?*

"Mr. Snow, I'm afraid I don't know. I'm sorry, but she's only been in approximately fifteen minutes."

Isaac looked at the clock. *Eight thirty. It couldn't have happened long ago.*

"A car hit her hard on the right side of her body. She may have several broken or fractured bones. Nothing is visually out of place, but the X-rays could say different. We are also doing a CT scan to check for head trauma. I called to inform you as quickly as I could."

Spinning out of control, Isaac's head felt like it might implode and explode at the same time. The unfairness of life was not in his thoughts at this point. He didn't ask the question, "Why?" to himself or God. He could only think of what needed done.

"Can you tell me anything else, doctor?"

Tom and Helen were right beside him. He stepped away for space to think. Everything closed in.

"I would recommend you get here ASAP. Until we've evaluated her further, we won't know how to help her. The need could arise for decisions pertaining to her treatment. As of now, our primary concern is the possibility of internal hemorrhaging, trauma to her head, or possible comatose. I just can't say at this point, but it would be best if you were here."

"I'm currently in Taos, but I'll head there right now. Please, do everything you can and keep me informed. We have health insurance. She's covered. I'll pay for anything."

Isaac conveniently left out the part about piloting his own plane. The doctor would vehemently object and he knew it. *It isn't the doc's problem though. It's mine.* If he didn't reach Sarah in time, he would never forgive himself. *Please, God, not her, too.*

"Does your wife have any medical history that might affect her treatment? She was in the Susan G. Komen Walk for the Cure when she was hit. Is she a cancer survivor?"

"No, no. Her mother died of cancer. She's never had any serious medical problems. No medications or allergies." He envisioned Sarah when they had dropped her off in Albuquerque, beautiful, vibrant, excited, and full of life. "She's healthy. Very, very healthy."

He hoped that was still true. His angel, mother of his children, lover, and forever partner was in the fight for her life. Could he live without her? Did he even want to? Never before, even with Caroline broken and bloody in his arms, had he been so aware of the physical pain emotional distress caused. *Hang on for me. For us. Don't leave me. Please, God, don't let her leave me.*

"Thank you, Mr. Snow. Be careful getting here. When you arrive, tell the ER desk who you are and that Dr. Ellison wishes to speak with you immediately. I'll leave instructions."

"Thank you." Isaac heard himself think it, but he didn't know if it actually came out.

The line went dead.

Chapter Forty-Nine

A long, thin finger ran across a paper map to occupy Ricky's mind. When everything went down, it was imperative he knew exactly how to get back to the cabin in relationship to his location. All the proper coordinates were plugged into his GPS, but he had seen too many electronics malfunction over the years. He was in the technology business and understood that nothing compared to a piece of paper for reliability. His finger retraced the route, point by point.

He waited. The next hour of his life had no room for mistakes. It was an all-in gamble. All he had to do was follow along and, at the appropriate juncture, play his part. He fidgeted at the thought. Once the final domino tipped, there was no turning back. His escape would be more intense than any he had ever experienced.

The roar of a racing engine thundered through his open window. He was positioned well off the highway in the shade of a tree grove along the airport road. The entrance was in full view. Tom's grey truck rocketed toward him and shot past the roadside rest area like a bullet.

My, my . . . In a hurry, are we?

Isaac drove. Ricky could see both his hands on the steering wheel through the binoculars. Helen sat in the passenger seat with Josie in the back. Helen's presence came as no mystery.

Someone had to drive home after dropping them off. But that was about to change.

Isaac's next move was the important one. Ricky had no doubts about the soon-to-come scene on the tarmac. Isaac would go absolutely bat-shit crazy when he found his destroyed plane. And when he did, his choice of action would release the pendulum. Ricky had a pretty good theory what would happen, but there were no guarantees.

Chapter Fifty

They banked into a hard left curve, and the force pushed Helen against the passenger door.

"Careful," she said.

"I got it, Mom." Isaac's tone left little to be deciphered. He was in no mood to accept driving comments.

After the phone call from the hospital, Helen and Tom had both tried to talk him out of flying. Instead, they offered to drive him and Josie to Albuquerque. But their words fell upon deaf ears. He had already made up his mind and would not deviate.

Once they accepted his decision, Helen tried to convince him to let Josie stay behind. She argued that they would only take a half hour to be on the road. By the time Isaac got to the airfield, flew to Albuquerque, and hailed a cab to the hospital, it would take a solid two to three hours. They would all arrive around the same time anyway.

Again, Isaac declined and explained that he was not going to let her out of his sight. If it came down to Sarah only having a few hours left to live, he wanted Josie there to say good-bye to her mother. The trouble of flying might only save him ten minutes. But it was ten minutes he wasn't willing to give up.

Helen reluctantly conceded, realizing she truly had no say in the matter. The only way for her to help was to put her own reservations aside and go with them. Josie needed looked after while Isaac conferred with the doctors and attended to Sarah. If a difficult decision had to be made, for better or worse, she knew her son might need support. Isaac agreed but afforded her no time to pack.

The final arrangement ended with Isaac, Josie, and Helen leaving immediately and flying to Albuquerque. Tom would stay, pack for himself and Helen, bring all the luggage, and drive down in their SUV.

Five minutes after bolting out of the driveway, Isaac brought the pickup to a screeching halt in front of the FBO (fixed-base operator) office at the airfield. They all piled out. Helen and Josie were to get into the airplane, strap in, and wait while he ran over the checklist. He walked toward the Cessna, wrist deep in his flight bag, when Helen broke his concentration.

"Is something wrong with your plane?" she asked with evident concern. She held Josie's hand, and they both stood motionless.

He looked up. It only took a second to see and smell that something was definitely amiss. He noticed the stench of aviation gas before the new paint job. Fuel had pooled underneath the bird. Wet asphalt shimmered in the morning glow. Fumes rose in the warming air and drifted to their noses.

Isaac narrowed his eyes and studied the scene. He found the flat tires and, finally, the crimson red spray paint that molested the otherwise white airplane.

"Does that say . . ." Helen couldn't believe her eyes.

"What does 'Suck It' mean?" Josie peered up at her, a curiously innocent expression on her face.

Helen turned to Isaac for instruction, and he subtly shook his head. "Well . . ." She tried to think. "I guess it means . . ."

"They're all vandalized," Isaac said with his outstretched arm pointed at the line of planes.

Glad to have the subject changed away from Josie's question, Helen observed the other two aircraft. She covered her mouth with her free hand.

"What's a rich dick?" Josie asked as she read the words written across the fuselage two spaces down.

Helen's mouth went agape. "Uh" was all she could manage while her mind spun to find an explanation appropriate for an eight-year-old. Again, Isaac came to her rescue.

"Everybody back in the truck." He stepped forward into the broad puddle of gas and tiptoed to a place underneath the wing. He found three punctures approximately the size of a screwdriver shaft penetrating into the overhead tanks. A single droplet of gas clung to a hole, not quite heavy enough to drip. "Son of a bitch," he softly muttered.

"Hon," Helen called, "what happened?"

Isaac's palms covered his face. He ran them back over his whole head absolutely dumbfounded as to what he should do next. The weekend had gone so well. Then without warning, the morning had turned sour. Sarah was in the hospital, hit by a car. He needed to get to her and fast. Now his magic carpet was destroyed, useless in his time of need. Desperation filled his cup and neared the point of spilling over. But he did have one more option. Although not entirely legal, he decided to go with it. Sarah was more important than any trouble he might get into.

Familiar with the airfield because of his job, he jumped into action. Spinning on a heel, he moved out of the gas puddle and headed for the night watchman's office.

"Wait for me out here," he directed to Helen and Josie.

Clear of the wet fuel, he began to run the fifty-yard stretch. The security guard's only job was to keep riffraff out of the airfield and assist any late-night pilots. At almost nine in the morning, the guard had no idea of what had transpired outside his window during the night. Otherwise, the cops would already be there to investigate, and Isaac would have been notified. A golf cart sat a few feet from the door so the on-duty guard could make regular patrols around the property.

The fuel tanks on Isaac's Cessna were completely drained, and with the holes as small as they were, he knew it would have taken at least an hour for all the gas to dribble out. Beyond that, all the guard had to do was look out his window and see that the visiting planes had new paint jobs.

The office door wasn't locked and burst open under the force of his urgency.

Arnulfo Chavez, the portly night guard in his late forties, appeared to have no interest in physical activity or even getting out of his rolling desk chair. Empty Pepsi cans, pretzel bags from the vending machine, and a Butterfinger wrapper littered his workspace. Despite the large window overlooking the grounds, Arnie hadn't noticed Isaac striding across the tarmac. Startled at the intrusion, he turned away from the small color television and toward the door. A tense silence filled the room.

"What are you doing here?" Arnie finally asked. His English was broken and had a heavy Hispanic accent. "I did not know you was on patrol today."

"I'm not," Isaac said tersely. He had known him for a couple years now. Arnie tended to be lax on the job, but there had never been any cause to comment on it. "Have you been here all night?"

The blunt question took him aback, and he answered defensively. "Yes. Why?"

Isaac pointed his finger at the window. "Then you should be able to explain why my airplane is trashed." He glared across the counter.

Arnie scrunched his brow in obvious confusion. At first, he thought it was a joke. But judging by the raging fire in Isaac's eyes, he decided not to respond with a dismissive remark. "I don't know what you're talking about." He sat forward in the chair and rested his forearms on the littered desktop.

"Maybe," Isaac bellowed with fury from Arnie's lack of concern, "if you'd get off your ass . . ." He waved his hand around at all the junk food trash. "You would have noticed that someone painted, slashed the tires, and drained the fuel from every single plane out there. Meanwhile, you sat here and watched TV." His face turned deep red, and a vein bulged in his neck.

Arnie finally rocked his squatty carcass out of the chair and moseyed to the window. The planes were a ways down the tarmac but close enough to see the obvious damage. A slightly green tint washed over his mahogany complexion.

"I . . ." He shook his head, incredulous. "I don't know nothin' about it. I was right here all night and didn't see nobody," he pled. "I swear no cars or nothin' came in."

"Exactly, Arnie. You were here. Planes don't vandalize themselves. That's almost a million dollars worth of aircraft out there, ruined because you didn't walk your patrols. You don't even have to walk." Isaac slapped the counter and roared, "You have a golf cart!"

Arnie's pallor continued to change. Now he looked visually sick, a nauseous shade of yellow with a neatly trimmed salt-and-pepper mustache in the middle of his haggard face. Jobs like his weren't easily come by. The night security position was a golden ticket. The city owns the airport, and government perks apply. With a screw-up this big, Arnie envisioned his salary and health-care benefits swirling down the drain. He had let his guard down with no excuses.

Harping on Arnie did nothing to help Isaac. It released some steam, but it didn't get him any closer to Sarah. He had to keep moving forward, go beyond what he couldn't change to what he could. His airplane was out of commission. End of story. No amount of ass chewing could change it. He needed a fast ride to Albuquerque.

The regional MedEvac plane was parked inside the FBO hangar attached to Arnie's office. Isaac stepped to a waist-high door and reached for a set of keys on a pegboard hook. The MedEvac plane was for medical emergencies only. A specially trained team of pilots and EMTs used it to transport critical patients out of the rural area and to advanced medical facilities in places like Santa Fe, Albuquerque, or Denver. Technically, Isaac did have a medical emergency, and the air ambulance was the only functional plane he had access to.

"Señor, you can't come back here." Arnie moved across the room. He planted his sturdy frame in front of the gate faster than Isaac thought possible for a man with so much extra girth. Arnie held both palms forward like a traffic cop.

"Get out of my way, Arnie." He stared down at the man six inches below. "My wife's in the hospital, and I need to get there. I'm taking the MedEvac in hangar one." He twisted the handle of the half door and pushed.

Arnie saw the determination in Isaac's eyes and realized that no amount of coaxing would detour him. He also feared for his job and refused to be accused of further dereliction of his duties. In an unreasonable panic, he turned sideways and jammed his boot against the base of the gate. His right hand shot into a belt holster and removed a can of pepper spray. Without warning, he pointed it at Isaac and let loose a jet.

Isaac saw it coming a split second before it happened. He turned away and absorbed the blast on the back of his shirt. "Dammit, Arnie! What the hell are you doing?" He stepped away and put his arms around his face before turning around. "Shit! That burns!"

"Señor, I cannot let you take the plane." Arnie continued to hold his pepper spray at the ready. The entirety of his outstretched arm shook from the adrenaline in his system. "Nobody takes the plane except for emergencies." His finger was still on the trigger, but he had stopped squeezing. The five-foot-six security guard was clearly in a level of stress far beyond what his decision-making skills could handle. He had the look of a desperate animal fearing for survival.

If Isaac caught pepper spray in the face, it wouldn't matter if he had the keys to the MedEvac or not. He wouldn't be able to fly until the effects wore off, and that could take quite a while. Soon the cops were going to be there because Arnie was already dialing their number on a desk phone with his free hand. Isaac had no desire to be detained after the police arrived. A series of questions would be one more thing to slow him down. He and the girls should leave while they still had the chance.

Back outside, he stripped off his shirt. The spray had soaked through the fabric and irritated the skin on his back. The fumes burned his eyes and sinuses. He pulled it over his head and threw it to the ground.

Helen and Josie stood by the pickup and watched with wide eyes as Isaac's tense, shirtless physique approached. Every muscle in his body stood in high relief, subconsciously flexed in anger.

Helen grabbed Josie by the shoulders and directed her to the backdoor of the gray truck. "C'mon, Jo. I think we're driving."

They all buckled in, and Helen asked, "What happened in there?" She crinkled her nose. "Whew. What is that smell?"

Josie coughed in the backseat from the leftover effect of Arnie's aim.

Isaac started the engine and pulled the gearshift into drive. He made an arching turn across the tarmac and accelerated out of the airport. He checked the gas gauge and found a satisfactory three-quarters of a tank. Then he explained everything that had happened in the office.

"Let's just drive there like we originally talked about." Helen placed a hand on his bare shoulder. "No more complications."

He nodded. "You're right. That's all we can do now." He took a deep breath to calm himself and glanced in the rearview mirror. "Jo, you okay back there?"

She had taken the filtered news of her mother's situation well, but she was quieter than normal due to the obviously strange turn of events. She was young, not dumb, and didn't have to be told that things weren't going well. "Yes," she said softly.

"That's my girl." Isaac tried to put on a reassuring face.

Helen turned around and gave her a tight-lipped smile.

"Mom, call Dad and let him know the change of plans. Tell him we're still going ahead and we'll see him there."

While Helen relayed the news to Tom, Isaac navigated his way through town and used the reprieve to take inventory of the situation. Since the unexpected phone call, the morning had delivered him one disastrous scenario after another. He couldn't help but wonder if so much chaos was in some way his own doing. He tried to think of his life and what decision could possibly have led him to this point. A killer had taken Caroline from their lives earlier in the summer. The same man now threatened to take Josie. What was supposed to be a weekend of refreshment had turned into a living nightmare and potentially life-threatening situation for Sarah. His most expedient means of transportation was destroyed, and to top things off, he now had a three-hour drive to relive everything. Three hours to keep the worst thoughts at bay. Three hours to reach Sarah, hopefully still alive.

South out of town, they traversed down Highway 68. The slow, winding route took them deep into the mountains.

The world felt like it had turned its back on him and hung his family out to dry. He didn't think it could get any worse.

Chapter Fifty-One

With the cunning of nature's best predators, Ricky stalked his prey. He blended in, pursued Josie from a distance, and gave no cause for alarm. His blue, avian eyes were poised for the kill.

Isaac, Helen, and Josie were headed exactly where he knew they would. There is really only one obvious route from Taos to Albuquerque, one way he confidently presumed they would go.

When he vandalized the airplanes, he knew Isaac would have to drive. The damage he inflicted on the Cessna was far beyond a quick repair. Now on a long, scarcely populated stretch of blacktop, he tailed his prize of all prizes from a quarter-mile back. Everything progressed famously.

Traveling south on Highway 68, Ricky began running the soon-to-come sequence of events through his head. He had practically memorized every curve, twist, and rise on the two-lane road. His GPS tracked the route on a screen. A little blue car represented his position.

In the seat next to him sat a bag full of trade secret tools. The cans of spray paint were long gone, disposed of for good. He still had the fireworks though and another concoction he had formulated in the night. The trap, like any good snare, needed camouflage. Everything had to look as authentic as possible. He felt confident it would fool anyone, even Isaac.

At approximately three miles outside of town, Ricky had not met a single vehicle on the road. Time for action drew near. Each rotation of the tires pulled him closer. All around, nature's stone walls rose up and funneled them into the narrow Rio Grande Valley. There were mountains to the left, the river to the right, and more mountains beyond.

He sped up and gained some ground. Isaac drove like a bat out of hell, and Ricky refused to be left behind. The winding road offered the sole sanctuary in the rugged terrain. Once off the beaten path, untamed wilderness stretched out for hundreds and hundreds of square miles.

He adjusted his grip on the steering wheel.

Chapter Fifty-Two

Life kept throwing punches below the belt. Sarah could die, and Isaac might not reach her in time to say farewell as she embarked on her final journey. He did his best to ignore the raw emotion in his heart and drive, focusing solely on the road ahead.

His foot floored the accelerator as they rounded a curve and hit a straightaway. A galvanized guardrail on their right separated the road from the river below. A rock face rose several hundred vertical feet to the left. The speedometer quickly climbed from fifty-five to eighty miles per hour. He wanted to go faster, but the snakelike track didn't allow for more speed. It followed the water-carved canyon and methodically rolled southward to lower elevations. With Helen and Josie in the pickup, he couldn't risk being reckless and taking the bends any hastier. Regardless of Sarah's condition, his mother and daughter's safety were currently his responsibility.

Helen said something. Whether she spoke to him or Josie, he couldn't say. He heard but did not listen. His mind was too busy retracing the plethora of radical events. His airplane was trashed. He clenched and unclenched his jaw at the absurdity of it. Three planes parked at a rural airfield vandalized beyond use. And all the while, a paid security guard sat on his butt nibbling candy and guzzling Pepsi. It was preventable, and they should be halfway to Albuquerque by now. That was what really infuriated him.

And how did a car hit Sarah on a closed course?

He relaxed his grip and held the wheel steady for the straight portion of the road. A vehicle in his rearview mirror tailgated him. Isaac looked down at the speedometer. It read eighty-five. It was all the urgency the skinny little pavement allowed for. But the white pickup behind them ventured even closer, like it wanted to pass.

What the hell? He let off the throttle to allow the maniac by. He hoped whoever the idiot with a death wish was wouldn't slow down after he was in the lead. One more second between him and Sarah was unacceptable. He had to be there for her. He would not fail like he had with Caroline.

Slowing down to fifty-five again, he hit the flat, left-hand curve. They all leaned to the right as Isaac steered the pickup around the bend. The guardrail ran parallel to the road, two feet out from the passenger side. The next curve went right, and everyone leaned the other way. And so it went for the next ten minutes. He looked at the dashboard clock. Nine twenty-five. They were making decent time considering the terrain and a three-quarter-ton pickup. After thirty more minutes, they could get onto a larger highway and really put the pedal to the metal.

Up ahead, he saw it, but Helen said it first. "Someone's blocking the road."

She was right. A pickup was stalled across both lanes.

"Are you kidding me? We don't have time for this."

They slowed, coming to a complete stop twenty feet out, and searched for a way around.

Chapter Fifty-Three

A massive ponderosa pine towered into the heavens. The charred, split trunk set it apart from the others, a result of lightning. Ricky admired Mother Nature's fantastic violence.

He had the tree marked on his GPS with a waypoint. The little blue car passed the dot on the screen at exactly the same time he drove past. All his desires and schemes were finally at a head. It was time to engage the target and put himself in the line of fire.

From his location, no more paved roads branched off Highway 68 until the little town of Espanola. It was a solid thirty-five miles down the valley and the only place for Isaac to go through on his way to I-25. Ricky had to stop following and take the lead. The narrow road and frequent blind curves made the task exceedingly difficult. Isaac also didn't make the chore any easier. He drove at a breakneck pace.

Ricky tried to go around twice. Each time, he ran out of road before the next curve and double yellow line. Nerves wet his palms with a clammy layer of sweat. He needed to pass Isaac. Now. Otherwise, he could end up short on time and unable to properly camouflage the setup. Preparations had to be made for everything to look authentic. At their current speeds, it would take several minutes to build a cushion.

Ricky took the next curve as hard as he dared. As soon as the road opened up, he put his front bumper within feet of Isaac's tailgate. The act went against the very core of his nature. He knew the difference between being seen and being noticed. It was impossible to live life without being seen. Avoiding notice, on the other hand, was a skill Ricky had refined to an art. But Josie called to him like none before.

He inched to the left and, with the road open ahead, hoped his Chevy had the muscle to quickly slip around. To his satisfaction, Isaac eased off the accelerator just enough to shoot past. He swerved back into his lane a mere instant before the next blind curve.

Ricky scoped them out with his peripheral vision. Helen and Josie glanced his way, but Isaac kept his eyes on the road. *Distance is what I need now. Approximately one minute of separation would do.*

Josie stayed at the pinnacle of his motivation. There was only himself, the road, and the prize that awaited him. Fortune was in his front pocket and had been all weekend. He threw caution to the wind and rocketed down the mountain road without thought of personal safety. He slowed as little as he dared on the curves and floored it on the straights.

His second marker showed up in perfect sync with the GPS, a boulder that had once broken off the cliff above. He took a deep breath. Sweat beaded on his upper lip and forehead. *This is it. I can do it.*

He jammed down on the brake pedal as if his life depended on it. The tires alternated between bursts of skidding and groaning as the antilock brakes fought to harness the momentum. Even through the anticipation, adrenaline flooded his system at the harsh sound and feel of a sudden stop. He went from seventy-five miles per hour to a dead standstill.

"Holy shit!"

He wished for a moment to collect himself, but seconds were precious.

Ricky parked the pickup at a forty-five degree angle to the road and checked the gap between his front bumper and the rock face. In his side mirror, he did the same with the rear bumper and guardrail. Both ends were too narrow for a vehicle to go through. He quickly killed the engine and left the keys in the ignition.

At the front of the pickup, he popped the hood. He did each task in the order he had mentally rehearsed, precise, efficient, and never frantic. As he put the finishing touches on the scene, the sound of an approaching vehicle echoed off the canyon walls, and anxiety overwhelmed him.

Deception beckoned his best poker face.

Chapter Fifty-Four

G iven the current predicament, Isaac was prepared to do something he would never do under normal circumstances, drive by a motorist in need and leave him behind. His main concern was not assisting the unfortunate person, but to get the vehicle out of the way so he could keep traveling.

"That's the guy who just passed us," he said.

Helen stared out the windshield. "Where's all that smoke coming from?"

Waves of billowing, gray smoke poured from under the open hood.

"Looks like a hose busted." Isaac unbuckled his seat belt. "We can't waste time. I'll help him off the road, and then we're gone." *His problems can't be bigger than mine.*

When the man appeared out of the smoke and walked toward them, Isaac's perception immediately changed.

"I know that guy." He put the gearshift in park. "He works at the grocery store."

"Oh my!" Helen exclaimed. She covered the lower part of her face with both hands. "That's . . . a lot of blood."

The sight of blood all over a familiar face softened Isaac's attitude. To not help this person would be inhumane, regardless of the rush. He jumped out of the cab and placed a gentle hand on the shoulder of the injured man he knew as Derek. "Are you okay?"

Ricky lifted his head and touched his fingers to his nose. He pulled them back and looked at the fresh coating of blood. "I think I'm fine. I hit my nose on the steering wheel. Damn thing surprised the hell out of me. Kind of shook me up."

Isaac scanned about the smoking pickup. "What surprised you?" His hand was still on the man's shoulder.

"A deer was right in the middle of the road when I came around the curve. I didn't have time to stop or . . ." He waved his hand around at the setting. "Room to swerve." Ricky leaned over, resting his shaky hands on his knees.

Isaac noticed. "That's the adrenaline. Take a few deep breaths. It'll wear off in a minute." He pulled a white handkerchief from his hip pocket. "Here." He handed it over. "You work at the grocery store, right?"

Ricky nodded and held the cloth to his nose, a look of recognition and gratitude in his eyes.

"C'mon. Let's take a look at your truck."

Isaac stood in front of the grill and open hood. An image of a warm, Fourth of July night and fireworks filling the sky skipped through his mind. He couldn't say why, so he pushed the thought aside. Smoke continued to roll out from the engine area. Across the grill and headlights, he found a generous slathering of blood.

Isaac let out a whistle. "Yeah, you nailed him all right." He swiveled his head around. "Where's the deer?"

Ricky pointed down the hill to the river. "It ran off that way." He sniffed and wiped his face with his shirt. "Sucker busted my radiator and didn't even die."

Isaac kneeled. He wanted to look under the Chevy. Whatever fluid caused all the smoke would surely have made a puddle on the ground. He placed one hand on the bumper for balance and the other on the asphalt for support. He craned his neck lower to get a good look.

As soon as Isaac's eyes were trained down, Ricky stepped closer. He drew a high-voltage stun gun from underneath his shirttail and pressed it firmly into Isaac's bare lower back. The prongs were centered directly on top of his spine when Ricky pulled the trigger.

Isaac's body arched as his muscles succumbed to the current of eight hundred thousand volts. He collapsed to the ground without a word, unable to overpower the onslaught of electricity invading his neuromuscular system. With his location in front of Ricky's pickup, Helen and Josie couldn't see.

Ricky zapped him again, this time at the base of his skull. A slight groan escaped Isaac's lips while Ricky held the pulse for a full five seconds.

Isaac wouldn't get to his feet in the next couple minutes; Ricky was certain. But after that, he couldn't say with confidence. To further safeguard the bait and switch, he put a heavy-duty zip tie around Isaac's wrists and cinched it unmercifully tight. Another went around his ankles and held them together. He reared back with his leg and planted the toe of his boot into Isaac's ribs for good measure. Satisfied that his foe could do nothing to stop him, Ricky readied himself to take out Helen.

From around the front of the pickup, he limped across the blacktop and went to her window.

She rolled it down with a look of concern. "Is everything okay? Are you hurt?"

"I'll be all right. Hit my nose on the steering wheel. That's all." He tapped it twice with his pointer finger. "It'll be good as new when I get cleaned up."

"What happened?"

"A deer was right in the middle of the road. Dumb thing must have had a death wish." He flashed his trademark smile, so gentle, handsome, and unsuspicious. Those bedroom blues bored right into Helen.

"I'm so sorry." Genuine compassion showed in her words. In no way did she feel in danger.

He motioned to his pickup. "I need to call a tow truck to get me back to town. I understand you guys are in a bit of a hurry?"

"Yes. Family emergency."

Ricky nodded. "I understand. I won't keep you, but could I borrow your cell phone?"

"Of course." She bent forward and reached into the floorboard for her purse.

As Helen leaned over, Ricky slipped his arm through the open window. The handheld weapon found a bare patch of skin between her ear and shirt collar. She slumped in response with a jerky spasm. Just like he did Isaac, he nailed her again at the top of her spine. Inserting the charge into the body's central nervous system via the spinal column gained maximum effect. Five seconds of treatment seemed like an eternity but ensured disability, especially with her smaller stature.

Ricky's finger pecked at the unlock button. He swung the door out and reached for her purse in the floorboard. Thin and nimble, his fingers rummaged through the contents until he found her cell phone. He spun around and flung it into the flowing river below. Isaac's cell rested in the center console's cup holder. Ricky leaned against Helen's body. His chest touched her side, and he grasped the phone. A swift toss sent it spiraling into the ravine.

He stretched across the cab again, and his body pushed Helen's limp torso to the middle. He twisted the keys out of the ignition and put them in his pocket. The idea of leaving them stranded on a lonely stretch of road with no means of communication or transportation relieved him.

All the weeks of waiting were over. It was just him and Josie.

He turned his attention to the backseat. She stared at his familiar face, wide-eyed, and scooted to the far corner. He opened the backdoor and reached out for her leg. Finally, his hungry fingers found her and latched on.

Chapter Fifty-Five

Isaac remembered kneeling on the pavement to inspect underneath the smoking pickup. Then a sudden blast of power knocked him to the ground. Now, lying on his stomach with chip seal gravel pocking into his shirtless skin, he tried to clear the fuzz from his scrambled head.

He rolled onto his back to get a better look at the surroundings. Every muscle in his body ached with the motion. But the discomfort was not nearly as sharp as the cutting sensation on his wrists. As he turned over, the weight of his body smashed his bound hands. Wedged between his lower back and the asphalt, the plastic flex cuffs dug into his flesh. He shifted, trying to release the pressure, and found his motor skills as sluggish as a reptile in winter.

Disorientation morphed into fear. *What happened to me?*

He could see his dad's truck sitting right where he had left it. Rotating his head in the other direction, he saw an open stretch of blacktop. The disabled vehicle was gone, disappeared somewhere beyond the next blind curve. *I have to move before I get run over.*

He tried to use his legs and, like his hands, discovered they were tied together. Lying on his side, arms behind his back, he pushed with his feet. A makeshift inchworm motion slowly edged him off the pavement. A portion of his ribcage and most of his upper arm succumbed to the abrasive surface. Tiny beads of blood began to seep from the skin. At the white stripe, he tucked himself into the narrow space against the guardrail. Sun glistened off a fresh layer of sweat from the effort.

He managed to sit up and look at his feet. The zip tie was thick—the kind police use to arrest people when they run out of proper handcuffs—and allowed no wiggle room. The plastic was too strong to break with brute strength, especially with his current lack of muscular cooperation.

He racked his brain, searching for a memory of how he ended up this way. An image of warm Fourth of July nights streaked through his head again, the same thought he had right before leaning over to check for a fluid leak. He attempted to shake the thought. Then realization hit.

"Mom!" Urgency filled his voice. "Mom! Are you there?" A breakdown of the last five minutes began to manifest. The so-called accident between the white pickup and deer was no accident at all. Rather, it was a carefully staged and effective ploy.

No answer came from his mother.

He slithered beside the wooden guardrail posts toward the truck. Gravel, debris, and asphalt continued to gnaw at his hands, left arm, and ribcage. Sweat made the rubble stick, and the bloody scrapes developed into road rash.

"Isaac?" A soft reply finally came.

"Mom, are you okay?" He squirmed with even more urgency. Too many questions remained unanswered.

"I think so." Her voice sounded uncertain.

"What the hell happened?" A kick of his feet sprayed loose rocks into the air, and they dinged off the galvanized rail. "Where's the guy?"

Disoriented, Helen sat up and peered out the windshield. "I don't know." She thought hard. Something was definitely off.

Her muscles ached like a bad case of influenza. "He wanted to use my phone to call a tow truck." She tried to sit taller, hearing but not seeing her son.

Isaac had almost made his way to the passenger side. The backdoor sat ajar. "Josie?" he called out. "Mom, is Josie okay?"

Helen slowly twisted at the waist to look over her shoulder. "She's right back—" Her pace quickened in panic. "She's not here!" A swift click with her thumb unbuckled the seat belt, and she turned completely around. Her knees were in the seat. "She's gone!"

Each piece of an intricate puzzle fell into place. The whole picture was there in black and white: Derek the grocery store clerk, the airplanes, the staged wreck, and Josie. Key points added up in an undisputable sequence. They explained everything.

"Josie, answer me," Helen commanded.

"She's not there."

Helen ignored him. "Josephine Snow, you answer me this instant." The demand sounded fearful, not adamant.

"He took her." Isaac was sprawled outside her door now.

Helen poked her head out the open window and looked down. Isaac lying on the ground didn't seem to bother her. "I don't understand," she went on. "He couldn't have taken her." She averted her stare to the backseat as if Josie might reappear.

Already on borrowed time, he didn't care to debate the validity of Josie's kidnapping.

"Dad keeps a multi-tool in the glove box." He put ice to his voice. "Get it for me."

"But she was right here. All he wanted was my phone."

"Mom, the multi-tool. Now! I'm tied up." He managed to kick the running board with a loud bang to gain her attention.

While he waited for the cutters, a clear display of events poured through his mind. He saw the eyes that stared at him from across Caroline and Josie's bedroom on the first night of summer. They were the same piercing blues he had seen at the grocery store. And they were the same eyes that had just played him for a fool.

A stream of grizzly abduction memories emerged as if he had been there himself. Letters and Polaroids followed, every one addressed to Josie. The graphic pictures were terrible, but nothing compared to the words of handwritten intent. The last one, "I'll be seeing you. Soon," rang louder than ever. No matter how much Isaac had hoped and prayed that it would be, the promise was not empty.

Lastly, the row of vandalized airplanes came to mind. All had been trashed, not just his. *The paint on mine was . . . red.* He felt disgusted with himself that he hadn't noticed the subtle clue, a jab to mock him.

And only moments ago, he had stood in front of the murderer's pickup and swallowed his bait. Blood covered the grill and headlights, but now that he recalled, not one dent marred the vehicle, and no blood trail from an injured animal was left behind. He had been so concerned with reaching Sarah that awareness fell by the wayside. Even though he couldn't place it before, the seemingly random vision of fireworks and Fourth of July festivals finally made sense.

The Independence Day memories were from childhood. As little boys, he and Charlie lit smoke bombs to play war and pull pranks. The odor was undeniable and, here and now, the smoke had poured from underneath the hood and flawlessly simulated a fluid leak.

Helen emerged with the multi-tool. She opened the wire cutters and knelt in front of Isaac. Slipping the plastic tie between the jaws, she clamped down.

He snatched the tool with his newly freed hands and clipped the bindings on his ankles. Helen reached out and helped pull him up by the arms. They both staggered, neither in full command of their muscles, and rushed to their seats. She slammed her door shut while Isaac teetered around the front. Bloody and dirty, he stretched an arm across the hood for support. His body was there, but his head and heart felt hollow.

Sarah was in the hospital, Caroline was already dead, and Josie drew further and further away by the second. Three girls—his girls—beyond the protection he yearned to give them. No matter how hard he tried, he couldn't stop the tide.

Helen said, "We have to get her back."

Without a word, he put his foot on the brake and reached for the ignition. His hand fumbled for the keys. They weren't there.

We are truly stranded, and Josie is on her own.

Chapter Fifty-Six

It took every ounce of discipline to drive on as Ricky struggled to control himself. Josie slept in a drug-induced state from the chloroform. Helpless, she rested in the front passenger floorboard.

This was, unequivocally, the most exhilarated he ever remembered feeling. He had to draw it out and savor the ride. Ending the adventure too soon would be a tragic disservice to his efforts. After he finished with her, it could take years to recapture the euphoric bliss.

Perplexed, he couldn't put a finger on why Josie demanded so much of him. If the situation called for it, he would pursue her to the ends of the earth. She was more than a minor obsession. Maybe because he had to go without her for so long. Originally, it had been because she and Caroline were identical twins. He had never had twins before. The fantastical idea excited him. Now it was just Josie. And somehow, he relished the notion of her, even more so than when there were two of them. She called to him in a way he didn't fully understand.

Despite his rushed escape, Ricky knew the stakes were about to change. Eventually, the chase would be on. Every law enforcement officer within a hundred miles on God's green earth was about to search for him. His best guess was that, currently, no one beyond Isaac and Helen knew anything. Their first opportunity to call for help wouldn't come until another motorist stopped or Isaac made it back to town on foot. Either option suited Ricky fine. One could take as long as the next.

The song "Time Is on My Side" played in his head.

He continued in a blaze up the mountain road. Confidence blossomed. By the time the police were notified, put together a plan, and finally exercised it, he would be nothing but a tiny speck hidden inside millions of acres of wilderness and uncharted roads.

He glanced down at Josie's little form. The last time he had seen her sleep was in her own bedroom in Ruidoso. He thought it odd how a dropped flashlight ended up the cause for so much.

Soon, she would pay for his troubles.

Chapter Fifty-Seven

An iron fist connected with the dash. Isaac clearly recalled leaving the engine running when he got out to help. He'd left his cell phone in the cup holder. It too had disappeared. Even a small break would go a long way, but the stars weren't aligned, at least not for him.

He gripped the steering wheel with both hands and violently shook it. "No!" he screamed at the top of his lungs. The wail was long and drawn out, the very essence of defeat.

Helen began to cry next to him. "I don't know what to do." Fresh tears ran down her cheeks. She loved Josie and couldn't bear the thought of what she would soon have to endure. "We have to do something. We have to go."

He lifted his hands from the wheel in a pose of surrender. Years of military training pulled him from a state of panic and guided his mind in the direction of focus and decisiveness. "Did he take your cell?" He held out his hand.

Helen jerked her purse from the floor. Her hands dove into the bag and found the phone pocket. It was empty. She dug to the bottom. Still nothing. Raking her fingers through once more, a jingle caught her ear. It wasn't a cell phone, but better. *Why didn't I think of this before?* She dangled a ring of keys into the air with two fobs attached.

"Please tell me that's a spare," he said hopefully.

"I forgot. I keep the second set to both cars in my purse."

He snatched them away and drove the master key into the ignition. The truck purred to life. It made the most glorious sound he had ever heard.

"I didn't think about it because I never use them," she explained and sniffed her runny nose.

He almost jammed the gearshift into drive but stopped short. He sat there, motionless, for a pause.

"What are you doing?" Helen pled. "Go!"

She was right, of course. The most logical choice was to give chase and hopefully catch up to Josie and her captor. But something in the back of his mind told him to act differently. He realized the problem and, as much as it defied rationale, made a judgment call. Josie's life hung in the balance of his choices. He didn't deny it and knew what had to be done.

"No," he told Helen.

"He's getting away!"

He executed a hasty three-point turn. "He's already gotten away." He floored it and started back down the road the way they had just come.

Helen looked at him like he had lost his mind. Desperation struck her face as she silently pled for him not to drive away.

"His pickup is faster than ours," he explained. "Dad's is built for work, not speed."

"But they can't be far."

"It doesn't matter." His voice slowly grew calm. The more he reasoned it out, the surer of himself he became. "I guarantee he's driving double-time now and we'll never catch up."

Helen stared ahead. She held onto a support handle and continued to fight off the after effects of the stun gun. "Then where are we going?"

Isaac rolled his neck around. He also tried to shake off the fatigued muscle feeling. "Back to the airport."

"We just came from there. We need to call the police. Somebody has to start searching."

"Yeah, well, we don't have a phone, Mom."

She reached up to the rearview mirror and punched a button with the symbol of a phone on it.

"What are you doing?" he asked.

She gave him an incredulous look. "Calling for help."

"It won't work. That's a Bluetooth connection. It's only compatible with your cell. Calls go through the car speakers so you can talk hands free."

Helen shook her head. "Not this one. There are too many places with no service in these mountains. Your dad buys minutes through OnStar. It's a satellite signal, and we can use it anywhere." She held the icon down until service engaged and then used buttons on the dash to dial. "At our age, it makes us feel safer to always have service."

Isaac was impressed with his mom's knowledge of the system. "Who are you calling?"

"Nine one one!"

He quickly hit the disconnect button before the call connected. A sigh of relief escaped his lips. "You can't do that."

"Why?" She scrambled to redial. "That's what it's for."

He grabbed her wrist and gave it a reassuring squeeze. "Stop dialing, Mom. That's not what I mean." He had to let her in on his idea. Otherwise, she wouldn't understand. "Look," he explained. "If you call nine one one, the alert will go to Taos PD. By the time they question us and finally realize the urgency, Josie will be long gone. And that's before a search plan has even been put together." The thought of never seeing her again constricted his throat. "I promise there's a better way to do this."

"I don't understand. What better way?" She had no knowledge of what happened the night before at the grocery store or the greater meaning behind the vandalized airplanes. The whole affair appeared one-dimensional to her. A man had taken her granddaughter. That was it.

"Call Charlie," he instructed.

"Charlie?" Now she thought he had lost it for sure. "He can't do anything from Ruidoso. It's too far away." She hit the phone button again. "You're not thinking straight. I'm calling the police, and I'm doing it right now."

"Dammit, Mom. Stop that." He hit the end button for the second time. "If you call the police, Josie is as good as dead."

She gave him a shocked expression, surprised that he dared talk about Josie's fate so bluntly.

"I mean it. Get Charlie on the line. We'll explain what happened, and he can call the Taos police. Everything will move ten times faster if another officer calls it in." He pushed for every millisecond of speed the cumbersome truck had to offer.

"Charlie," he went on, "knows who to contact at the FBI. Their people can come in on a chopper from Santa Fe or Albuquerque. If we do it this way, Josie stands a chance. If not, we can forget it. The cops will keep me from getting involved."

It never crossed Helen's mind that Isaac would help. She assumed he would leave it to the professionals. "And what is it, exactly, that you plan on doing?"

"Never mind that."

Isaac gave her Charlie's number by memory, and they waited for an answer. It felt so wrong to be driving in the opposite direction of Josie, but the plan was her only hope of rescue and his chance for redemption. He pushed the accelerator harder. The truck devoured the pavement. Finally, after three rings, Charlie's voice came over the speakers.

"Chief Biddle."

"Thank God," Isaac spoke into the ceiling mike. "We really need your help."

"Isaac?"

"We have an emergency situation. Listen to what I have to say before you ask questions."

There was a brief pause. "Okay," he agreed seriously. "Shoot."

He relayed everything that had happened from the time Dr. Ellison called to inform him of Sarah's accident, to the vandalized airplanes, and, ultimately, the kidnapping of Josie. Helen jumped in occasionally to give a detail Isaac left out. Charlie made good on his agreement. He didn't say one word until they finished.

"*Now?*" he asked in disbelief. "This is happening right *now*?" He wanted to be crystal clear.

"As we speak," Isaac assured.

"I'll call it in immediately and relay everything you just told me. It should expedite a search."

Isaac and Helen shared a glance. This was exactly what they wanted to hear. Helen nodded approvingly. The story Isaac told Charlie had come as a revelation to her. She understood the depth and elaborate planning it took the kidnapper to pull this off. One by one, they had jumped through his hoops. No matter how absurd Isaac's actions seemed at first, she realized he was right. They would never catch him by driving.

"Then," Charlie said, "I'll call the hospital and find out about Sarah. I'm a chief of police, and they'll let me know what's going on. Don't worry. I'll head to Albuquerque and look after her myself. As for you, do whatever needs done to find Josie."

"I will."

"Go get the bastard."

Chapter Fifty-Eight

T wenty minutes after Helen's spare set of keys saved them from despair, they made it back to the north side of town. A police cruiser in the oncoming lane blew by. His flashers whirled in circles, and the siren blared.

Isaac watched him speed in the opposite direction. "That would be Charlie," he said. "The call's gone out."

Helen looked in her side mirror. The cruiser was almost out of sight.

The officer's urgency pleased Isaac. More people knew about Josie's plight now. She had help on the way, but none that would find her in time. He hoped to solve that with his next dubious move. And to succeed, the officer had to be gone from the airfield. Only a gun would stop Isaac at this point. Had the officer not been called away, he would have come face to face with a serious conundrum, shoot Isaac or willingly allow a felony to happen. Isaac had no delusions to the likely outcome of that showdown.

"Mom, listen to me carefully." He averted his focus from the road to look her in the eye. Satisfied he had her attention, he said, "When I get out, you need to leave immediately. Do you understand?"

She nodded.

"Good. Call Dad, and have him meet you at the police station. When you get there, tell them who you are and that you're a witness to the abduction. They already know what's going on from Charlie. Tell them everything you can possibly remember." He glanced at her again. "Are you following me?"

"Yes."

"Don't go anywhere else. Drop me off, and go directly to the station."

"I will." She wiped moisture from her eyes. Isaac had her intent on action, not sadness. "Are you sure this is a good idea?"

He took a deep, contemplative breath and slowly exhaled. "It's the only one I have. If Josie and that . . ." He trailed off, too focused on the task at hand to find a choice word for the kidnapper. "If they stay on the highway, police in Espanola will be ready. The first thing that happens with abductions is a perimeter setup. Espanola is the gateway to larger corridors. I seriously doubt they could make it through without being spotted."

"Then why are you doing this?"

"Because I don't think he'll go through Espanola. It's too far away from where he took her. He's a smart one and won't take that risk. And he didn't double back to Taos."

"How do you know?"

"He left skid marks six inches from my head when he drove away. They were headed south."

"Where else can he go from there?" Helen knew no other real roads branched off Highway 68 between the two towns.

"There are a million and one mining tracks and logging trails that lead off the highway. My guess is he took one into the mountains. If I were him, it's what I would do."

"Why didn't you tell Charlie about that?"

"None of those roads are mapped. To anyone on the ground, it would be an endless maze and impossible for the police to effectively search. They don't have the manpower." He gave her a weak smile for reassurance. "That's why I'm the one who has to do it."

She reached out and touched his arm. Even though he stood a head above her and could grow a full beard, he was her boy, her only son. She felt pride that he was brave and selfless, a person willing to risk his life to protect those he loved. He did not fear for himself, but she did. She feared she might never see him or Josie alive again. "Isaac, promise me you'll be careful."

"I have to stay alive, Mom. I'm her only chance." He said it with absolute conviction.

"What about the guard with pepper spray?"

"I'll handle him." They raced down the tarmac, and he could see her concern over Arnie. "There's nothing you can do here," he added. "Go to the station. That's where you're needed most."

The FBO came closer and closer. They were only a hundred yards out. He wheeled the pickup in a semicircle. Less than five feet from the office entrance, they came to a stop.

Isaac bolted out of his seat and swung the pickup door closed behind him.

"I love you," Helen shouted. She watched him disappear inside, unsure if he heard the last words she might ever say to him.

He twisted the knob to the office door and threw his shoulder into it. Arnie, he figured, was probably still ruffled from their previous confrontation. The best way to take out an enemy is by surprise. That was Isaac's philosophy to handle the unpredictable night watchman.

Arnie sat behind the desk, face buried in his hands. No doubt he was fretting over the recent events and pondering the security of his job. His head sprang up at Isaac's sudden intrusion. Immediate recognition changed his languid expression. He must have also noticed the determined nature to Isaac's actions because he reached for his hip holster of pepper spray.

Before he could get it out, Isaac reacted. He grabbed a logbook off the counter and flung it across the room. Papers and notes scattered. Next, he took a coffee mug full of pens and pencils and hurled it at Arnie's head. The paunchy fellow had to duck to avoid the projectiles.

With his nemesis in full defensive mode, Isaac put a hand on the counter and vaulted over the top. He landed in front of the desk.

The guard's eyes were so enlarged, the whites showed all the way around. He did his best to back up and put distance between himself and Isaac. A couple more seconds was all he needed to unleash the fiery liquid.

In a last-ditch effort to overtake Arnie before getting hosed, Isaac leapt headlong over the desk. Pepsi cans and snack wrappers scattered as his body flew forward.

Arnie had the canister in his hand now and raised his arm to defend himself. But it came a split second too late. Isaac's shoulder drove into his chest, and they went to the floor. Arnie's head bumped a file cabinet. A model airplane toppled off and crashed beside the flailing dog pile. Arnie, sprawled on his back and out of breath, sucked in sharply. Precious air filled his lungs. Dazed from the solid collision, he peered up toward the ceiling. Isaac's dark, angry orbs occupied the space.

He straddled Arnie's rotund midsection with both knees on the ground. He'd managed to wrestle the pepper spray away. "Now you listen, and you listen good," he growled. "My wife is in the hospital, and my little girl needs help." He aimed the nozzle straight at the rent-a-cop's face. Blood and sweat were dried in crusty rivulets along Isaac's left bicep and forearm. His shirtless physique rose and fell with heavy breaths. "I'm taking the MedEvac, and you're not going to give me any trouble. Is that clear?"

Arnie shielded his face and nodded. He nervously licked at his lips, eyes darting around in search of a makeshift weapon and betraying his otherwise cooperative demeanor.

Isaac saw the defiance and knew he had to disable the man. It was the only way to keep him from interfering.

"Don't struggle if I let you up," Isaac baited.

He came off his knees a few inches. Arnie dropped his hands and used them to push up into a sitting position.

Isaac didn't hesitate. He squeezed and let loose a stream of liquid pain before Arnie knew what hit him. He howled in agony as the burning solution seeped into his eyes and sinuses.

The spray earned Isaac a few minutes of solitude. It would take at least that long for Arnie to compose himself and do anything useful. With that in mind, he snagged the MedEvac keys from the pegboard. Through the dividing door and into the hangar, he found a black void. Light from inside the office exposed a green button mounted to the wall. It controlled the bay doors. He pressed it, and sunshine flooded the dark space with a brilliant glow.

A finely polished Cessna Caravan waited in the middle of the concrete floor. It had a single turbine engine, overhead wings, and the Star of Life running up the tail, a blue, six-pointed star outlined with a white border and the rod of Asclepius in the center.

Isaac dashed to the wheels and removed the chocks. He climbed into the cockpit and took a second to familiarize himself with the instrument layout. He had never flown a Caravan before. But thousands of hours in trainers, jets, and other planes gave him more than ample preparation. He ran over a mental list of functions. Confident in his ability, the engine roared to life. Chopped air from the propellers bounced off the metal walls of the hangar. It sounded ominous and powerful.

He opened the throttle, taxied outside, and prepared for immediate takeoff. A windsock indicated a southwesterly breeze. He was about to fly solo in a completely foreign aircraft, a testament to how desperately he wanted to save Josie. The moment stood out, and he hoped it wasn't too late.

"I'm coming, Jo. Daddy's coming. Be brave."

He recalled Caroline's last few minutes on earth, how he held her but couldn't save her. He envisioned her tiny body on the gurney during their frantic rush to the hospital. Two EMTs fought to save her life. Blood covered the ambulance floor. It ran from her neck, saturated the gurney sheet, and steadily dripped off. He remembered wanting to scoop it up and put it back inside of her. And when they wheeled her away, he was left alone to stare at the crimson pool. Those were the last moments he had spent with his baby girl. The memory tore him apart inside.

God, he begged, *please don't make me go through that again. Not with Josie.*

He pulled back on the yoke and lifted off. The chase officially began.

Chapter Fifty-Nine

Back tires fishtailed across loose gravel and dry dirt. The last Ricky saw Isaac and Helen, they were unable to help themselves, much less come after him. But he imagined the ridiculously resilient Isaac somehow escaping his makeshift handcuffs and rising to the challenge. Odds were another car wouldn't show up for several minutes at least. If one did though, it might be the spark Isaac needed to ignite a torrential flood of unstoppable rage.

Ricky squelched the thought, confident he had every angle covered. The road he traveled—if it could even be called a road—had dozens and dozens of arteries splitting off into no man's land. Even the splits had splits. It would be absolute pandemonium for a group of police cars to search the twisted quagmire. The reality gave him comfort as he navigated a one hundred and eighty-degree turn.

To complicate the search even further, every rutted track and winding pass ran directly through the middle of thick, pine forest. Some trees grew so closely that their limbs stretched out and covered his route. Each time he traversed, the line of sight changed. For chasers to see him, they would have to be right on his tail.

The further he drove, the less anxiety he felt. Every minute that lapsed increased his odds of a clean slip.

He ogled Josie in the floorboard. She was his for a reason, like their paths were crossed by fate, not coincidence. His thoughts trickled away from escape and veered toward lust. The ember of desire began to smolder.

Reaching out, his fingertips stroked her hair. A premonition of sweetly fragranced shampoo filled his nose. *Patience*, he cajoled himself.

When they approached the cabin, he noticed that nothing had changed since leaving in the early morning hours.

Nearby, a natural brook trickled through a garden of giant boulders. He hauled Josie from the cab and carried her to the tune of running water. Her body hung limp in his arms. At the low-slung, rear door frame, he stooped to enter. The primitive structure had never seen, nor would it ever see, the invention of a central heating system. Small doorways were to preserve warmth in the winter. He could almost see Robert Redford playing the role of Jeremiah Johnson, a fresh batch of furs hanging from his belt. But romantic fantasies were not part of the itinerary. At least not that kind.

He gently placed her on an old, wooden cot. Blankets and a pillow were already in place from his prior visit. A Polaroid flashed to document her arrival. He slipped it inside the journal where several pages were dedicated to her alone. Blonde hair, soft skin, and body—all four-foot-three inches and fifty-two pounds of it—rested there motionless. Bailey, Lindsay, and Mindy had all been fine stand-ins, but their draw held no comparison.

As he stared, his body shook with intoxicated desire. He wanted so badly to take his time, document, and film every millisecond of the experience. But immediate appeasement weighed heavily. The battle raged. Suddenly, he could take the burn no more. Physicality took control.

In the middle of the one-room space, he pulled his shirttail over his head and dropped it to the floor. Practiced fingers fiddled to undo his belt. A quick tug and bend had him disrobed. The buckle made a loud thump against the floor, an eerily familiar and unwelcome sound. His flashlight had made the same noise that rainy night in Ruidoso.

He poured his hands over Josie. The back of his knuckles caressed her arm so softly. If ever he felt love, this was it. Or perhaps obsession. Maybe both. But he knew he would do anything for her. Even wait. And so he turned away until she woke of her own accord.

Across the room, on the other rope bed frame, Ashley lay bound and gagged. Attentive, her eyes flashed wildly with fear. Yesterday evening, she had worked her shift at the Taos grocery store. She went out back to find Derek in hopes of sharing a cigarette and woke up in the dark, deserted cabin.

Ricky had to keep his emotions down to a simmer, and Ashley was there to assist. She was disposable, a useful tool to help him maintain control, a mere appetizer to prevent him from devouring the main course.

He slithered onto her body, each of her limbs drawn into his trademark spread. The razor-sharp hunting knife cut through her clothes, damp with terrified sweat, as she struggled to scream. Despite her pleading tears, he did not stop.

Chapter Sixty

The MedEvac Cessna passed one thousand feet AGL (above ground level). As much as Isaac didn't want to admit it, the man with Josie had the upper hand. Her captor knew exactly where they were headed and how to get there. Anyone clever enough to pull off such a ruse would. Isaac, on the other hand, had only a general direction to canvass.

He tried to think like his formidable adversary. *Where would I go?* Elusion was first on the agenda. *Where's the best place to hide?*

Isaac had flown countless times over the very ground he now searched. When wildfires burned, it wasn't orange flames that first appeared to patrol pilots. Gray, ghostly wisps of rising smoke were the earliest signs of trouble.

But he wasn't looking for smoke. He wanted dust. If the white Chevy had abandoned pavement and was still on the move, a disturbed trail of dirt would betray it. He prayed it would be that easy.

Breaking the landscape into grids, he searched each one, top to bottom and left to right. The river was his guide. Below, he saw the spot on Highway 68 where it had all gone down. He had been too focused on Sarah at the time and wished he'd seen with his eyes, not his emotions. Every warning bell had sounded loud and clear, but fell upon his deaf ears. Now it came to this. In less than two hours, he had gone from coffee to felony. He had worked hard to leave his days of war and violence behind, not ashamed of what he'd done, but relieved to be finished. This felt like war all over again. All the elements were there: killing, innocent deaths, turmoil, and deceit. Where he'd always cared about order and composure, his "give a shit" regarding right and wrong slowly leeched from his psyche. Bloodlust festered in his soul, and he drew power from the poison.

A brownish cloud rose from a mountain in the east. He adjusted his heading to get a better view. High above the logging corridor, he found the source, a white pickup. It barreled along with its tires spitting fresh earth behind it. His heart leapt with hope. Further up the ridge, he spied their likely destination. He had seen it before, a forgotten place tucked miles from civilization. The more he thought about it, the more it made sense. For the first time in a long time, he thanked God for his unique skill set. Only because he was a pilot and knew the topography did he stand a chance of finding Josie.

A brief shroud of placidity settled over him as he scanned the radically undulated globe for a place to land. Trees, slopes, and jagged granite dominated. And as suddenly as the breaks came, so did the obstacles.

Chapter Sixty-One

A long pause filled the headset of Isaac's radio. He had just finished communicating his predicament to an air traffic controller in Santa Fe. It was not the normal type of transmission ATC operators received, and was met with silence.

"Santa Fe, do you read? I am a civil air patrol pilot in pursuit of a kidnapper and an eight-year-old girl. I need you to report my coordinates to all local and federal law enforcement. Do you copy?"

Finally, "Roger that, Civil Air. I . . . will pass it along immediately."

Isaac conveniently omitted the fact that he was in a stolen aircraft. The last thing he needed was the FAA running interference with the chase. They did not take thefts, commandeering, or hijacking lightly.

With his headset quiet again, he tilted to the left for a better perspective of the landscape. Josie already had the police on her side, and soon, if the Santa Fe controller delivered, they would know her whereabouts. Regardless, the new development lacked expediency. Only Isaac had the means to beat the clock. And he couldn't very well swoop down and buzz the killer, alerting him to his presence. That had the potential for a hostage situation. If Isaac held him at bay until the cops showed, Josie was the man's prime bargaining power. The only thing to stop him from harming her was a surprise attack. For that, he had to get out of the air and engage him on foot.

Small victories. One battle at a time . . . Where the hell am I going to land?

The nearest flat spot, large enough for an airplane to set down, was a straight stretch of logging trail. He wasn't concerned about damaging the aircraft. If he could walk away from the landing, that was all that mattered. In this environment, a few bumps were inevitable. But as he descended and made a line with the road, the trees encroached to a space narrower than his wingtips. The towering ponderosas would rip them off and send him crashing. An impact that violent might kill him.

He pulled up and deliberately searched the terrain for something wider. Every open space was too sheer with cliffs and solid rocks to try. Finally, a clearing of tall grass ran in a semicircle across a shallow grade. It appeared to be a grazing meadow for high country elk. He vaguely recalled seeing it on patrol flights but never had cause to scrutinize it. Getting on the ground within close proximity to Josie was the sole objective, and this was his best option.

Isaac approached the barren swath. It was wide and short with no room for error. He had to instantly set down the Caravan as soon as the woods gave way. Flying low, a screech sounded from the belly of the Cessna as it skimmed the treetops. The wood on metal contact shrieked like nails on a chalkboard.

Nose up, he controlled altitude with power. The task was like trying to land on the deck of an aircraft carrier but first having to clear a forty-foot wall. At night, it would be suicide.

With flaps set to full, he broke over open ground and cut the juice. As expected, the far side of the clearing rapidly drew near, a lush thicket, dark and beastly with death in its maw.

He struggled for control. Beneath the grass, the earth was anything but smooth. If he didn't stay perpendicular to the slope, gravity would snare him, and the plane would tumble like a tin can down the face.

Using depth perception, he gauged the distance to the treeline, pressing the brakes as hard as his legs could push. For the briefest instant, he thought he had it made. Then a monstrous jolt rattled him to the bone. The high-winged Cessna rolled over a hidden tree stump. What appeared as a meadow from above was actually a clear cut of harvested timber. Early summer rains had helped the grass grow tall and conceal the leftover stumps.

Nylon fabric on the seat belt cut into his neck where it passed over his shoulder. The friction of synthetic material burned his unprotected chest, holding him in the seat. His hands gripped the yoke to brace against the relentless pounding. But his head bounced freely and smashed against the window. Blood oozed over his ear from the contusion.

Gritting his teeth against the bucking, he stomped the brakes with new fervor. The mass of trees advanced with each rotation of the propeller. If they collided, fragments of jagged shrapnel would fill the air.

Bouncing once more, the top of Isaac's head hit the ceiling and jammed his neck. Little flashes of light—fireflies twinkling in a world asunder—filled his vision. And just as suddenly, a robust stump tall enough to take out the front landing gear somersaulted them forward. The turbine prop chewed into the mountain like a weed eater from hell as the fuselage went vertical. It threw Isaac into the yoke and instruments. He heard a sputter erupt from the exhaust pipe, and then everything went silent.

The plane rested, rudder to the sky, for a pause. After a creak and then a groan, it toppled, the tail section coming to a halt in the upper branches of the forest.

Warm, thick blood poured from Isaac's face and covered the gauges. He hung, almost completely upside down, by the seat belt. Darkness at the edges of his periphery crept in. The strength to move eluded his will. Before the tunnel of sight closed, he apologized to his family, wishing they could have seen how hard he tried.

Peace beckoned, and he gave in.

Chapter Sixty-Two

A soft, steady thump reverberated in the otherwise noiseless room. With his ear pressed against Ashley's sternum, Ricky's head rose and fell with her rhythmic breaths. The cadence of her heart soothed his turbulent nature.

She was not the day's pièce de résistance, but details were never to be omitted. True to form, he took her picture and wrote a few words in his leather journal. An outburst of wrath typically followed, but his unbridled violence spawned from frustration. With Josie in his possession, he felt satisfied. A more creative prospect was in store for Ashley.

He smoothed her hair back. Long, steady strokes tucked loose strands behind her ears. Using his pointer finger, he tapped the tip of her nose. "That helps a lot." His smile was genuine and wicked all in the same.

Ricky sauntered to the back porch. Safe in privacy, he stretched in the warm sunlight, naked as the day he was born. He felt relaxed. It was hard to believe that so many people were searching for him.

The only fresh water source flowed in the neighboring creek. He walked barefoot across the dirt and stuck a toe in the clear stream. The near freezing temperature caused him to jerk back. Gradually, he submerged his whole foot. Dust and pine needles loosened in the current. He squatted, sat his bare butt on a flat boulder, and immersed both legs up to the knees.

The hydrotherapy was an unexpected gem. Cupped hands washed him until all traces of sin were gone. Then he splashed his face with cold water to close the pores.

Feet and calves still in the creek, he leaned back on his elbows and rested for several minutes. The breeze caressed his wet body, and he closed his eyes to concentrate on the invigorating sensation. The evaporative effect puckered his skin. When his feet went numb, he stood and shook like a dog.

Josie consumed all of his attention. He had a special destination in mind for her, a setting even more remote than the cabin. It wasn't far, a short, quarter-mile hike up the mountain.

He rock-hopped all the way back to the rear door. It kept dirt from sticking to his clean feet. Inside, neither girl had budged. Josie slept, curled on the cot while Ashley stared at the ceiling, silently weeping.

Ricky anxiously put his clothes back on and began constructing a booby trap. The idea wasn't complex. Fishing line, a couple nails, two pieces of rope, a chair, and a shotgun completed the devious contraption. He and Josie were leaving, and the next person through the front door was in for a big surprise.

Chapter Sixty-Three

E verything was black. Isaac opened his eyes, or at least thought he did. A blank canvas filled his vision. For a fleeting instant, he wondered if he were dead. Then pain. Death was supposed to be painless. What he currently felt was the antithesis of comfort.

Just as the channel of light had closed upon crashing, it began to expand. Daylight slipped in and, with it, an abysmal throb between his temples. It overwhelmed his ability to concentrate. He squinted, trying to filter the brightness. It helped, if only slightly. Worse, taking a breath seemed near impossible. The full weight of his upper body pressed into the shoulder harness of the seat belt. The aircraft, tipped perpendicular to the slope, held him suspended.

Isaac had personally witnessed a handful of plane crashes during his career. The first priority after going down is for pilots and passengers to escape the wreckage. He had no idea what kind of damage the Caravan had suffered. Fuel could be leaking and only a spark away from total annihilation. There was no way for him to tell how long he'd been unconscious. He had to move.

His fingers grappled for the seat belt release. It gave way, and he plunged face-first into the cracked windshield. His chest collided into the double-handled yoke. The impact knocked the wind out of him.

A sharp gasp refilled his lungs. Lying across the instrument panel, he curled into the fetal position. An agonizing groan permeated the otherwise hushed space. He clenched his jaw and tried to sort through the onslaught of abuse. Feeling short of breath and dizzy, a new kind of agony set in. He felt defeated.

The soles of his hiking boots kicked against the door. After the third contact, it flopped open. He went out feet first, scooted along, and pulled himself onto the mountain face below.

Now on terra firma, his equilibrium did not agree with the upright position. After two gangled steps away from the door, he fell over. Everything rotated around him, the sky, trees, and earth. Even his body seemed to spin on a perpetual merry-go-round. On his elbows, he army-crawled to a hewn trunk and managed to lean against it for support. He closed his eyes, tilted his head back, and did nothing. Each push and pull of his diaphragm discovered more satisfaction in the thin air. Slowly, his breathing steadied.

Isaac touched his scalp, right at the hairline. A wet feeling—something like tepid water pouring—covered his face. He knew it was blood, but had no idea how much. When he drew his hand away, it was saturated.

"Shit," he said with quiet desperation.

He wiped his bloody palm down the side of his olive cargo pants, reached up, and gingerly probed around for the source. A loose flap of skin hung from above an eyebrow. When he pushed it into place, it fell back down. Without a shirt to use as a bandage, he had nothing to wrap the wound. Too much blood dribbled down his face and off his chin to go on without a compress.

In the fuselage of the Cessna, medical bins were stuffed with bandages, gauze, tape, and other emergency materials. The only way to help himself was to crawl inside the precariously propped remnants. He willed himself to act.

Inside, Isaac stood on the dash and climbed behind the front seats. Medical supplies were scattered everywhere. He found a roll of gauze, hurriedly wrapped it around his forehead, and immediately squelched the flow. He used a second roll to clear his eyes and face. Even though more places hurt and screamed for attention, none of them was the type he could treat on the fly. Bumps and bruises needed time, and time he did not have.

Every well-equipped aircraft carries a top-notch survival kit. Isaac located the bright orange bag with shoulder straps and yanked at the zipper. Within, he found the necessities for one to subsist in the wilderness.

The contents spilled onto the grassy earth. He only needed certain tools to get him through the next hour: a personal locator beacon, flashlight, knife, and water bottle. Bearing a light load would help conserve energy. He stowed the four items, threw in a trauma kit just in case, and closed the bag. If Josie were wounded, he wanted the means to treat her.

With the backpack over his shoulders, Isaac groaned and forced his legs into a jog. His throbbing head intensified in sync with each pump of his accelerated heart rate. Three minutes in, his lungs grew hungry. The physical demands on his body were worse than he'd thought. But he refused to use the burning lungs and wobbly legs as excuses to rest.

The terrain was rugged. He ran in the direction of the road, nearly twisting his ankles on shifting, slope-side rocks. If he could make it to the logging road—even with the added distance of a winding path—it would be faster than a direct line through the bush.

When he reached the hard-packed track, he relished the humble victory, and quickened his pace. Resolute, he vowed, *I will save Josie or die trying.*

Chapter Sixty-Four

Josie's hands slapped against Ricky's backside. She was slung over his shoulder like a sack of potatoes. Each step he made up the ridge toward the ghost town swayed her arms back and forth. The coincidental contact was not lost on him.

He walked into the clearing and surveyed the ancient settlement. Several single-room shacks were scattered about, built of logs from the old resident miners. Long years and hard seasons had faded the crudely erected walls to gray, drafty wood. Uninhabited for decades, only the wind spoke here.

A few more paces brought them to the glorified hut he had pre-selected. It was the sturdiest of houses, and all his documentation equipment was inside.

They passed under barely recognizable fragments of bison hide nailed to the door frame. The primitive inhabitants had used the skins as door flaps.

Ricky laid Josie on a padded, blue shipping blanket that covered the earthen floor. He flipped on a battery-powered headlamp and sifted through his supply bag. Two-foot-long pieces of rebar were placed at each corner of the blanket. A three-pound mini sledge drove them into the dirt until they were well seated. As much as he wanted to have Josie without restraints, he remembered the rejection when Mindy had tried to escape from his home in Colorado. Certain he didn't want to endure a similar experience, he began to wrap her wrists and ankles to the steel rods.

He made four slipknots, spread her arms and legs, and bound each one to the nearest stake. Josie stirred at the tugging. When he pulled at the braid on her ankle, it cinched the coarse, grass fibers into her Achilles tendon, and her eyes flashed open.

"Welcome back," he offered.

Josie remained fixed, her eyes darting around the dark space. Sunlight poured through cracks and holes in the walls. She could see the lit doorway, but not who spoke to her. He was just a silhouette, and when he faced her directly, the LED lamp on his head was blinding.

"Don't try to move. The ropes will get tighter if you pull." He drew her other ankle snug and tied it to the post. A satisfied smirk curled his lip. "Okay?"

Josie didn't respond. Nothing made sense, and she couldn't reason it out. Her natural instinct was to flee, but his warning proved true. When a jolt of panic swept sensibility away, she writhed to gain freedom. The coils tightened in unison and sharply quelled her attempt. She grimaced in agony.

"Told you," Ricky reminded her. "I don't want to hurt you, but if you hurt yourself . . ." He shrugged his shoulders.

Josie tried to say something, but it caught at her lips.

Ricky pinched the gag between his thumb and pointer finger. "Yeah, about that." He motioned out the open door. "Sound can be funny in the mountains. Sometimes you can't hear things that are ten feet away. Other times, it carries for miles." He winked. "Sorry. Can't take any chances."

Scared out of her mind, Josie began to cry. Unfamiliarity with her location, situation, and the man holding her hostage, not a single thread of hope presented itself for her to latch onto. The tears came steady. The gag muted the crooning.

Ricky ignored her and readied the camera equipment. He took a few snapshots, fully clothed, and continued to the video. He placed the recorder on a tripod and adjusted it until satisfied with the frame. Its lamp cast a cozy, yellow glow upon her. This particular footage was going to be the masterpiece of his collection. It had to be perfect.

Finally, with everything situated, Ricky was ready to begin. *Make it last. This is it for a while.*

He rummaged within his bag. It was near impossible to deny the physical any longer, but not writing his feelings down would haunt him forever. His hand probed deeper, searching for the diary. He glanced to his left and then right. "Where is it?"

Soft illumination from the video recorder revealed the small room in its entirety. He couldn't locate the journal anywhere. "Son of a bitch!" he lashed out. A frustrated leg kicked at nothing in particular. *I left it at the cabin.*

Ricky reached a stalemate. He studied the warm, supple skin of Josephine Snow and made the call.

Chapter Sixty-Five

The aggressive tread on Isaac's hiking boots chewed into the dry soil and carried him up the rugged mountain. A slight hobble made his stride uneven from where he'd twisted an ankle on loose scree. He ran along the road's shoulder, just in case he had to sidestep into the trees for cover. The last thing he wanted was for Josie's captor to know he was onto him.

For twenty minutes, he kept a grueling pace. If it meant rescuing Josie, he would graciously sacrifice his body a thousand times. Footfall after footfall, pebbles crunched beneath his weight. Lack of oxygen caused him to feel faint. He had experienced blackouts before. It was part of air force fighter training. They'd put him in a centrifuge to build his body's tolerance to g-forces. He recalled the "hic" maneuver, a diaphragm exercise to keep blood in the brain. But this was different. Training or no, ten thousand feet did not cater to an oxygen-starved system. He wasn't sure how much longer he could keep it up.

Bent on endurance, he rounded another curve and was taken off guard. The cabin came into full view, and he dove into the woods. He crawled across the needle-strewn floor, nestled between two pine trees, and devoured as much atmosphere as the altitude allowed. Forty yards ahead, the tailgate of a white Chevy truck protruded from beneath a fallen pine. This was definitely the right place.

Charging the shelter, while tempting, would not work. Isaac could hold his own in a fight, but busted up and exhausted, physical confrontation with a wily man was too risky. When it did come down to a scrap, shock and awe were his best advantages. That would take some thinking and slick maneuvering.

There was only one shot at this. No tiebreakers. No ribbon for second place. Ultimately, Josie would live or die by the outcome.

The cabin's door stood in the center of a dilapidated front porch. One window sat to the right of the entrance. The remaining walls were solid. He couldn't see but guessed there was also a rear door and considered which one to approach. No noise or motion was detectable from within, and no smoke rose from the chimney.

All was quiet and still, his stomach the one exception. It growled with a vengeance, perhaps from physical exertion. Or maybe it was an omen of the rumble to come. Either way, he pushed it from his mind, but not before heeding the warning.

Josie was in there. He was sure of it. And the instant he barged in, the struggle for her life, his life, would ensue. It made him think of Sarah and wonder if he would ever see her again. He had to harness every ounce of focus and callousness. It had been years since he had taken a human life. Once upon a time, he struggled with the idea of it, wondering how it would feel to kill. He approached his commanding officer with the concern, a man he trusted and deeply respected, and was given an answer that ingrained itself into his character.

"Isaac," his CO told him, a firm hand on his shoulder. "You're a pilot in the United States Air Force. Your job entails doing things that others don't want to do or don't even realize needs to be done. It brings safety to our country and freedom to our people. You bear the burden others cannot or will not. Don't think of the few lives you're ending, but the many you're saving."

The wise commander had delivered the words without a single emotion, and Isaac had never questioned them. Now with the lesson ringing clearly in his mind, he understood the responsibility staring him in the face. For the sake of every innocent child in America, including his own, the man he tracked needed to die.

His thoughts turned primal and violent. Instinct came to power and reigned over exhaustion.

Sitting between the trees, Isaac gathered himself. He quietly shucked off the backpack and reached in. The personal locator beacon was wrapped firmly in his grip. His thumb slid toward the activation button while he weighed the options. *If I activate it now, search and rescue will come. If they get here before I have Josie, she might end up a hostage.* The notion was less than appealing.

He put the beacon back inside the canvas and decided to risk going it alone.

The rubber handle of the fixed-blade survival knife found his fingers. It was firmly seated in his right hand with the blade facing outward from the bottom of his fist. He slashed the air to get a feel for it. Within an arm's reach, he noticed a broken limb lying among fallen pinecones. Roughly an inch and a half thick and five feet long, the branch was perfect for a spear. He used the knife to whittle a tip at the narrow end. Wood shavings dropped steadily with each stroke. The point was crudely shaped, but if thrust with enough force, it could easily penetrate flesh. Double weapons made it easier to deliver a lethal stab.

With his spear in his left hand and knife in his right, he scrambled for the left wall of the cabin, certain to avoid any loose footing or dried sticks. The windowless barrier provided cover from anyone inside. He wished he hadn't put the heavy-duty flashlight in the survival bag. It bounced with every stride and eventually became a painful nuisance pounding against his vertebrae.

At the wall, he pressed his ear to the logs and listened. Silence. The lack of sound unnerved him, like the last seconds of stillness before a predator pounces. He wondered if his presence were known and, if so, who was hunting who.

He stared at his fists, both wielding potential harbingers of death. His dream of retribution for Caroline's murder neared reality. The idea wasn't sadistic but practical. Anyone who trampled on the rights of others, especially children, should no longer have rights of his own.

The floor of the porch was assembled of wide, timber planks. He poked his head past the corner and waited. Some boards might hold his weight, others not. He tested each foot placement, creeping along before submitting the full weight of his body. A single squeak was one too many.

Without incident, a heavy coat of sweat polishing his torso, he made it to the door. Adjacent was the small, square window cut into the logs.

He let out a shaky breath. The gauze around his head kept sweat out of his eyes. Once again, Sarah entered his mind. *If this goes badly, I'm sorry. I love you.*

He didn't want what was. He wanted what used to be: Caroline and Josie running barefoot in the green grass beneath the shade of the old cottonwood tree; Sarah cooking in the kitchen, the warm smell of food drifting through the screen door onto the back patio; Charlie, his best friend, enjoying the day with them; and even little Jason doing something crazy. All had once been. Now he would give his life if he could put it back in place for everyone.

In that pause of reflection, it felt like Caroline was with him. He could sense her presence all around.

"Please help me," he whispered, hoping she could hear.

He crouched, passed in front of the threshold, and knelt under the hazy window. Steady as the tide, he rose and leveled his eyes with the bottom of the pane.

Covered in soot from the fireplace and years of dust, only the vague outline of shapes presented themselves on the other side. A dark spot in the middle of the room stood out. He could see it was a chair, but the opaque glass obscured his view. Squinting, he scrutinized it harder, and then something moved.

It was a girl, facing away from him and bound to the chair. She was small and shook her head from one side to the other. He couldn't see her face, but it didn't appear like she was wearing any clothes. Fear and hope swelled, fear that Josie had been raped and hope that he could keep her alive. He struggled to contain the relief.

A quick scan didn't reveal anything else of concern. Josie appeared to be alone. Regardless, he was ready. He worked the knife and spear in his hands in anxious preparation. *Swift and strong.*

The front door had an old-time, wooden latch, the kind that lifts and lowers into a slot. He used the knuckles on his knife hand to carefully raise the lock. In one seamless motion, he flung open the door and sprang into the room.

A shotgun erupted, and Isaac froze. The thunderous boom rattled him to the core. Fresh blood exploded. He pictured Josie and wished he could have held her, like Caroline, one last time.

Chapter Sixty-Six

Time was not to be wasted. Ricky grabbed the rifle and headed back to the cabin. This would be his third trip, including the two he had already made to haul the equipment and Josie. He was at the apex of his life and now had to take a nonsensical pause to retrieve the journal. The delay irked him.

Rifle in hand, he crabbed his body sideways to help with the steep gradient and hustled down the trail. Bears and mountain lions lived in the wilds of New Mexico, and in case of a chance encounter, the firearm gave him security.

The stacked log walls came into view, and Ricky eased his pace. He kept his eyes on the path. In minutes, he would be back at the ghost town with the journal, Josie before him. Then a shotgun blast shattered the silence.

He stood tall, alert, frozen on the trail. Few things had ever shaken him so suddenly. Fear surged through his body and prompted action. He leapt from the footpath and into the woods. A granite outcropping shadowed by trees offered concealment and an ideal perspective of the cabin. He scrambled the few yards, low to the ground and catlike.

Nestled within the stony fortress, Ricky reviewed how he'd rigged the shotgun inside. *The front door must be opened for the weapon to fire.* Ashley was tied to a chair and unable to move.

That he was certain of. He had nailed the chair legs into the wooden floor so she couldn't topple over by swaying her body. The concept of her escaping was also implausible. The ropes binding her to the chair were wound in a cruel, uncompromising way. She would die of dehydration long before she could wriggle free.

He was dumbfounded to think that the police or a search party could have sniffed him out so quickly. Besides, if the person responsible were a vigilante, Ricky would have heard him coming.

Curiosity drove him mad. He considered other options as he sat in wait. *Maybe a gust of wind pushed the front door open.* He looked at the surrounding trees. Even their tops were perfectly still. *No.* He pictured the latch in his head. *It has to be lifted too far to open by accident.*

The more he thought, the more it became clear. Ashley and Josie aside, he was no longer alone. Whether they'd found him or an unlucky soul had happened along, someone was there.

The location was one grain of sand to an entire beach. *What are the odds?*

Ricky took his rifle and rested it across a flat spot on the granite rock. He adjusted himself until the rear entry of the cabin was directly in his crosshairs. Whoever was inside posed a direct threat and had to be eliminated for good.

He kept the shaky scope trained down the hill, ready to blow a hole through anyone who stepped outside.

Chapter Sixty-Seven

No sensation came, just empty silence. Isaac blinked repeatedly, expecting death, or certainly pain, to take over at any moment, but there was nothing. Physically, all seemed well. Yet he knew the gun was intended for something . . . someone.

Ashley had been part of the living only seconds before. She had moved her head from side to side, searching the room for anything that might help her escape. Now, chin hanging to her chest, Ashley's brains and blood were splattered all over the wall, and all over Isaac.

The shot had come from somewhere in the room, but he saw no one hidden within the small space. A mechanism was the only thing that could have taken the place of a human finger. His eyes darted around. Judging by the direction of the blood spatter, it had come from almost straight in front of him. It only took a second to surmise what had happened.

The scatter gun was tied to a bed frame and pointed directly at the girl in the chair. A strand of clear fishing line was attached to the trigger. The opposite end ran across the room and connected to a bent nail hammered into the front door. The concept was basic. When the door opened, the string tightened and pulled the trigger.

A void the size of a man's fist had blown through Ashley's skull and removed her face. Blood poured in a massive wave through her blonde hair, down her naked chest and arms. The gruesome sight sickened Isaac. The scene before him was of a young, dead girl. He realized the contraption had not been set to kill him, but instead, the person he thought was Josie.

I killed her. Isaac's knees hit the floor. His spear and knife dropped to the old, wooden planks, and the dull thump brought about a sense of déjà vu. The last time he had heard that sound was just before Caroline died. It was once again a reminder of death and loss of a daughter. He couldn't understand why—perhaps exhaustion—no tears came to his eyes. Failure was the only thing he felt, failure to protect what he loved most, failure to be a man, a father, a husband.

On hands and knees, he crawled to the side of the chair and dared not look at her face. He had a flawless mental picture of Josie's bright eyes and didn't wish to erase it with what he knew would be a grizzly sight. Instead, he took the survival knife and cut her ropes loose. Even in death, it didn't seem right for his beloved girl to wear restraints. As he freed her, her bare body slumped and fell from the seat.

Isaac pulled her limp hand to his face. Blood smeared on his cheek. He didn't want to let go or say good-bye. He just wanted to sit there with her broken shell for the rest of eternity. Caroline was once again with her sister, and it gave him a small measure of comfort.

Kissing the hand, he tried to keep his heart from bursting. He forced his unfocused eyes to open and look at her. Josie deserved that much. If her spirit were still there in the room, watching as her father held her earthly body, he didn't want her to think that he was ashamed to see her. It was himself with whom he was ashamed.

Isaac no longer cared for the chase. The goal was always to rescue Josie first, then exact retribution on the killer. But retribution without gain had lost its appeal.

As his vision trained on the bloody hand, he tried to notice every last detail. He wanted to remember Josie, just as she was. Her soft skin. Each individual finger. Even her chipped, hot pink nail polish seemed preciously important.

Pink nail polish? A tiny ray of hope pierced his gloom. Josie had not been wearing pink nail polish. In fact, as of that morning, she hadn't been wearing *any* nail polish. The neon paint on this hand was flaking from days of wear. The sudden observation spurred closer scrutiny and another vague feeling of familiarity.

The hand was not that of a child, but of a young teenager, probably fifteen or sixteen. The size, texture, and shape were all wrong for Josie. Relief washed over him. This meant she might still be alive, but the new hope was mixed with reverence. The girl in front of him, violated and dead, was someone's daughter.

Isaac studied her with more intensity. As he took in the fullness of her corpse, it became infinitely clear that it was indeed not Josie. The mangled girl was too tall, closer to womanhood than childhood.

He checked her face and got exactly what he expected. An empty cavity stared back at him, and he could see the floor on the other side of the scarlet flesh. The remnants of her eyes, mouth, nose, and upper lip were scattered into a million pieces. Whoever she was, even her own mother would not have recognized her.

Nausea churned in his stomach. Polaroids of brutalized victims were once the extreme. As Isaac held the abused teen in his arms, the reality was far worse in person than in pictures. He cradled her like she was his own, wishing he could have arrived early enough to help. Instead, he'd become the linchpin to her demise.

He laid the girl down and draped a blanket over her nude body. She had suffered enough indignation. Josie was out there somewhere on a path toward a similar fate. He didn't know where, but she had to be close.

Once again, with spear and knife in hand, he moved toward the rear door. He checked for additional stratagems and found none. Cautiously, he raised the handle and stepped onto the back porch, looking for sign. All was calm.

One more tentative stride forward and a bullet struck him. It collided with his chest at over three thousand feet per second, and he stumbled backward in pained disbelief. He collapsed, coming to rest beside the girl under the blanket.

Chapter Sixty-Eight

Watching Isaac perish from the direct hit was one of the most riveting experiences of Ricky's life. He had never shot a man before. It was new, utterly unexpected, and he immediately liked it. But questions rolled through his brain like a cigarette factory, and he squelched a rising panic.

What the hell? How did he know where to find me? Is he alone? This should be impossible. The list had begun the instant Isaac's battered, shirtless body came into the crosshairs. The fact that Isaac was even there encroached on the realm of inhuman. *Did I leave a trail?*

A quick mental recap confirmed that all the precautions Ricky had taken were completed without failure. At the feint on the highway, he had taken Isaac and Helen's keys and cell phones and left them with a serious case of fried circuits. That should have held them at bay, but here Isaac was, and the timeline numbers didn't crunch. *What am I missing?*

The 30-06 round pierced Isaac through the ribcage, surely ending his life. Ricky had no qualms. The rifle scope was sighted perfectly. The shot had been less than one hundred yards, easy for a novice shooter, and he'd watched Isaac topple like a stone statue. *He may be a supernatural badass, but he's not bulletproof.*

Ricky emerged from his hiding place and snuck down to the cabin, cautiously bobbing from tree to tree for cover. Retrieving the journal was still priority, but for practical purposes, he had to make certain his nemesis was defeated once and for all.

Ricky wondered what Isaac's secret means of transportation was. If he'd driven, dust from the road or the sound of an engine would have easily given him away. A helicopter came to mind, but that didn't add up either. The noise alone—steady, unmistakable thumps from the long blades—would have carried for miles. There was nowhere to land an airplane. Besides, Ricky had destroyed that option. The only other explanation was for Isaac to have arrived on foot, but the distance from the highway to the cabin was far too great for such a hasty appearance. Ricky put the riddle aside.

He leaned against the passenger fender of his white pickup and used it as a safety barrier. The back porch was on the opposite side of the hood, its wooden door ajar. Everything past the threshold was cast in dark shadow. Rifle at the ready, he stood with an alert posture. There was no detectable movement from within, just as he expected.

Chapter Sixty-Nine

S earing, hot pain rippled from the wound. Severed nerves worked in overdrive, sending arduous messages to the brain. Isaac felt like he was being branded with a fiery poker with no relief in store.

The copper-coated lead had passed between his torso and left bicep. A mass of muscle on his outer ribcage, the latissimus dorsi, had an aperture through it, just below the armpit. Agonizing as it was, he much preferred it to the alternative. Two inches in either direction, he would have suffered a punctured lung or a missing appendage. Death might be something he sought before the end, but he wasn't there yet. *Josie. I have to find Josie.*

He shuffled across the floor toward the front entry of the cabin, keeping low in fear that another bullet might come whizzing by. Thus far, Derek, the alleged grocery store clerk, had proven rather shrewd.

Isaac inspected his weapons. *Shit. A knife and stick against a psycho with a rifle.* He squeezed them tightly. They felt so inadequate. *C'mon. I need a plan.* He turned and faced the old bed. *The shotgun!*

After a couple quick slices from the knife, it fell off the frame and into his hands. *Please have extra shells.* The shotgun was an auto-loader, Remington 11-87, and the breech was closed. It was the best news he'd had all morning. A closed chamber meant the weapon had automatically ejected the spent round and pulled a live one from the magazine. It was cocked and locked.

Quickly, he slid back the breech to confirm. It was loaded. He glanced underneath and checked the magazine. Brass and the unstamped primer of another round shined back at him. *Two shots.* He urgently searched for a box of ammunition. No extra shells were in sight. He would just have to take what was given and get the hell out.

Before escaping the same way he had come in, Isaac briefly took one last assessment of the room to make sure there was nothing of further use. A leather-bound book atop a plywood table caught his eye. He probably never would have noticed, but the space was so vacant of décor, the object demanded his attention. He hurriedly secured it in his grip, not bothering to look inside.

The sanctuary of the forest was only yards from the porch. Refuge was in its shadows, and he concealed himself within. *Where are you, Josie?*

"Where has he taken you?" he quietly whispered and searched the surroundings.

Keeping his senses alert, curiosity told him he should open the journal. Pictures and rows of detailed notes filled the inside of the book. The contents were meticulously organized, and nothing short of eye-popping.

Polaroid pictures of little girls, vile words of intent, and abduction jottings were all neatly laid out, page by page, each labeled with a name. The chronicle was laden with more victims than Isaac imagined possible. This was not the work of an opportunistic pedophile. This was the doings of a cold, calculated sadist with a very long track record.

He quickly flipped through, bile rising in his throat, until two familiar faces stared up at him. Next to Josie and Caroline's picture was an article from the *Ruidoso News* editorial. It pertained to their brilliant rescue of Jason Smith. Following the publication were detailed descriptions of their daily routines and schedules, each listed by date. The printed composition was carefully glued to the page, and the notes were written in clean penmanship. He immediately recognized the handwriting. It matched all three of the letters they had received over the summer. It proved what he already knew. This was the property of the man who had killed Caroline and promised to return for Josie almost three months ago.

The smell of fresh-cut grass, the sound of children's laughter, and scents of a home-cooked meal drifted through Isaac's memory. A photograph of Josie and Caroline running in their Ruidoso backyard was clipped to the page. Josie had a Frisbee in her hand, and Caroline gave chase. The side deck off the kitchen could be seen in the background. Two people were on it. He squinted closely and saw himself. The other person was garbed in tan clothing.

Charlie. He remembered sitting on the porch that evening with his friend, having a beer while the kids played. Sarah was out of sight, just inside the screen door.

It sent chills down his spine. They had been stalked, tested for weaknesses. It was not by chance that he had come into their lives. If the twins had never saved Jason and made headlines, life would have gone on as usual. The canvas was much larger than he ever fathomed, sobering yet enraging.

He continued through the pages dedicated to Bailey Davis, followed by Lindsay Watson and, finally, Mindy Kessler. After Mindy, the next sheet of paper was devoted to the young teenage girl in the cabin. Now that he could see her face, he placed who she was. She was the cashier from the grocery store, Ashley. He had taken her sometime between yesterday evening and that very morning. The man posing as Derek was the culprit, and he had snared her out of convenience.

The last page before the blank sheets began was titled "Josephine Snow." There was a photo of her, Isaac's Cessna, an outline of the weekend's events, and a short synopsis of intent. The final inscription was the most recent and meaningful. It read simply "Ghost Town."

There was no question that the words implied Josie's current locale. Without a second to lose, Isaac closed the journal. A flicker on the front flap caught his eye. In the lower, right-hand corner of the leather cover were three letters, each stamped in gold leaf: R.E.D.

Do you like . . . red? Isaac recalled the unwelcome posts, all ending with the same unexplained question. *We've had his initials from the beginning. He was asking if they liked . . . him.*

Isaac bolted up the mountainside in a flash of raw power. R.E.D. had to be somewhere between the two locations. This was the pivotal wormhole in time, an opportunity to find Josie without the dangerous tension of a standoff.

He had flown over the ghost town multiple times on patrols. In fact, the reference point was often used in his flight logs. She was there. He could feel it.

The device inside Isaac's pocket was now an invaluable form of communication. He tugged at the flap on his cargo pouch without breaking stride. With sure fingers, he activated the personal locator beacon. Somewhere, a dot on a screen was about to start blinking. Search and Rescue would scramble and arrive at his exact whereabouts. Isaac was no longer off the grid. He was at the center of a map and screaming for help.

Hopefully, word of the crisis had spread to all local authorities by now, and the rescue signal would bring more than just a search team. He wanted the whole damn cavalry.

Chapter Seventy

As an adolescent, Ricky never imagined he would be brave enough to stash an extensive porn collection in his bedroom, but he had. And while he obsessed over magazine prints, he never fathomed the audacious task of buying dirty videos from a stranger on the street, but he had done that too. It definitely never crossed his mind that child pornography would become his addiction. One lustful pleasure after another morphed him into a predator.

His history was one of repetition. The quest for stimulation was in his nature, and new sensations led the way to satisfaction. His bored, neglected intellect always craved something to do. Someone to do.

Now, a grown man apart from his humble beginnings with an X-rated magazine, he was a cold-blooded killer many times over. And with the shot to Isaac, he had laid waste to his first non-target victim.

New gusto flowed through every step he made from behind the pickup and toward the cabin. Adjacent to the back landing, he pressed himself against the exterior log wall. Isaac was cunning, and for his own safety, Ricky aired on the side of caution.

Slowly, his sharp, aqua eyes peeking around the corner, he bolted into the doorway, gun in front and swinging left to right. Instantly, things didn't add up.

Ashley's body was there, covered and alone. *Dammit! Where is he?*

Chapter Seventy-One

The ghost town appeared very different at ground level than from above. Everything seemed smaller from the air, more manageable. The perspective on foot was much larger.

Isaac estimated there had originally been twenty or more buildings in the old mining camp. Maybe five of them were still in fair enough condition to safely enter. One in particular looked to be in better shape than the other four, and it seemed the logical choice. He decided to begin there.

Finally, he had some hard-earned time on his side. The play-by-play of events had been the most intense of his life, even beyond those in the air force. But in the last five minutes, the tables had turned. Even if it were only marginal, he was in the superior position.

Still, the clock ticked. Short of breath, Isaac raced into the clearing of the ramshackle town. He held his left arm snuggly against his shredded rib muscles. The wound bled enough to leave a dribbling trail if he didn't apply pressure. He clutched the shotgun in his right hand with the barrel pointed out front and ready for a fight.

The rickety shanty was not airtight, and the single entry point stood permanently agape. Cracks in the walls let in tiny beams of filtered light, but not enough to spy into the inner hollow. He desperately wanted to call for Josie. In the mountains though, a voice could resonate and he thought better of it. *What if he's already in there? No, he can't be. Not yet.* Only the intonation of the woods whispered.

The operation required stealth, and stealth meant complete silence. Soft earth and sparse blades of grass cushioned his approach. Fear begged the obvious question. *What will I do if she's not here?*

Enough natural sunlight came through the doorway to reveal two separate tripods. One supported a camera; the other had a camcorder. Both were pointed to a pallet of bedding. And there, in the middle of it all, Josie laid bound and gagged. She appeared unharmed, but her eyes were wild with trepidation.

Isaac's silhouette, the outline of a man holding a gun, revealed itself in the backlit portal, and she thought it was her captor. The sound of gunfire from down the hill had heightened her terror.

The roughly spun ropes that fixed her in position were excruciating. Her hands and feet throbbed with each rapid pump of her heart and swelled with a bluish tint. She tried to scream. The grass-rope gag gnawed into her cheeks.

Relief blossomed inside of Isaac. The angst he had of losing Josie relinquished its grasp and pulled the corners of his mouth into a grin. Water filled his eyes, and joy flooded his heart.

Moving further into the room, he went to his knees beside her. "It's me, baby," he whispered.

Josie wriggled hard, not realizing who it was.

"Shhhh!" he demanded, holding a finger to his lips. "It's okay, Jo. It's me." He leaned over, put his face in front of hers, and gave the best reassuring smile he could muster. "He can't know I'm here," he said in a hushed murmur. She needed to stay calm.

The distress was still there, visibly emanating through the passages of her eyes.

"We're getting out of here, kiddo." Their departure needed to go quietly and quickly. "I'm going to cut these ropes." His hand ran along one of the taut cords marring her young skin. He couldn't bear to see her tied like some wild, untamed beast.

He leaned the shotgun against the wall and immediately took out his knife, grateful that he had kept the tool and not abandoned it after the weapons upgrade.

As badly as he wanted to whisk her away into the forest and be done with the killer forever, Isaac snapped back to reality. What he wanted and what was necessary were entirely different. R.E.D. would continue to hunt them and haunt their dreams. Just like he had done all summer, he would pursue them relentlessly, never retreating until he fulfilled his purpose. Running and hiding were no good.

With knife blade ready to cut away the painful restraints, he had to make a judgment call. Footsteps from outside were heading their way. He would have never heard them, but the swirling sierra breeze blew in the right direction and cemented his decision. To liberate Josie now would alert the huntsman, and battle would surely ensue.

He held his finger to his lips once more and gestured for Josie to be silent. The appearance of her solitude was the best way to save her life.

"Jo," Isaac whispered. "I am not leaving you." He gave her a hard, uncompromising stare. "Don't . . . move."

She nodded.

"I have to hide. Do not look at me. We can't let the bad man know I'm here, okay?"

She nodded again, so brave and trusting of her father.

"Good girl," he said, barely audible. He stroked a lock of hair from her face and assured her with another smile. "I'm going to get him. He can't hurt you anymore."

They were on the edge. One blunder could end it all, this duel to the death. No rules.

Isaac rose and pocketed his knife. He took up the shotgun and backed into the darkest corner of the room. It was against the same wall as the entrance. He stood rigid in the nook, gun pointed at the doorway, safety off, and finger on the trigger. All the maniac had to do was walk into the line of fire.

Josie trained her eyes on her father, and he tilted his head toward the door. She moved them appropriately.

Good girl. Don't give Daddy away.

A shadow of a man materialized along the outer wall, opposite where Isaac hid. The figure blocked sunshine from passing through pinholes and cracks in the wood. It slid forward and crept to the corner nearest the entry.

Isaac watched, unblinking, each calculated step. At such close range, the lead projectiles would rip through R.E.D., much the same as they did Ashley. There was no way to prevent Josie from witnessing the slaughter.

Isaac could hear his own heartbeat. Intensity bled from his pores, and sweat slicked his palms. He feared that his presence might be sensed. The frozen moment lingered, an undetectable lapse in time. The stalker loomed, his silhouette obstructing shafts of sunlight. Isaac wondered how long he would wait there. *C'mon, you bastard.*

Then a solution rang crystal clear.

Chapter Seventy-Two

I f he were going to unleash a barrage through the thin wall, Josie had to be completely free of potential harm. Isaac gauged the direction of his aim. The dark shape was on full alert, and Isaac suspected the least little noise might send him running.

I'm going to kill you, you son of a bitch. In a seamless motion, he rotated at the hips and aligned the shotgun barrel, high enough to dispatch the man's vitals. The trigger clicked, the firing pin struck, and a deep concussion filled the tiny room with thunder. It blew a silver dollar-sized hole through the brittle timber.

A frantic holler immediately followed. Isaac manifested outside the hut like a crack of lightning. The semi-auto shotgun had already loaded the next shell into the chamber and was ready to fire again.

R.E.D. was curled on the ground, his rifle negligently dropped two feet away. The lead discharge had passed through the dry-rotted logs, entered his tissue by way of shattering the right shoulder blade, and exited the front of his torso, just below the clavicle. The resulting aperture was the circumference of a baseball. In addition to an exorbitant amount of blood and tattered flesh, the wound was littered with fabric from his shirt and woodchips from the shack.

Isaac reached down and tossed away the rifle. R.E.D. was on his back, drawn into himself and moaning in pain. His discomfort was too great to consider fighting.

Isaac stood tall over the only person he had ever truly wanted to kill. Hate swelled in his heart, and a sense of pleasure from the man's agony warmed his blood. He had dominated his opponent and felt powerful. He aligned the shotgun with the murderer's face and pressed the barrel against his lips. One shell was left in the chamber. R.E.D. stopped his display of misery and froze. Isaac pushed the tip of the barrel harder until he opened his mouth and let the warm metal slide past his teeth. Both of their orbs burned hot, one with dismay, one with malevolence.

Isaac's features fell expressionless, and Caroline filled his mind. If not for this man, she would be alive and well, a happy, vibrant child with lots to offer the world in the long years to come. He wanted to kill the bastard badly, and had he not found the leather journal, he would have gladly done so without hesitation. Now he wrestled with the notion.

In retrospect, Caroline was only a small piece of the puzzle. Numerous families across the country had lost their children to the hands of this butcher, and none had found closure or even a body to bury. Isaac flinched. To be the parent of a missing child—not knowing if she were lost or dead—had to be one of the worst feelings imaginable. When Caroline died, Isaac, Sarah, Josie, Tom, and Helen had all suffered for it. But at least they knew her fate and had a vessel to place beneath the earth.

Isaac realized he played but a single role in one scene of a much larger drama. Maybe he was the hero to finally track down the villain, but others deserved justice as much or more than he did, to stand in front of R.E.D. and watch as his punishment was carried out. Isaac stared at the agonized creature below him and waited for the scales of consequence to tip in favor of life or death.

"What's your name?"

The man's shoulder drained clabbered gore onto the dusty soil. He didn't reply.

Isaac extracted the barrel from his mouth. "I have your book, and I know your initials, R-E-D. Now," he repeated flatly, "tell me your name, or I'll kill you and find out anyway."

His eyes darted around, but there was nobody there, no one to help him or intervene. He was alone in the hands of an enraged captor, like his own victims had experienced.

Isaac pressed the gun to his forehead this time, finger never leaving the trigger. He shoved his foot down on the wounded shoulder. The knobby, rubber soles dug in, and the killer shouted in anguish.

Isaac's voice was eerily calm and resolute for the circumstances. "Last chance. Tell me your name, or I end your pathetic life."

Sadness lingered in the man's baby blues. He was defeated and scared. "My name . . ." He wheezed and coughed. "Ricky."

"Your full name." Isaac pressed his boot down again.

"Richard!" He shouted in a torturous wail. "Shit! Stop! My name is Richard." He moved his gaze away, seeking anything to look at besides Isaac's black, torrid stare.

"R-E-D?" Isaac jabbed the muzzle against his forehead with enough force to break the skin.

Ricky shut his eyes and trembled. "Richard . . . Edgar . . . Doors. I live in Colorado." He whimpered like a scolded dog. "I'm sorry. Please don't kill me."

The salutation on each of the three letters was crisp in Isaac's mind. *Do you like red?* He actually wanted approval and validation from the girls he raped, a wretched desire for acceptance by a child. Isaac almost felt sorry for him. Almost.

The distant thump of helicopter blades cut the air. The sound came in and out with the varying strength of the wind. It was getting closer, maybe a mile or two away. He remembered engaging the personal locator beacon in his pants pocket. The signal must have been received.

"It's not safe for you to live," Isaac said flatly.

"Please, no! I'll do anything you want," he begged. Panic boiled rampantly in his voice.

Isaac removed the tip of the barrel from Ricky's head and pressed the stock to his own shoulder. He sighted down the length of the gun and studied the face of Caroline's murderer.

"Please," Ricky whispered. "I'm sorry."

"You're not forgiven," Isaac countered. Then he pulled the trigger.

Chapter Seventy-Three

The twelve-gauge semi-auto ejected a final shell casing onto the grass, and this time, the breech remained open. The gun was empty. A plume of dust rose from behind Ricky's head and drifted away. His body shook from heaving sobs, and a dark, growing stain saturated the front of his pants.

Isaac considered if he might regret the decision to let him live. For months, he'd craved vengeance, but he no longer felt like he had the right. He wanted other families to find closure and have the chance to move on with their lives.

Threads of torment unraveled. Isaac roared like an enraged lion. Through pain and numerous near-death experiences, he had prevailed, and Josie was safe. All cords of composure popped, and he lost it.

He turned the empty shotgun around in his hands and gripped the barrel like a baseball bat. It ascended to a pinnacle, and he swung down with all his strength. The walnut stock collided with Ricky's temple, knocking him out cold. Under such force, the gun dismantled itself, parts scattering in all directions. Isaac dropped the blued cylinder of the barrel. Exasperation and tears of an overwhelmed nature blurred his vision. He held his hands in front of his face—examining the palms with fingers spread wide—and wondered what they were capable of. A jerky surge of air left his lungs, and he ran both hands over his face and hair. The feeling was indescribable, like nothing he'd experienced before.

He pivoted in an agitated circle, fingers clawing into his scalp. His foot, like it had a will of its own, lurched and smashed into Ricky's ribcage. It felt so good that he did it again.

"I hate you!" he wailed in a disembodied voice. His feet flew, possessed with frenzied rage. With each strike, he yelled, "You killed her, motherfucker. You killed her. You killed her. You killed her."

Strings of spittle flew from Isaac's lips. Droplets of sorrow poured down his grimy cheeks. Blood dripped from an array of wounds.

"Why . . . Why . . . Why?" he bellowed. Tears of a broken man soaked his face. Isaac lifted the sole of his hiking boot and stomped into Ricky's groin, again and again and again. Still in a fit of violence, he straddled his chest and sent an iron fist into his jaw. "Piece of shit!"

Isaac clawed at the loose earth and filled his grip with dirt, forcefully cramming it into Ricky's open mouth and nostrils. "Eat it, you bastard," he demanded through gritted teeth.

It went on until he had nothing left. His legs buckled from exhaustion. Right there, he let it all go and wept mournfully and heavily. For how long, he couldn't say. Then he heard it. A voice called, soft and sweet, one he'd never forget. It carried on the wind and pulled him from despair.

"Josie needs you."

Caroline? Isaac sat up and wiped his face, making brown smudges across his cheeks. He searched the sky for her, but only the big and blue stared back.

Whether an interjection from his conscience, or a true message from his beloved, he was grateful. There was still work to be done. He struggled to his feet, limped inside, and knelt over

Josie. She tried to speak, but the gag prevented it. He lifted her small head and undid the grassy rope knot.

"Daddy!" she exclaimed.

Isaac hugged her tightly against his chest. "Everything is going to be okay."

Chapter Seventy-Four

The bright red helicopter made a big circle above them, its Search and Rescue emblem painted in white along the side. Out in the open, Isaac waved his arms in the air to signal their presence. He'd left Josie sitting against the hut. One of the walls provided a few feet of shade.

When the pilot set the bird down, he idled the engine and remained in his seat. Three other men exited the cabin door and tentatively approached.

Isaac went to step forward and greet them. Instead, he froze and raised his hands. One of the crew was a uniformed police officer with his sidearm drawn. It was pointed at the ground but ready to use if the need arose. Isaac kept his arms up as to not give any reason for confusion.

"Isaac Snow?" the officer asked from a distance.

"I'm Isaac Snow. Am I ever glad to see you guys."

"Mr. Snow, I'm Deputy Sheriff De Leon. Where's the medical evacuation airplane you stole?" The officer kept constant eye contact.

Shit. He's going to arrest me.

"Down the mountain." He used a thumb to motion in the direction he had come from. "I crash landed and ran up here."

The policeman nodded at the other two men who wore paramedic jumpsuits and carried medical toolboxes.

They came prepared for the worst.

"I was at the airport investigating vandalized property— some of which, if I'm not mistaken, is yours—when a missing person report pulled me off." He raised an eyebrow. "Then we get another call from the airport that says you have stolen an emergency transportation vehicle to find your daughter." He shook his head back and forth in a show of incredulousness. "Do you mind if I see some identification?"

Isaac lowered his hands and slowly extracted his wallet from a rear pocket. The olive cargo pants rode low on his waist, and he tugged them up. When he flipped open a clear flap with his driver's license, the officer studied it.

Finally, Deputy De Leon returned the handgun to his hip holster. "Thank you, Mr. Snow. With all that's going on, I need to make sure you are you."

"I understand." He gestured behind him. "Can one of you look after my little girl?" he asked the two paramedics. "Her wrists and ankles look pretty bad."

Josie watched them from her seat in the shade.

"You've got her?" De Leon asked, stunned. "You really found her?" He tilted his head to glance past Isaac and saw Josie.

One of the paramedics enthusiastically hustled to her.

"Yes," Isaac confirmed. He wasn't in the mood to go into the story. Josie's plight was over. Now he had Sarah to worry about. "Do you know anything about my wife?"

"I'm sorry?" he asked with evident confusion. "Your wife?"

"She's at a hospital in Albuquerque. Has any word come through? I'm friends with the chief of police in Ruidoso, Charlie Biddle. He's supposed to be checking on it for me."

"Apparently I don't know near enough." He shifted on his feet. His eyes roamed the landscape. "So where's the kidnapper?"

Isaac pointed to a motionless lump hog-tied on the ground. Officer De Leon had been so preoccupied that he hadn't noticed the brutally wounded man. He wasted no time redrawing his pistol. Without a word, he trotted off toward Ricky.

The second paramedic pointed to the worst of Isaac's injuries. "Is that a bullet wound?"

"Just a graze." He shrugged.

The mobile medic moved in and leaned over. "That's a considerable amount of damage for a graze."

Isaac didn't respond.

"What'd you do to your head?" he asked about the self-applied gauze wrap.

"Cut it when I crashed the plane."

He sidestepped and opened the way for Isaac to walk. "C'mon. Let's sit in the chopper, and I'll clean those up. I need to get a closer look."

Inside the helicopter, the circulating air was cool on his exposed torso. He sat patiently, drifting into a zone as the man worked. The other paramedic was still tending to Josie. Isaac watched him ask her questions and wrap soft bandages around the damage. Once finished, the EMT carried her over, gently lifting her inside. She sat down in the seat next to her father.

"How is she?" Isaac asked.

"Well, she has the nastiest rope burns I've ever seen. Her hands and feet are fine, but they'll probably be sore for a few days." He gestured toward her ankles. "She says the Achilles tendons on both legs hurt. I'm sure they'll want to get X-rays in town, but it's most likely just severe bruising." He reached up with a latex-gloved hand and smoothed the glob of salve he'd applied to her raw mouth and cheeks. "In no time at all, her smile will be as good as new."

Isaac's paramedic lifted Josie's legs and shoved a stack of pillows and blankets under her feet. "Keep that under there on the ride back. They need to stay elevated." He then tapped the pilot's shoulder in the cockpit.

A man in Ray-Ban Aviator sunglasses turned and gave the thumbs-up sign.

"Pete here will take you back to Taos. From the looks of it, you two fared way better than the other guy. We're going to stay and see to him." He gave Isaac a knowing grin. "They're ready and waiting for you at the hospital." He jumped out of the helicopter, took hold of the door latch, and went to close it.

"Wait." Isaac leaned out. "There's a cabin down the hill." He pointed to the trail that would lead them. "Tell Deputy De Leon he should see it. Also, there's a leather journal in that building." He moved his outstretched finger to the hut where Josie was held. "There."

"Will do," he agreed. "If I'm not mistaken, the FBI is already on the way."

Isaac nodded. He understood perfectly well that the whole place was about to be one massive crime scene. Their injuries were almost lucky breaks. It enabled them to leave and delay talking to the investigators. Otherwise, they might have been forced to stay and go through the lengthy process of statements and interrogation. Both needed a modicum, at least, of medical attention. And more importantly, they had to find a ride to Albuquerque.

The paramedic winked at Josie and slid the door shut. He gave it two hard pats with his hand and began walking to where the deputy stood over Ricky.

Pete applied power to the engine. Soon after, the chopper was back in the air. It banked to the north and picked up speed.

All Isaac could think of was Sarah.

Chapter Seventy-Five

Taos Medical Clinic used a vacant lot across the street as their helipad. A sidewalk ran into the middle of the landing area where it connected with a square, cement pad. A giant "H" adorned the center mass. The helicopter hovered and sat down on its mark.

From overhead, Isaac peered out the window. Two law enforcement officers stood in the street. He undid his harness. Next, he unbuckled Josie. Her feet still rested on the heap of pillows. The swelling in her calves was less severe than before, but the bruises around her ankles had darkened. She had to be in a considerable amount of pain. Other than signs of mild discomfort though, she never let on or fussed.

Pete the pilot opened the hatch. He hauled Josie from the seat and gingerly laid her on a gurney that a group of medical staff had shown up with. Helen was with them. She stayed out of the way, looking on with both hands cupped over her mouth and nose. Isaac gave her a weak yet encouraging smile. She shook her head in disbelief and turned her attention to Josie.

He wondered how his mother must have felt over the course of the morning. After giving her account of the Highway 68 incident, it must have felt like an endless wait.

The team of people carrying Josie started back across the lot to the clinic. Helen followed the huddle closely.

"Mr. Snow?" The gentle voice came from a nurse with a second assemblage of staff and another gurney. "Let's get you on here and inside." She reached up, offering Isaac support.

"I'm fine," he confidently replied. He tugged on a handle, steadied himself, and hopped three feet to the ground. His legs were stiffer than he'd presumed.

Pete stood nearest, mirror lens aviators glinting, fully prepared to catch him if he lost balance. There was no need, but he did notice Isaac's cheek crinkle as his feet hit the hard concrete surface. "You sure you're okay? You might as well let them carry you."

"No, no." Isaac straightened his posture. Every muscle in his body was suddenly noticeable. "I'm just not as flexible as I used to be." And it was true. Only a couple hours earlier, he had been much more flexible, but that was before he'd succumbed to electroshock therapy, crash landings, high-altitude mountain sprints, and bullet holes.

Another nurse shook her head at his stubbornness. Blood had soaked through the fresh layers of gauze. "You're lucky to be alive, Mr. Snow. That's what you are."

Isaac started walking, refusing all attempts at assistance. Standing there and arguing was no way to pass the time. Up ahead, Josie had already crossed the street. The two cops he had seen from the chopper stood in the middle of the road, prepared to stop any traffic that might happen along.

At least I can walk. Tomorrow I'm going to be sore as hell.

Tom came jogging out of the clinic. He stopped to watch as they carried Josie past. Helen took his hand and said something. Then she pulled away and disappeared with Josie through the automatic glass doors.

Tom quickly crossed the street and ran to Isaac's side. A man of practicality, he didn't bother asking the obvious questions. Instead, he whistled. "Damn, son. Where's your shirt?"

Isaac raised his arm a few inches. The image spoke for itself. In addition to the saturated bandage, deep purple bruises colored the surrounding flesh.

Tom whistled again. "What happened?" He scrutinized the area with big eyes.

"Son of a bitch shot me." Isaac kept moving, trying his best to put rubber back into his stride.

"So?" Tom was at his side, matching every step.

"What?"

He knew his son was in fair condition and didn't bother with coddling because experience said it would do no good. But beyond the ludicrous story that Helen had shared, he was in the dark.

They stepped off the curb and onto the asphalt. Tom put a hand on his son's shoulder. "Did you get him?"

Isaac looked down and gave a curt nod.

"Good. Good." He paused. "Is he alive? Where is he?"

He nodded again. "A deputy has him in custody. He used logging roads to access an abandoned cabin." The picture was burned into his psyche and would remain that way for the rest of his life. "There's an old silver mining ghost town a little further up the ridge. That's where he took Josie."

Isaac didn't mention Ashley. He couldn't shake the logic that he had been the one to kill her.

Tom didn't know what to say. He sensed there was more to the story. "You okay?" The question did not imply Isaac's physical well-being.

"Fine." He grimaced as he stepped up the next curb.

"I know this isn't what you want to hear, but we don't have any word about Sarah. I spoke with Charlie a few minutes ago, and he's still trying to run her down. None of the hospitals seem to know anything about her, and no one will pick up her cell phone."

Almost to the front doors of the clinic—before Isaac could ask any questions—the sheriff came striding out. He was tall, dark-skinned, and in his mid-forties. A thick, neatly trimmed head of hair showed signs of gray around the ears.

"Mr. Snow," he said in greeting, "my name is Roberto Gonzalez. I'm the sheriff." Other than the pronunciation of his name, he had no accent, only a firm, decisive tone. "We'll get you and your daughter treated immediately. Then, as you can imagine, I will need a statement."

"I'll give you whatever you want while I'm here, but I'm on the first ride to Albuquerque."

Sheriff Gonzalez complied. "We are aware of the urgent matter pertaining to your wife. I want you to understand that we are here to help in any way possible."

A nurse showed them through the emergency room to an examination station behind a curtain. Fresh paper covered the top of a patient table. "Please, sit."

He climbed onto a stool, turned around, and gently eased his frame down. The paper sheet crunched under his weight.

A young, clean-cut doctor in a white, mid-length coat entered. Whereas Isaac had the look of a soldier who'd just been to hell and back, the physician's button-tab collar and slacks were pressed to perfection. "Hello, Mr. Snow. I'm Dr. Alvarez." The doctor leaned in close to analyze the gunshot wound. "Can you lift your arm for me?"

Isaac swallowed the discomfort and gently did as he was asked.

"You're a very fortunate man. Another inch over and you're looking at broken ribs or worse. When a bullet collides with bone, the results are rarely favorable."

"How long is this going to take?"

Dr. Alvarez stopped his inspection and smirked. "Is there somewhere else you need to be?" Sarcastic humor filled the question. He pinched a piece of tape on the gauze, peeling it away from Isaac's skin.

"As a matter of fact . . ." He clenched his teeth and let out a closed-mouth groan.

"Yeah." Dr. Alvarez scrunched his nose as he meticulously removed the bandage. "This is going to be . . ." He enunciated the next words. "A little tender."

Isaac shut his eyes and gritted his teeth to another long pull of tape. The adhesion stretched the skin away from his ribs with each tug. He huffed in irritation and referred to his previous question. "So? How long?"

The doctor came to eye level with Isaac. "Are you serious?" He looked to Tom and then the sheriff. "Is he serious?"

Sheriff Gonzalez interjected. "Look, Doc, his wife is in the hospital in Albuquerque. She's been in an accident." Conversation was casual. They clearly knew each other before this. "I know it's not ideal, but we're trying to get him there. Just do what you can, and they'll take care of the rest in Albuquerque."

"You want me to let him leave without fixing it?" He was stunned.

"I didn't say that."

"I don't know if any of you are aware," the doctor said tersely. "This is a *gunshot*. I have to sterilize it, assess the severity of the damage, and then . . ." He held up a single, rigid finger to make a point. "Stitch it up." He put sarcasm back in his voice. "It takes more than hydrogen peroxide and a Band-Aid."

Tom could see Isaac's frustration building. Dr. Alvarez didn't know that Sarah was, most likely, unconscious and unable to make decisions for herself.

"Doc," Sheriff Gonzalez grumbled, "he'll be at a hospital this afternoon. What can you do that's quick?"

The doctor scurried out of the room, muttering something unintelligible. It was plain to see. He thought they were all fools not to allow him proper time with the injury.

Tom took the liberty of following and got his attention in the hallway. "Doctor Alvarez?"

He spun on his heel, stopped rambling, gave a snippy look, and waited to hear what Tom had to say.

"A car hit my daughter-in-law. When my son spoke with the ER doctor this morning, she was unconscious. He told him to get there as fast as he could because decisions regarding her treatment might need to be made. Her prognosis isn't good."

His perturbed face loosened perceptibly. "Why are you telling me this?"

"Because we're the only family she has. There is no one else. When . . ." Tom considered how to put it. "Everything went haywire this morning, it delayed us a bit to say the least."

"I see."

"If you would just do whatever you can to speed things along, we would all be very grateful."

He acknowledged in understanding, but didn't look too keen about sending a patient out the doors without proper care. In a moment, he returned with two syringes, each with measured amounts of liquid.

"What's that?" Isaac scrutinized the counter where the injections waited.

"Morphine and antibiotics. If you're determined to leave, no one can blame me if you get an infection."

"Do I need the morphine?"

Dr. Alvarez made a quizzical expression. "Don't you want it?" He shook his head, dumbfounded. "You're either too tough for your own good or have a very high pain tolerance."

"I'll manage," Isaac assured.

"I have no doubt. But it's my job to treat the patient. I'm not giving you much. Only enough to make your ride to Albuquerque more comfortable."

Tom's cell phone rang. As he dug it from the case on his belt, he left the room.

Isaac shifted his attention to the sheriff. "How's my girl doing?"

"Your mother is looking after her. I think she's recovering nicely."

"She is," Dr. Alvarez chimed in. "I got a report from a nurse in the hall."

"What was it?"

His head was almost in Isaac's armpit, busily working. "She said there is heavy bruising and lacerations on both wrists and ankles. Nothing is torn or broken."

He sighed with relief.

"Hope you're not scared," the doc teased and held the syringe in front of Isaac. "Relax your arm."

He was just about to stick the needle in when Tom abruptly yanked the curtain aside. "Hold up a second."

Dr. Alvarez rolled his eyes. "It's just morphine, people," he said, exasperated. "I swear. This is the first time I've had anyone with severe injuries that didn't want my help."

"It can wait." The expression on Tom's face was unreadable. "I think you should take this." He handed the phone to Isaac.

Chapter Seventy-Six

I saac's heart pumped into overdrive. There was a gut feeling, something telling him that the call had to do with Sarah. The already tiny space shrunk to a fraction of its size. Claustrophobia enveloped him. His whole body thumped like one massive heartbeat, and he prayed. *I don't know how much more I can take.*

"Hello?" It came out shaky and dry. He swallowed and tried again. "Hello?" he asked, more clearly this time.

Background noise filled the earpiece. There was a band playing or a radio. It sounded like a band. A man's voice on a PA system called out names. Whoever was on the line was at some sort of party.

"Hello?" he repeated, trying to hear over the racket.

Finally, an answer. "Can you hear me? Honey?"

Even through the commotion, Sarah's voice was unmistakable. It was her. Not a voice mail or recording, but truly her. Wherever she was, whatever she was doing, she sounded strong.

"Yes." Isaac had no capacity for emotion left. His heart was full. His mind was full. There were questions, so very many questions he had no answers to. But they didn't matter. Sarah was alive, and they were still a family.

"It's me," she came back. "Can you hear me okay? I just finished my walk. There's a live band, and it's really loud." Her excitement of accomplishment was evident.

Isaac envisioned her. There in her workout gear, running shoes, and hair in a sweaty ponytail, he could see her. He had never been more proud or relieved. There were no words, only a picture of the woman he loved with every ounce of his being.

Eyes closed and through the lump in his throat, he replied simply, "I love you."

Epilogue

Leaves on the aspens trembled, and the poplars were deep green. The temperature stayed consistently warm enough that lawns required a weekly mowing. Shade was becoming a prized outdoor commodity, and the long awaited summer had everyone around town in a chipper mood. Ruidoso was alive.

Charlie pulled his police cruiser to a stop at the curb of Isaac and Sarah's home. It was impossible to miss the sign staked in the front yard by a local realtor. A "Sold" banner was attached to the top.

Charlie knew it was coming eventually, but the idea of his best friends moving away was going to take some getting used to. It wasn't that he blamed them, not after everything that had happened on this very piece of property. But it was still strange. He had been coming over for sleepovers, meals, and visits since he was a small boy. He felt as much at home in their cozy Craftsman-style house as he did his own place. *All good things must come to an end.*

As was custom, he showed himself inside without knocking, removed his utility belt, and hung it on the coat rack. Many things in the Snow's life had changed over the last twelve months, but some traditions were still observed. Having their bachelor friend over for dinner on Wednesday nights was one of them.

What had once been a sanctuary to a family was now just another address on the street. All the womanly touches that transform walls and a roof into a place of comfort and belonging were stowed into boxes. They were stacked here and there, the contents of each one labeled with a bold Sharpie marker. Only the large pieces of furniture were recognizable. And even they didn't appear as welcoming as they had a week or two prior.

The kitchen felt no different from the living room. Boxes were piled in high stacks. All the pots, pans, plates, silverware, and cooking utensils were neatly tucked away, not to be used until reopened at their new residence. This marked the first time Charlie had entered the kitchen on a Wednesday night that Sarah was not bustling around a hot stove, putting the final touches on a culinary masterpiece. The meals were not generally fancy, but they were always warm, tasted great, and served in large portions. The latter, of course, was the most pleasing part to Charlie. His rotund belly growled at the thought of no longer having his weekly treat. He longed for the day when he would find a good woman with whom he could share his life with.

The quiet space had an eeriness about it, somehow queer without people. He listened for any sound in the void. Chair legs scooted across wood. It came from the patio, drifting through the screen door, an inviting noise.

The hinges squeaked as it swung open, and he walked outside. His jovial smile showed at the sight of his friends.

"Charlie," Sarah welcomed. "You made it."

"C'mon out here, buddy. Here." Isaac pulled a chair out from the patio set. "Take a load off."

"Don't mind if I do."

Charlie took a seat and immediately put his focus on a thin, square box. The label was one he recognized well. It put to rest any concerns about what was going to be served for supper.

Sarah stood from her chair, grabbed a paper plate, and lifted the lid on the pizza box. "We have half supreme and half pepperoni. What'll it be?"

He leaned forward, observing the portions to make sure he wasn't taking all that remained of one kind. The amounts were equal. "How about one of each?"

Isaac reached into an Igloo icebox and fished out a beer. The top twisted and gave off the refreshing hiss that only comes from popping a carbonated beverage. He passed it across the table, and it was received with grateful eyes.

No one spoke much as Charlie put the hurt on two enormous slices of pizza. Trying to speak to him during mealtimes was a one-sided conversation.

The yard sat idle. A few leaves rustled in the light breeze, and birds chirped in the forest to the back. The surrounding mountains were serene.

"Where's Josie?" Charlie asked through a full mouth.

"Some friends are having a slumber party," Sarah answered. "They wanted to celebrate her last night in town. We're picking her up on the way out tomorrow."

Charlie contemplated. "So y'all are really doing it?"

"Yep, we're really doing it." Isaac let out a long sigh. "I'm sure going to miss the place, but it's time to go. Time for a change."

He didn't press the issue. They had talked about this at least a dozen times, and he knew what his friend meant.

Sarah told him, "You'll have to find another woman to cook for you."

"I suppose I will." He rested a hand on his belly. "But I seriously doubt she'll hold a candle to what I'm accustomed to."

"Don't you dare tell her that."

Charlie chuckled. "Yeah, you're probably right. Who knows? Maybe I'll find some spicy little thing that needs a man to take care of. That wouldn't be so bad." *No telling what time can change.*

Twelve months ago, upon laying Caroline to rest, Isaac and Sarah had entertained the possibility of moving. It was going to be difficult living in a house, day after day, night after night, that reminded them so much of her. Starting a new life in a fresh place seemed right. But as the days went by and time slowly glazed the pain, they realized that running away was not the answer, not yet anyway. No matter how far they went or what they changed, the hurt was inescapable.

Josie needed to attend the same school for another year. She had friends there. Taking her away from them—separation from familiarity—didn't seem fair. She'd been through enough. And honestly, they weren't sure where to begin their next chapter. The stress of a quick move, fire-selling the house, and trying to find a replacement at the same time was too much.

Now, nine months after Josie's abduction and twelve months after Caroline's death, it was the last night Isaac or Sarah would spend on Valley View Lane. As the sign in their yard implied, it was no longer theirs. The new owners would be moving in next week.

Charlie slugged down the final drops of beer and leaned forward in his chair. "I don't mean to change the subject." He hesitated. "But have y'all heard anything lately about . . . him?"

Isaac shook his head. "Other than he's serving life imprisonment without the possibility of parole?" There was an edge to his inflection.

Sarah didn't respond. Her jaw locked in a less-than-thrilled expression. It had been a quick, but not altogether satisfying, trial. Most, if not all of the families who had been affected by Ricky, wanted the death penalty. The prosecution lawyers pushed for lethal injection. The amount of ironclad evidence was undisputable. Capital punishment seemed conclusive, at least for one of the multiple counts of abduction, rape, manslaughter, and murder.

Ricky could not mask what he had done or come up with any grounds to bargain. The leather journal that Isaac discovered was just the starting point to a long and precise trail of damning evidence. Numerous pictures and videotapes of his victims had been uncovered at his residence outside of Denver. It linked him to several other disappearances over the past few years. The irrefutable documentation progressed toward execution. Then, on the day of the first hearing, Ricky pulled one final rabbit out of the hat and requested a plea bargain, one they could not resist.

The defense knew anything short of death row for their client would be a resounding victory. In exchange for a guarantee that he would not be tried with the death penalty, Ricky offered to reveal the burial locations of each child. For so long, fear of rotting in prison had kept him out of trouble. In the end though, the will to survive outweighed living like a caged animal.

The prosecution, in conjunction with the families of every victim, agreed to drop the death penalty. They could finally bring their lost children home.

Charlie, uncomfortable with the topic, wanted to get it out of the way. He despised Ricky just as much as anyone did. Caroline, after all, was an honorary niece. He loved her unconditionally.

"Well," Charlie clarified, "he *was* serving multiple life sentences. But not any longer."

The shocked, enraged faces of both Isaac and Sarah told him that he'd better rephrase the story.

"I don't mean that he's been released or escaped," he hurriedly corrected. "Richard Doors is dead. Dead and buried."

Sarah was confused. "What do you mean he's dead?"

"Murdered."

"Someone killed him?" Isaac drifted forward in rapt interest, laying his hands flat on the table.

"That's what I'm told. His convictions were kept private, private from the other inmates, that is. But it appears someone leaked the information."

Isaac felt delivered. The man who had taken so much from them was no longer on this earth. It seemed cruel to celebrate his death, but there was no denying the comfort it brought.

"How?" Sarah wanted to know.

"Well," Charlie said and drew out the word, "it's complicated." He thought about how best to say it. "They found him in his solitary cell, given a similar treatment as his victims. Someone—most likely a gang of prisoners—raped him. Violently. They used a handcrafted knife to cut him up. A medical examiner confirms that he was alive through everything."

"How do you think they knew the specifics of what he did?" Isaac asked.

"That's the million-dollar question." Charlie shifted in his chair and inhaled the fresh, evening air. "See, child molesters—they call them chomos—have it the roughest in prison. Even the worst, most sadistic convicts have no respect for pedophiles. Your run-of-the-mill drug dealer, armed robber, you name it, has little trouble sharing with other inmates what he is in for. Pedophiles, on the other hand, know how they will be treated if anybody finds out. So, to protect themselves, they isolate and stay tight-lipped on any personal details. It's a catch-22. Keeping quiet about your crime eventually gets the other cons suspicious, and even in a super maximum prison, guards can be bought."

"So a guard probably told?"

"It's possible. Somebody had to unlock his cell." He shrugged a set of hefty shoulders. "If it weren't a guard, there's other ways to find out. Ricky's trials were major news. In prison, word travels like wildfire. Inside those walls, there are no secrets. Just like that." He snapped his fingers. "The gig is up."

A long silence followed. It was a lot to digest.

Isaac leaned back. So much was changing. So much had changed.

Charlie looked as if he were deep in thought, preoccupied.

"Anything else?" Isaac probed.

Charlie averted his eyes toward Sarah and imperceptibly nodded.

"I know you're trying to protect me," Sarah said, "but I can handle it."

Divulging was the right thing to do. He knew it was, but it felt awkward in front of a lady.

"He actually died of asphyxiation, a blockage in his windpipe. The homemade knife," he went on, "wasn't just used to cut him up. They severed his uh . . ." He took a short pause. "Genitals— all of his genitals—and shoved them into his mouth." He shifted again uncomfortably. "The way it was explained to me, somebody pinched his nose and placed a hand over his mouth. It closed the airway. A body's natural reaction is to swallow and gasp. When he did, it . . . or they . . . got stuck in his throat. After passing out, resuscitation was his only chance. As you can imagine, that didn't happen."

*   *   *

The world can be cruel. No one knew that better than the three of them sitting around the table. It was hard to fathom that such beauty can be filled with such evil. Isaac, in particular, exemplified what a human is capable of. He had been there when the unknown man dove through a window with Caroline. She was left behind, bleeding and dying in his arms. The sorrow nearly ripped their family apart. Then a new crisis arose and united them. Josie was being hunted. Protection for her weighed even more heavily on their hearts than the pain of loss did.

After weeks of taunts coming in the mail, Isaac had to endure the abduction of his only remaining daughter. The groundwork

had been laid when Ricky placed a phony call to Tom and
Helen's house, impersonating a doctor. He contrived a story that
led Isaac to believe Sarah was in an Albuquerque hospital, very
likely on her deathbed.

As the tumultuous timeline unwound, Josie was taken, and
Isaac had no choice but to give chase into the wilderness. There,
the confrontation came to an apex, and he prevailed. But the
victory was not without sacrifice. Even though Ricky had set the
death trap at the cabin, Isaac was the one who tripped the wire
and added Ashley to the total body count.

That occurrence was the most unsettling for Isaac. Deep
down, he knew it was not his fault, but the guilt stayed. When
he finally met Ashley's parents, because of his own feelings, he
expected them to blame him. Instead, they'd forgiven him and
showed genuine gratitude for capturing the man responsible.
They harbored no ill will toward Isaac. With tears of anguish
running down her cheeks, Ashley's mother pulled his hands to
her lips and kissed them.

"Thank you," she said in a sure voice. "Thank you for what
you did." She reached up and lifted his chin. "Don't ever hang
your head because of what happened to my Ashley. Because of
you, she can rest in peace. We can *all* rest in peace."

It was a moment he would never forget. Even a brokenhearted
mother had the power to forgive. And that forgiveness set him
free.

As he sat there and contemplated, a phrase kept coming
to mind. "If everything on earth was perfect, then what is the
point of heaven?" The preacher had said the words of comfort
at Caroline's funeral. And just now, Isaac understood the gravity
of their meaning. Life is about the good and the bad. Good is
easy. Bad is hard. Finding a way to make good from the bad is
the secret. The few who discover the ability within themselves—
nothing can stand in their way of happiness.

* * *

"It's a long drive to Taos," Charlie said and drew Isaac back to the patio. He took another piece of pizza from the box. It was cold, but that had never stopped him before. "Y'all want some help loading in the morning? I think I could pull a few strings."

"Sure!" Sarah didn't hesitate. "What'd you have in mind?"

Charlie smirked. "We just got a couple of young guys in. Our motto is to serve and protect. I can't think of a better way to serve our taxpaying citizens than by helping them load boxes."

"You can do that?" Isaac asked.

Charlie gave him a hurt look. "You would ever doubt me?"

"I am the chief of police. The title comes with a few useful perks, like making the newbies do exactly as I say."

"Seriously?" Sarah snickered. "You would really make them?"

"Hey, you're paying their salaries." He raised his hand like an American Indian in an old Western and mustered his best baritone voice. "Chief say; brave do. Not other way around."

Everyone broke out in laughter. Isaac couldn't wait to tell Tom what Charlie was going to make the new recruits do. Talk about serving the community. It was nice having friends in high places, even if that place was a small town in New Mexico. Besides their beloved Caroline, Charlie was who they would miss the most.

Acknowledgments

This is my simple expression of thanks to those who have helped me on my way. Though it may be small, my gratitude is true.

To my parents: You instilled a strong sense of morals and ethics into my character from an early age. I know it wasn't always easy. Thank you for your unconditional love.

To my in-laws: Your generosity knows no bounds. Even when you had no idea what I was up to, your support was unwavering. Thank you.

To my advance readers: Your honest feedback is exactly what I needed. Thank you for taking time out of your busy lives to help with mine.

And finally, to my wife: I don't know where to begin. If not for you, this book might be a pile of papers at the bottom of a landfill. You pulled it out of the trash, and patted me on the back. You told me I could do better, and saw it through to the end. Thank you—for everything.

On my journey, I have enjoyed the lessons of countless individuals. Watching and listening has oftentimes taught me what *not* to do as much as what *to* do. Characters, visionaries, friends, and enemies: subtly or severely, you have shaped my life. Thanks to all.

L andon Parham lives in Dallas, Texas. He operates an e-business with his wife while working to become a full-time novelist. His hobbies include mountain biking and distance running. The majestic, rural expanses of America inspire his visions and will continue to show up as integral parts of his work.

For more information, visit Landon's website at:
www.landonparham.com